By the same author:

Tree (1969)

Mountain Paradiseological Physiolatrical Aestheticism, 2 vols., (1971)

Dhaulagirideon (1972)

The Neolithic Paradox—Reflections on Landscape & Language (1973)

Tsā (1974)

The Moses Fragments (1974)

The Anthropology of Ascent (1975)

Adore (1976)

Shelley: A Biotopography (1976)

Biography of Self-Consciousness, 2 vols., (1977)

The Premise (1978)

Autobiography of a Boy—The Life & Times of a Beginner's Mind (1978)

The Waterfall (1979) & screenplay

The Mountain Spirit ed., (1979)

Nikos Kazantzakis (1981)

Ice Bird (1981)

Humanity & Radical Will ed., (1981)

Mountain People ed., (1981)

DÉVA

A NOVEL

MICHAEL TOBIAS

Prelude by
Kimon Friar

AVANT
BOOKS

Published in 1982 by Avant Books
3737 Fifth Avenue, Suite 203
San Diego, California 92103

Distributed in the British Isles by Wildwood House, Ltd., London

Cover design by Dalia Hartman

Photos: Front cover, pp. 1, 44, 47, 55, 61, 63, 68, 89, 98, 110, 132, 142, 168, 178—Michael Tobias.
P. vi—courtesy of the National Palace Museum, Taipei, China.
P. 122—cave painting, Dordogne, France.
P. 174—courtesy of the Louvre, Paris.

Library of Congress Catalog Card Number 81-67849
ISBN 0-932238-10-6

First Printing
Manufactured in the United States of America

For Gretel

"Mountains lie all about, with many difficult turns leading here and there. The trails run up and down; we are martyred with obstructing rocks. No matter how well we keep the path if we miss one single step, we shall never know safe return. But whoever has the good fortune to penetrate that wilderness, for his labors will gain a beatific reward, for he shall find there his heart's delight. The wilderness abounds in whatsoever the ear desires to hear, whatsoever would please the eye: so that no one could possibly wish to be anywhere else. And this I well know; for I have been there."*

*From Strassburg's *Tristan Und Isolde*, Middle High German text, translated by Joseph Campbell.

PRELUDE

In my freshman year at the University of Wisconsin, struggling among Apollonian and Dionysian dualities in a study of ancient Greek culture, I wrote a sonnet to "The Rock" in an anguished attempt to bridge the gap between the animate consciousness of man and the inanimate unconsciousness of things. Rock and man, I concluded, differed only in the degree of their participation in an eternal movement of atoms, in a rhythm, a dance, a combustion, an energy. I identified motion with the state of being alive, and man's particular form of consciousness as a degree of distillation in that eternal movement that seems, at least to man's mind, without beginning or end. Many years later, on the island of Corfu, as I stood on the edge of a plunging cliff looking out over the Ionian Sea, I accidentally kicked a stone over the rim and gazed at it hypnotically as it repeatedly struck the cliff's undulating verticals, lunged toward the sea and, with a final muffled splash, jetting a corona of rainbow spray in its entrance to a watery world (its familiar and its opposite), rested finally on the sea bottom, there to be covered by sea moss and nibbled at eternally by fishes until it became one with the fluidity of water. I identified physically with that plunging stone, winced with it every time it struck some protuberance of the cliff, disappeared with it in a world the reverse of my own, and to this day am dually with it in an atmosphere of fluid and not of air.

There are many ways to approach this fantastic first novel by Michael Tobias: as a saga of mountain climbing, as a fairy tale, as science fiction, as an exercise in self-exploration, as ontological masturbation, as a dissection or autopsy of asceticism, as an incrustation of phantasmagoric language—but my own predilection impels me to isolate one aspect, perhaps the most central: man's confrontation with The Rock. The apotheosis of rock is, of course, the Mountain, whether as granite or as glacier, for ice is water turned solid, the static fluidity of rock in abeyance, energy petrified. Why, however, should man feel impelled to grapple with it, to start on a long trek of incredible hardship, physical suffering and imminent death? The banal answer most often given with a tone of utter finality is "Because it is there," but this disclosure has always seemed to me like a ferocious paper dragon guarding the entrance to some inner sanctum where true illumination glows softly in an alabaster vase tended by silent devotees. This answer, like the paper dragon, like the mountain itself, is but an illusion and must crumple away to vanish and unveil the face behind the mask.

The problem ultimately to be faced concerns the true relationship of man to the phenomena of nature beyond the apprehension of his own individual consciousness, to the thing-in-itself as it really is, to the Mountain as the most solid and sublime representation of phenomena within man's immediate environment on this planet. Man has often pointed out in his pride that he is unique in our planetary system (and, so far as he knows, in the universe) in the intense degree of his consciousness, greatly superior to that of animals, birds, insects, plants or "inanimate" things. This, in conjunction with his atavistic memory, has arrogantly set him apart as lord and master of his immediate environment at least, but at the same time it has tragically set him apart in an ever-increasing isolation. It is the abyss of this isolation which man struggles to bridge every time he confronts an object outside himself, whether it be a flower, a mountain, or another human being. His trek up a mountain, therefore, becomes a pilgrimage of ascent toward lost origins, toward that Lost Eden, that Lost Paradise, that Shangri-La, that Déva where there is no longer any distinction between animate and inanimate, conscious and unconscious; where there is only a pulsing, radiating energy in an eternal flow.

Ascension, however, is erotic, whether it is in flattening out your body against solid rock, grappling it with fingernails and toes, or erect in twined embrace with a woman in an ecstatic struggle to resemble that Platonic beast with two heads, four arms and four legs, that monstrous two-backed beast that in its final orgasm, for an eternal moment, not only becomes one perfect identity once more, neither male nor female, but also One with the entire flow of the universe, with nature, with what has been called God under one name or the other. In this final, mystic communication with Nature, in this rapturous sublimation, there is complete unconsciousness, complete forgetfulness, a pure Nothingness where space and time are neither within nor without, but all about. There is nothing but *Tsā*, an eternal flow, the Watercourse Way, a dance of primal elements, an energy whose essence is heat, is fire. Man knows that he will enter into and become part of this eternal flow when the heat leaves his mortal body, when he dies—that is, when he disintegrates into it—but so intense is his desire to experience his ultimate destiny while he is still alive and retains his individual integrity, his unique consciousness, that he has often attemped throughout history to attain subliminal states where his mind is so intensified and heightened that under the incandescence of its rapture it may attain a Nirvana in which all dualities are resolved in paradox, in a living death. It is the only method man has of cutting away from his normal existence as *simile*, in which his relation to things is always *like* something else, and becoming *metaphor*, in which he is no longer only one half of a comparison, in which he no longer *exists* existentially but *is* what he no longer confronts but has *become*. Man strives to live as Metaphor.

This is a view, I strongly suspect, which will be opposed in particular by many mountain climbers themselves, for whom mountain climbing is not a mystique, not a form of spiritual ascension, but an exhilarating form of exertion that primarily taxes man's physical capacities to the utmost and leads to an exaltation that is the result of mental and bodily conquest, a purification not so much of man's spiritual as of his physical wastes. For them, indeed, the mountain is to be climbed because it is there, and therefore a challenge to man's supremacy. There is glory and sublimity in this view, but it does not obviate an approach such as this one by Michael Tobias and which has its counterpart in many Eastern sages as well as in such Western imaginations as Shelley or Kazantzakis. It is essentially a poet's approach to the universe, a poet's attempt to understand the world as Metaphor.

Kimon Friar
Villa Giornata
Ekali, Greece

CHAPTER ONE

I love this world, love it so much that I'll never get my fill, and when I think about that, and what we're doing to dear old Gaia, why I nearly go berserk.

The English art critic, William Hazlitt, spoke out in defense of mist, of atmospheric indistinctness, of emotion borrowing "a more refined existence from *objects* that hover on the brink of nothingness" (*Why Distant Objects Please*, 1821). I also love nothingness, the feeling I get of it up on a mountain.

Those *objects* engender lovely stanzas, the metrical kind which frustrated undergrads at the Mount Holyokes are apt to dote upon. But in real life, those same objects manifest satchels of surveyor notes down rivers with news of discovered Everests. Ill-equipped but invincible, the explorer sallies forth. Whitman, Kipling and Ibsen each hailed this process of discovery: Homo plorares, man who seeks outward, who cries out—whose vision is, by definition, aloof, ever ahead of itself. Or mine is, anyway.

The valley which, from afar, graces the eye with presentiments of Claude, of the *Georgics*, up close accosts that hapless dreamer with horseflies unrelenting. The mountain philosopher, Wilfred Noyce, managed that *of such dreams is boldness born*. But then this eminent British spokesman for all outdoor nihilists foundered one day off an icy ridge in the Pamirs in the early 1960s. Long before his fall, Geoffrey Young, walking on one leg, would emphasize the fact that explorers return time and again to their ordeals only because it is their strange proclivity to forget pain and hardship and remember pleasure. The explorer remembers the vagueness—twilight moments where the brunt of candescent noonday has given over to chalky evening, awash in orange desert horizons. His eyes alight like hornets along shadowy brooks and drink there of safe evanescence. This he recounts in any dozen of his ways, from botanical reports to the founding of legends about himself, comme T.E. Lawrence.

The old photographs give something of the style and dauntlessness; black and white, obscure and worn—a medley of half-forgotten Royal Geographical Society archives—names, and with them, dangerous dreams and feverish expenditures all lost. The permutations of dizzy stance, the amusing bivouacs and gripping blizzards, the agonizing deaths—Merkl on Nanga Parbat, Kurz, archetypically, on the Eiger. A graphic legacy of aerial ardor rendered all the more dramatic and philosophical in this strange montage which seems to isolate each epic in its turn. I feel a masochistic allegiance to all of this, a nearly forlorn contagion, not just because most of these men have disappeared or gotten old, but because they were, for all their strength and awesome mobility, merely human after all.

Piercing the black-and-white congruence of effort atop rock and ice is a grim halo of achievement, a mathematical morbidity of altitudes, desperate pendent nights and long wild days. Such mythography is remote from our present era of equipment sophistication, travel and approach ease. Even at the time of Herzog's ascent of Annapurna in 1951, there were no reliable maps of the area. When William Green, Boss and Kaufman nearly pulled off the North Ridge of Mt. Cook in 1882, it was only after a 24,000-mile journey by land and boat to New Zealand. We forget what it meant to come to India in 1900. For all of his incurable technological superiority, the modern adventurer has lost most of the wildness of his forebears; of William Graham on Changabang, Professor Parker on Denali dragging his fourteen-foot dry spruce to the North Summit; of the ravished, giggling Herman Buhl subsequent to his lone hallucinating descent of Nanga Parbat; the backwoodsy Matthias Zurbiggen soloing the interminable scree of Aconcagua, and of the happy-go-lucky 1924 Everest team in corduroy jackets on deck chairs, Norton bearing a haggard radiance from the otherworld where he had just been.

He reminisces on a slough of precious spells: wintry eves alone in Antarctic quonset huts strumming the dead radio transmitter; of those final throes preceding obscure rigor mortis; blind bivouacs on the exposed passes of the world, spine-cindering stones spalling off high aiguilles; arrows raining down in neck-deep Matto Grosso swamplands; flailing to the tune of West Irian mosquitoes on the slurp; exercising the last unction of sinew as beady-eyed and hankering captors partake communal, jovial chews, a faint chill polka-dotting our explorer's neck and loin to recall him from his confusion in a moment's last swoon: Oh, how it *might* have been. To rakehell destiny; *let the devil take the hindmost!* he had laughed to friends and family upon his departure months prior, all resolve, and giggles of farewell.

He is a man no more candid than Odysseus, and his heart is breaking. With each gambol he becomes increasingly embittered, inarticulate about his pain, not because he is so overwhelmed with experience that his vocables are limited to megalithic grunts of awe; but that his words gloss over boredom in a deadly brush of *This Is How It Went*, and too rapid-fire a hysteria, a heart-rending, to minutely convey, without losing his reading, the compass of it all. If the fish story grows and grows, the actual fish—all petite and fine with iridescence, reduced to mere myth—is gone in the nameless flock of out to sea. His one ambiguity is the woman he has loved. He'll die of her, tangled in remorse for not having lived his life differently, when such a massive chance to be normal presented itself. Under slow moving fans, repeatedly; in the maw of horror, until her name is hallowed and inside him like a cancer.

No one will know, at the end, who she was, what Salome, what she thought, with whom she took up new cohabitation. She'll quiver when his name, in later years, appears. Her mind will see a mirage, scintillating, of a ghost in oversized shoes, trudging over purposeless expanse. She'll remember all of those nights, before he had set off on the fateful last expedition, when they'd sat up in bed defining truth.

The more remote our surroundings, the more imperiled the situation, the more perfect my credentials. I had only to be consumptive to enlist the recommendation of all nineteenth century Weltschmerz, with its pale moons and tuberculosis. I felt the thrust of a nameless syndrome: When you're here, you want to be there, and thus postulated, the *topoparadox* ("When you're there, there's no there," said Gertrude Stein) feeds off exile, allowing each respite, every moment's contemplation to stray from its stance.

When washed by pleasant times, love-muttered, ensconced in those sweet sibilants that mucous-brained, lust-smitten poets have paraded era after era, I fell solemn, angry, pushed obnoxiously toward limits of unkindness, singularity. During such times I wanted angst like it was a juicy apple, or the Empty Quarter; to be sundered. And when so separated, when desolate, I'd start thinking all over again, get rational and more moderate. That's when I needed her most, damnit—Ghisela.

CHAPTER TWO

With platinum-blonde pubic hairs and a nasty smile, Ghisela was my mentor. Before that time my life had been as pure and becalmed as the early Rousseau's.

She had coconut tits, a Paul Newman face, muscles brazen and taut, the body of a twelve-year-old Nuba, a ten-year-old Kirghiz. A sabra's voluptuousness. She kissed with cliché lunges. Waist-length sandy hair. Flawless, whipcream-white buck teeth. A flirt. Half the day she did her yogas, just breathed. Her world was like a juke box, an aerosol can of organizations and puny efforts. At least in the mornings.

Of course she was also twenty-seven, mood and morass, a complainer, spoiled, M.A. in Anthropology from Princeton; drove motorcycles, aloof, consolidated. She stood five foot nine, and had an intensity which defied easy playing around.

She changed my life our first night out. I had poison oak at the time, my genitals were oozing, but when she heard me say that I'd never—never—masturbated, didn't even know how, well, she had that Princeton degree and all.

Her hands slimy with shampoo and spittle. Slowly fondling my anus, sliding in and out her loving finger, sudsing, squeezing, reconstituting my groin by tickling maneuvers until erection. Feigning a womb with her palm, voraciously, like a piston. I crouched, stooping out of control, a gazelle brought down by hyenas, slobbering. Umphing myself, flailing backwards in my throat. And bending deeper over with some atavistic need to swallow, to feed on my own bowels.

Her devilish eyes ablaze with anticipation, my member now rampaging in its peril, lost in the spiraling overthrow of throbbing, her force, her elegant expertise, her lust, had elicited.

Hips now exploding, water running into my mouth, in hyperanguished rhythm I grabbed onto her, probing desperately to come inside her as she yanked harder and harder. But then she turned, she stopped, withdrew and a cold shadow flooded my loins. I couldn't stand it. Shuddering, cock bristling defenselessness, I had to think fast. Standing there giggling, adoring me with cruelty in the imposed distance between the senses, she'd help me no longer. Frantic, like a fish-out-of-water, I was an idiot of ineptitude. Afraid to touch, embarrassed to look at it. How could I do it? And before another? Impossible chemicals of thought went racing towards reaction. She placed my left hand over it. I'm righthanded. I was clumsy. Like an invalid gunny-sacking, dumbfounded. This fabulous discovery was breaking out all over with a genetic, moral, ontological rash. Had anyone ever done it? Aristotle had not mentioned it. No friend had ever spoken of it.

The sudden succulent resourcefulness in my hands was an unprecedented miracle. To consummate oneself. Eyes closed. Groaning with adroit hubris. As if digging a trench between my legs. Squatting before her, angry, proud for the first time of such open-souled happiness. If this all sounds tragically antiquarian, for me it was a philosophical breakthrough. An immediate, categorical refutation of every beautiful woman, and sexual frustration I'd ever known. As it burst in drooling ringlets over the quaking hand. Pain in my swollen penis, now fast wrinkling. I couldn't believe it. What was next? And then she assured me, with diligent practice, with keen sensual reverence (she used those words) it should require only seconds, anywhere, anytime. This was God, I thought, reaching for a towel to hide my dizzy baptism.

And nearly every night thereafter for years. St. John in the wilderness of loins, eking out each possible pleasure from myself. Faster and faster. Feeling guilty but knowing intellectually it was a purer, safer form of relief. Relief I'd never needed before. Hence, wherefrom the guilt? I didn't know. I didn't need to know, fortunately. It took generally twenty seconds of hard going. Preferring soap to saliva, outside my pants to inside. No longer needing women, I began seeking novel locations for the ritual to enhance its flavor.

First on the floor, then in caves, state parks, on top of rock pinnacles at sunset, in public facilities, in an elevator. The possibility of being seen doing it provided a richer source of enjoyment than any other method. I understood at once the radical nature of exhibitionism, the environmentalism of it. Stretched out on a rock in a creekbed near Sante Fé, slowly sliding myself towards ejaculation, two young female hikers, probably in their mid-teens, came wandering around a corner on the trail before me. They stopped convulsively, thinking I could not see them yet. They could have gone around. They didn't, deliriously condemned to watching. I continued humping myself aloud now, moaning with my legs pulled back over me, my tongue fondling the air between my sex and torso. Until I came boisterously, gagging between exclamations, exaggerating the wailing claims to orgasm, breathing in loud bursts. And then I turned to face them directly. This was a double paradise.

In a cemetery outside Des Moines. With a younger cousin whom I took to see an X-rated movie. My hand slid down my pants. And then I went to work in the congested darkness. She muttered something, tossed to-and-fro, then quieted down and tried to ignore me. I came evenly, my pants wet, and then I put her hand over it. She fondled my warm, sticky crotch for the rest of the evening. Women needed only this slight aberration to plunge them from their own social stultifications.

In the lap of a young Frenchwoman busy relating the grisly details of her husband's death. It was a beautiful spring morning. We sat in a private compartment of a train moving quietly through the Jura. Limestone cliffs were catching the sun outside. Cherry blossoms were in full bloom. I burst over her dress. There was eminence in such boldness. A woman respected noble abandon, could identify with audacious pleasure and the liberation of the loins, provided the man was no pervert. I wasn't sure. But she too had been kept back from expressing her clitoris for millennia. Female generations had come and gone without ever having openly delighted in orgasm. And here was full-fledged youth, ripe, with blue eyes, sinewy dark eyebrows, and a complexion from some *Death in Venice* of the heart, innocently representing their plight. *Don't help me, I told her. Man must learn to come on his own terms, by his own nature.* And she listened. Hearing poetry in it, Shelley, or Sappho. There was conspiratorial appreciation that struck at her fondest roots.

Off the Golden Gate bridge during a full moon. In a wastebasket of Merrill-Lynch in New York. On letters to the IRS.

I left my seed at random, despite the warnings of Rabbis and Aztec wisemen, who felt it withered the insides. It was not a squandering, however, but an easy, adventuresome delegation of excess energy destined to dissolve lest I nourished it. It simultaneously developed wonderful muscles in the thighs and I was puzzled why that facet of the experience had not been hailed by health junkies. I could see it on "Good Morning America," before devotees who simulated the motions, squealed and sweated, and splattered the glass with a satisfaction unprecedented in the annals of sociology. The very latest in interactive cable TV.

With less ardor but greater sophistication and elegance of delivery, as the years went by the pleasure of masturbating took on new and subtler dimensions. I discovered there had been no history book written on the subject, no formal anthropological papers, no philosophical or religious disquisitions on the matter other than in keenly suggestive liturgies by obscure Spanish saints. Little mention in literature outside of the Portnoy genre. Inconsummate glossy lesbian play in *Penthouse*, puns by Freud, or William Styron, or sketchy statistical allurements in a Kinsey or Hite Report. No consistent provisions for it in science, in psychology. Why, I wondered, was such accessible joy, such rugged individualism, publicly verboten?

But I had my own invaluable techniques by now. Outside a mosque near Lahore. In the Paris underground at the Louvre stop, one late evening, in the peripheral presence of a single other human being, the two of us alone in a desert of emotions, all humanity, it seemed to me, concentrated on my last-ditch efforts. An Algerian woman, I suspect. For her side-glances were earnestly offering me support. But mostly I did it alone.

I had noted animals doing it. And knew its basis to lie in a racial intimacy that suddenly swells up, with overwhelming sexual suggestiveness in the intolerably inspired immediacy of easy physical consummation. But of greater import was the complementarity it offered the intellect, so prone otherwise to losing itself in odorless, insensate pursuit.

Three right lines of Whitman could do it; a glimpse of Makharova on the dance floor, the paintings of Lucas Cranach. The experience proved nearly as rewarding as the writing of poetry. By analogy, it was the physical equivalent of autobiography.

I felt certain that there were earlier efforts in this vein: in his *Meditations*, Marcus Aurelius did it; Gibbon in his own summing up, staring out at Mont Blanc from his terrace; John Donne, in his *Devotions Upon Emergent Occasions*; and, most spectacularly, in Darius's *Achaemenid Acts*, inscribed to the God Ahuramazda on the 1,500-foot cliff of Mount Behistan.

Women never tired of it. I thought I'd like to die doing it.

Ghisela was from Alabama. Her mother was born-again and her father a multi-millionaire who'd started out as a child leading cows to pasture for a nickel a day in the Cumberland Mountains. It took him twenty years to escape the forced routine of his ancestors. He learned the engineering trade and secured a job with the TVA. Ironically, Ghisela's brother ended up on a commune in the very county of his father's upbringing.

Ghisela's mother, a martyr to the cross, considered me a martyr to the crotch. She could not forgive my having killed Christ, nor my sleeping out of wedlock with her baby. She lived bouncily in a festering maze of the other world, going off on Bible tours to Africa, promulgating her Pauline harangues. But she was a good woman, lending zeal to her daughters.

Ghisela knew to leave home by early adolescence; went to boarding school in Steamboat Springs, Colorado, was thrown out for smoking dope, eloped, divorced, moved to Arizona, then to Princeton, and ended up in California dancing. She was a peculiar woman, I thought. Strong, striking to behold; hard to pin down.

Through the mad night haze of Kashmir, I dreamt and longed for opposites. Nothing was sufficient in itself save this outward pull. I wanted a name for it, for all the mounting desiderata. *Tam horosho gdye nas nyet!* There it's good, here it's not, say the Russians. Next year in Jerusalem. I wanted the whole thing. And no universe was enough. Ghisela and I could lounge in total undemand upon each other with willowy figments of desire. We would suds one another, sexualize rear end-wise like crocodiles or butterflies, and delight in our totality. Then slowly my grip dissolved. I wanted just what I now had, a Tibetan before me seated pensively and stalwart, on the edge of lost absolutes. How, from lofts in Manhattan and Big Sur, jetstreams overhead, I had expressly configured the elaborate journey, to inspire, to flush the balance of life: to live! To have my immensity of song before me, palpably. I wanted everything. To hold up the passage of events with one event so paramount, so rock solid and impedimental as to alter the course or stop it altogether. I wanted one blue unceasing element; the direct firmness of an idée fixe; not to let the thing slip by; to whimsically enter the domain of heartsickness.

To outreach the obvious and the normal, to define my own fate. If life was controversial, fraught with the minute, the petty, I would wrest a glory from the abject, a burglar take of each precious instant from what most human beings were satisfied with, as if life were just there before them, potatoes on a plate. I wanted more. Even if there was nothing out there, I wanted to want. And this weight of destination separated me, this obstinate unacceptance of life on the basis of a greater appreciation of it, in the middle of the day, in the heat of offset, while my legs still shook and wind blew the sky off.

In this serviceable kind of recognition I hoped to probe perimeters, to find redemption. I'd been confined for years in New York to the milder extremity of jobs and passages, and the gnawing tedium of unfulfilled plans. I'd hunted after impulse, not knowing it, but wanting it. To breathe, to move all dislocate, and nothing to undermine my falling away. Which is such a man's one option, all at once in a turnabout that broadens a desire for escape out over the plains of heaven stretching before such an eye, as in those John Masefield seas. Toward a vista that touches the bare toes, he sets off, abrupt, determined as a run away waif, with bed wrap and solemn pledge; he will extricate himself. There is no money he needs there, no conversation in the beginning. He is gone after his original soul, the first flower, in a heresy of sniffing and devolution. Who wouldn't go there? Within a matter of weeks his face has blackened, his bones smoothed down, there comes the swell of recognition—*Insist on yourself!* said Emerson, saith Muir—that he has arrived in a locale long ago evacuated by all mankind. Left to the gooseberry and upholstered mossy plush; to a place reinhabited by five-foot tribal nomads, kinks in their hair, men before the time of penis sheaths, who glided after howler monkey and bharal, aboard cliffs where prickly poppy threw up jets of violent silky calyx. There he breathes free, has intercourse with wiggling callipygian women, eyes darting phosphorescent all night long amidst the trembling broad-leaves.

No single experience had done for me quite handsomely enough, or with the store of almighty everything. To look out one morning and be quite jubilantly aware, plastered, to a *fern*. For all of my mind I lacked a theme. Until the restlessness for one became that very thread.

I had the ore; I needed rift. The center would not hold because I longed for *periphery*, wilderness, context.

I tore at my insides, raging after that Woman, after significance. Painfully, because no one lived like that. But how else? I sought high resurrection. There was none, not in New York. No job suited me for very long; each scheme became unaccountably familiar. An editing job for the trade; a promotions job; a research post in ethnography. I made no headway, met no person of patience.

I was doomed, save for a single other intimate who bolstered in me what Ghisela dissipated. His name was Allain Balladeur. And I was never sure who, or what he was. To this day he is an enigma, myriad, so divested, so all-embracing, as to verge toward that cobalt hue which encompasses—in haloes—the mythic and the insane.

He'd taken it upon himself to convert from Congolese to Hasid. He went all the way with his changeover, taking up residence on a bunk in Williamsburg, mumbling Talmud half of every day, walking with new stoop, growing whiskers on his French face. It was a Breughel peasant face, muffin, callow, garnered with Ezra Pound's tarantula eyes and Gurdjieff's high Mongol cheekbones; brushy eyebrows and razor lips. His chest and belly were a confusion of strength and excess. In his furniture-moving dungarees he lacked particular definition, his physique lost in Japanese handshakes and Mexican concessionaire appeals. Out of his work clothes his form and muscle tone were rather unimaginable. His body showed disproportionate furrow, transition. He was on his way to evidencing life, though I was never able to obtain his age—twenty-five, thirty, forty?

Balladeur's father died when he was young. His mother lived on, still young, in constant fits of alcoholism. Balladeur went to her ill-humored but beaten, with quavering propriety each time she faltered, blathering by phone, begging like a weasel for her son, like Apu's mother. She resided in the upper 60s around Second Avenue, with another man, Balladeur's apparent stepfather, also alcoholic, unmanageable. *The situation is not exactly handsome*, he'd tell me.

Balladeur now lived in an apartment over a Chinese picture framer near Penn Station, having abruptly simmered his Judaica. He slept with the framer's daughter, Renee, whose sister had six fingers and a withered left foot; all the more tragic because of her otherwise tremendous appeal, narrow stunning face and braids to her waist, like Renee's whose own sparkling snatch was never, *Never!* dry, Balladeur insisted. The sister helped the father frame kitsch and used her eleven fingers skillfully.

A dimpled fat lady cellist, who'd cut an album in Kansas and sold it for eight dollars, shared the flat along with a sixty-year-old animal trainer named Bumorvsky, a Rumanian who would come home smelling toxic and send a monthly pittance to his great aunt in Bucharest who wrote him only *I am dying, Bu, dying!*

His specialty was the toilet training of cats. "I order them to crap and they crap!" he crowed. "I tell Lilly, piss in that guy's face, and Lilly do for me." Lilly was a cheetah, his prize. "Cheetah's nearly extinct, you realize. *Extinct!* Can you imagine?"

Balladeur spent most of his time writing poems and short stories then, one a week, which he fired off to *Atlantic Monthly*. Nothing had been published. I assumed that he was poor (only later did I learn of his wealth) and I felt acutely responsive to him, fluent in his needs. Together we could spar and emotionalize about our studies, gab generously on one another's behalf: "Schmuck, you'll sell it! They'll come clamoring. I see the boat coming in now, on the horizon. Lord there's smoke piling out of it, covering the distance. It's the biggest boat anybody ever seen!"

Balladeur's mind worked with resonance, could sustain speed over and against doubt, haste which recorded its obsessive parlance in every idiom. His days could be blue and moping, or brilliantly comedic—Menander or Murosaki, Alsatian wood, or nobiliare as a margrave—all in an unmincing mood. He had nothing to live on for but his one achievement, we both agreed. His depressions and half-intimated flights had the Romain Gary look to them. Occasionally he would debauch, as with his Chinese, though it was something habitual, unconsidered, and took, he made quite sure, little of his time. For his time was the crucial thing. Joyce did it when he was twenty-six; like Bishop Berkeley; like Keats. His discipline was his altar and it was Dostoevskian, devouring all. He had a chance for the big one. Both he and I understood that to be so. And it was a bit frightening. His brilliance was a real, a tangible quality, becoming quantity, in the number of pages filled day by relentless day. A certain goddess editor at the *Atlantic* sent missives to him, all esoterica, abrupt with ever kindlier colophons and truncations, Allain acquiring a knack for interpreting her tentativeness, still unsure, but trembling, that knack, on the brink of sensing her secret urgings and their meaning: so close to fruition was he, to getting landed. In the beginning, the stricken writer had deduced and bungled oddly unassociative directives. Now he was learning.

His writing was a pithy kind, disjointed, moving fast, masterful. He sat at his Bombe desk, inherited from a first class gentleman farmer grandfather and like a real scrivener from Sanhedrin times sent flurrious irony, greatness, out into open markets upon an otherwise bleak, universally dumb page.

Month after month like a Kerouac or Miller or any such American giant who was or might have been, he drifted like this, all art. His modesty and chagrin and quiet soughs and nearly cropped style allowed his meanders to go on uncurtailed; he sank slowly, in other words, away in high spirits, incognito justifications, smelling the gutter with perspective that made all the difference—in theory anyway.

I recognized potential tragedy, knew it by name, a fate peculiar to the meek. But I said nothing, sensing at the same time the tremendous voice emerging. Balladeur had grown impatient his last year. Twice he raced uptown to help his mother recover from suicide attempts. She was giving in. She threw her face into a mirror, took thirty Valium, killed alley cats and couldn't remember. Allain fondled the cats. A horrible night. Later he learned that his mother hadn't done it, but his stepfather. At that time Allain was reading Heinrich Böll, and writing a novella about Afghanistan in 1917.

We were sage to sage, veterans out on memorial drive, all kibitz, out to commemorate world visions. It could be pavilion palaver, Duns Scotus jibe, or richly edifying trivia, imbued with etiquette, japery and agreed-upon allusion to depths. There was incoherence in it, but a kind of jazz impromptu, rhythm with direction. Linguistic lovemaking, Poppea and Nerone, proffering their self-conscious preeminence.

He had green eyes that held back the onrushing tide of failure. "The routine," he grizzled; "the routine starts to break me occasionally." And when it broke he'd be back staring down at the street from the second story of his building dug out, with its signature of bugs and cracking linoleum and coffee-stained food stamps.

One night he had stepped onto a table in an Indian restaurant and recited Robert Browning. He had a grasp of the momentary occasion. But he was suffering. That night in particular, not long after we'd met and he'd eaten an Indian chile pepper. His look remained glowering and happily gazy. He was laboring under my same deficiency: lack of theme, delight in self-infliction. His life had neither the storyline nor prospect enough to satisfy cravings which were both religious and theatrical. He couldn't bring himself to get on a bus and leave New York. He was lethargic save when with pen. He'd get worse, go cawing, grey-haired, Delmore Schwartzy, develop chancres, and finally take help from those able to ignore his talents. Maybe he'd sell pencils.

I knew others who were in trouble because of their brilliance. Ghisela, who yearned for any art at all, was weak and fitful for the absence of some compatible expressiveness, but suffered less for the handicap, having probably never known exactly the nerve of what she desired, unlike Allain, who was a living exposé of artistic candor and spewn gut. He was his own catch. In both cases I rallied clear. I was out, adventuring on a level that defied easy negotiation. No one could attend to my details nor grasp the unknowable outline. If I wanted to shape the breath and utterance, to be, foremost, a writer, I wanted also to live my own life. And to climb.

On a snowy morning, traffic-swept, amid the multitude of dead, dumb and dying monoliths rearing up their icy flanks, I lay down famished, my spirit laggard, thoughts hemmed in. Until I wobbled, queasy with a gusher of angry knowhow. And only the airport had meaning.

"You've got to have something to say!" I'd preach to Allain. "Some original thing. Something *outside* yourself, outside!"

"What's original! Was Johann Fausch new? No. Was Goethe? Only with respect to his theory of an ice age. And what of Upton Sinclair, Gaudi. Who has really invented something! Huh? It's the *way* that I'll say an old thing that everyone's forgotten."

"Will Rogers."

"Huh?"

"Will Rogers was inventive."

"They don't know him in the Congo."

"Your theme, Allain. What is it after all? People want lurid stuff, TV teasers, intimate histories, precious politics. No Afghan fables. You're poor, you dummy. And you could be rich. With the little time allotted mortal man, you're wasting."

"So I take ten days and put out my Gothic memoir. I can't even do it. I'm hopelessly elegant. You know that."

Allain fiddled uncomfortably. His denims were always too tight, which gave him the thigh-bound handyman look, or the circus barker putting up tarpaulin stanchions in ogre weather. He hauled furniture up narrow Williamsburg stairwells for pinched old women of dainty skin, pursed lips, and jellyfish mobility; retired Yiddishers going on about this one who ran off to Hartford with *that schikse*. Allain sweated and counted each twenty minutes. Twice a week he sank into this profession so as to pay his hundred-dollar rent, to buy books, bulk grains and vegetables. His Chinese habit, Renee, required some cultivation. She had a hankering for cheap painted dishes.

"Your life's a shambles!" I'd enunciate with a squeeze while Allain supped on Norwegian flat bread and a dip of taxini, Miso, and hit of vodka.

"You got all the mazel! With that rich family of yours. And what have *you* done with your luck? With a little more money I could write."

"It's not that simple."

"It is! Damnit. An extra $250 a month. I could write then. Even if for a single nonplussed month, a straight shot, no crapping out, no cockletting. I mean discipline."

"Get out of New York. Let's go climbing."

He lunged after the idea, revealing a whole new madness to his madness. And he got good, fast. At the Gunks in upper New York State. Then out to Colorado in my '68 Bug. He lost himself, going at it with the same unyielding intensity. We were 2,800 feet up a snow climb. I was belaying him. The wind was gusting. He reached a traverse. No place to fall. Rotten chunks of metamorphic, smokey striations.

"What do I do?" he voiced nervously.

"Mark the sequence in your mind. Once you start, you've got to go for it!"

I rubbed sweat off my hands.

He started, reached the critical edge, made a shuffle, squirmed, and then was gone.

"Allain?"

He dropped. The rope tautened against the sharp gape. But no word from him. A flush of slackness in the rope. I started pulling it in.

"Allain?"

Silence.

Across the verglassed slabs, his body shot out into space, smacked the slope and began rolling down a chute. I was mesmerized.

The body plummeted at high speed, hit an outcrop, broke in two, and continued bouncing. I squeezed shut my eyes and held on.

It was over, had happened so fast there was no fodder for consideration. I gazed out over the snow-born Rockies, pulled in the rope, feeling an extraordinary anger. Allain's body lay severed on the snow a half-mile below. Ceasura.

Suddenly, I spotted movement!

One of the two fleshy pieces stood up, walked over and re-fitted the other piece onto its shoulders.

He'd forgotten how to tie in; and had miraculously survived the fall because his rucksack buffered his back from initial impact.

One day, "Can you help or not?"

"How much?"

"You bother asking?"

"Three hundred?"

"I'd produce *the* definitive idyll."

"About?"

"Colitis! Pilpel. How do I know!"

I felt as if he were testing me, to see if I would give a disguised saint some milk.

He was one of those mortals translated before his time to the thin air of heaven. We were together in a sort-of-infancy. To be a young writer without wit, with high seriousness, begged frustration. I soared with my little bit of work, so plugged and elevated I could scarcely speak though it was my supreme end. But Balladeur had nearly arrived at literary coherence.

"Write like unleavened bread," my Mother had waxed. "Write with the easy stride of a Bedouin's camel."

"I will Mom."

"Just let him finish his studies already," Dad interceded. "Then he'll have something to say. No shortage of good writers. No one's begging for you until you're you!"

"And when are you you?"

"I guess you finally reach a plateau which is sufficient, although you recognize greater heights in yourself. At least you'll get paid for sufficiency; everything else is luck, extra fortune."

I see him teaching himself languages—Hopi, Sanskrit—and disappearing in a twilight. He hears the clapping of wings, the incessant traffic, sees the striae of skies, porous with the misgivings of all who breathed in that morning. A door slams. Chilean children next apartment dash about, spilling tricycles; an iron falls, and old Pontiacs warming up spew loud in the pre-work day. Balladeur looks at his carpenter hands. Examines a 35mm Kodachrome slide, of some Muromachi *luftmensch* left dangling by its painter over the fabric heights of Fuji, no longer pinned in time and space. He's inordinate this morning. Feeling the urgings of imipramine ($C_{19}H_{24}N_2$). The slide, the drug, he left very little. His recollections are pure thickness, from Monaco to Aspen; his surroundings bear no cogency; a woman wanders fretful through oil slicks, fairgrounds, chic parlors. She is lavender-irised, flaxen. On his mind.

He takes spotted pants to the cleaner. Fills up a car with gas (I didn't know he had one, a Lotus, yet; kept in a garage at his mother's building—she owned the building), looks at the newsstand, sees breasts, singles magazines.

A copy of Émile Cioran's *Prècis de Décomposition*; a vial of *Marrubium vulgare* extract, given him by the odd disciple of an Apache shaman, a New Jersey boy; electricity bills; an epic poem in the works; several articles and screenplays, a musical composition, a love letter and a history book; a few other papers peppering the old quarantined cubicle of dry walls and sooted kitchen and three sickly plants, Chinese plastic furniture, moldy tupperware and other exaggerations—and an emergent plan, as far off as the rumor of a deserted mountain village—littering the mind of that man. Buzzing.

He has been retyping an address book and taking agonized view of the countless slices of life. Selfish memory, pincushioned, blimp-like, inflated with the greedy gainsays of a life lived. He has been wondering about the thread. Boldly, wondering about the meaning. And sees instead a peacock's markings, his childhood fontanels—closed softly in the twilight.

On this day he is convinced that the names of Nerval, Averröes, Tristan Tzara, Emiliano Zapata, Sir Walter Raleigh, Cato the Elder, and Michael Faraday—an odd assortment of authentic heroes—will survive no more prominently than an ivory thimble or paleolithic tooth. He feels as meaningless as psi, or Albania's smallest denomination, the qintar. Unrecognizable in the feeble groping light of urban day.

Phone callers. Hours measured. The shirt increasingly constricts. The day darkens. He nears the edge, feels weight where once there was none; unmuscled. Post-schooling, post-those delirious Belgian Congo upbringings on a plantation, beyond the time when he could cry comfortably.

And then the night and lack of immortal partner, of *even* things, where the need and dream meet the thing-in-itself.

And another day.

Gaggles of philosophers will sigh over these matters.

The Veronese, wine-dark blazons will not do it; the library books will not do it; the sounds from Elizabethan Europe will not. There are countless scavengers who rummage through the possibilities. Until they say that life goes on. Like intestines or fettuccine. Or coyotes afflicted with tics and midges and lice and fleas and bludgeoned paws and thirst and constant awares. And always confronting barbed wire for the first time.

He's just ill-tempered; just gesticulating. Young man Balladeur has this manner of venting God's little hurts. Is stymied by Antarctic zoology; wanting to wear bermuda shorts, or troubled merely by the long ago. His one hankering is to budge.

Anything can happen at any time, said Plotinus. And as a result, anything can happen at any time. Therefore be prepared—continued Plotinus's astute and vigilant follower, Porphyry—for anything! And at anytime! We never hear mention of Peking Woman, or Cro-Magnon Woman, or Neanderthal Woman! Take heart, our evolution is a miracle. So said Heraclitus, Roger Bacon, Harry Truman, Balladeur.

In New York he spat on someone's shoes and was knocked on the head. In this little incident the length, the stature, the role, the full reason of mankind—from pavement to heaven, from cause to effect—is enunciated. The man was from Bismark. His mother had come haggardly from Hamburg, once. She carried with her a handbag full of saints' pictures. She married a grain distributor. Had two miscarriages. Her adopted boy studied homiletics at Loyola. Went to a meeting in Brooklyn. Encountered Balladeur just as the latter was releasing a buildup of phlegm which he associated with the first half of the nineteenth century, and then with *The Magic Mountain*. And finally with his grandfather who studied in Munich and got TB himself. So there was importance to it (the getting hit on the head and all) in that respect. The memory.

Until—in this way—there was, in fact, *no* importance, none whatsoever. The edges blurred, and the morning impinged resolutely, and young man Balladeur stopped answering the occasional phone call, put down his pen, walked out the door and away.

Balladeur disappeared. I went to his mother's apartment. We'd never met, her son always arranging things for secret reasons. She was immensely wealthy. I asked her why Allain preferred to live, and act, impoverished. She said he was funny that way. I saw photographs. He had been a race-car driver, and deeply involved in the commodity exchange. Balladeur was not so much a pathological liar as a man who could not control easily the dualities of his purpose. He foundered with brio, then shot out like a meteor.

She had no idea of his whereabouts. "Maybe Africa," she sighed. "Or Jordan." He was impulsive. Always on the sly. "You'll hear from him," she warmed. And I thanked her.

Sometimes in the Urals during winter a farmer could get lost in the sudden onslaught of a blizzard, in that space between the back door and the outhouse. He would pull up his trousers and start off on the last journey of his life, towards the house but unaligned. Such a man was later found huddled solid a hundred yards away. He'd finally collapsed there, having wandered awry in broadening circles, his screams never penetrating the snowfall. I had no compass, on my own, in circles risking increasing extension from my center, which Allain shared with me. Later on, it would be a true base camp. No confusion.

The city faded slowly, dissipating like the tenement smoke in winter. Even the slow grinding smash of garbage trucks on the street making their routine course at five a.m. on Thursdays, even they lumbered on and left the sidewalk below purer, stray milk cartons loitering the cracked pavement, an occasional swoosh of a vehicle, early commuter flights to Washington, the city waking up and a sun shivering above the slate sky. My one friend in New York had vanished. It was over. There was no reason for me to stay on.

In my mind was firmament; wind, sea, and lavish disarray. I prepossessed, verged towards all of it. Nature was in me, somehow by chance.

Unbridled, egging the spirit, a champion, I slipped from the bed to a soft tune, strode out into desert under violet darkness, this dream alone sustaining me. Quaking cacti, flagellant salamanders wriggling through the still-warm sands, meteorites, rings around the planet, and a vacant whistle hallowing nocturnal privies. All of Asia . . . beside myself with urging; the osprey, sedge tussocks, blueberries, migrating caribou, whales, I went out and left. Happened all of a sudden. I called Ghisela, said I was coming for good, that I loved her, gave her to understand that this time, in the space of a look, something mutual and ab-solutely affirmed had to happen.

I triple bolted my apartment, and with only a rucksack, trained to Kennedy Airport. A copy of Miller's *Hieronymous Bosch and the Oranges of Big Sur* in hand.

CHAPTER THREE

Big Sur, California
Spring, 1976

Orgasmic, electric, multiplied inexorably on the edge of a continent, the immense waves would burst against the cliffs rumbling earthbound in ultramarine geysers of spume. Heart-hugging cliffs of yellow sandstone. A sea riddled with whitecaps. In that collision was a delirium of unease. Within a week I was at home there.

Ghisela and I lived above, in a small hermitage of hanging plants, stoneware, shells, pieces of glacier quartz, books, a stereo and sink, with redwood steps leading to a downstairs study. Huge bay windows brought the full expanse of the sea indoors. A garden of overwrought succulents engulfed us. Every day a miracle transpired. White-tipped ivy, ice plants, fluttering palms, azalea, and rhododendrons: Always new flowers were emerging, new hues of heaven, scents and insects. The shed of a snake, topsy-turvy in the moist crumble of leaves and nuts broken open. The wavering suspensions of hummingbirds feeding on the nectar of trumpet flowers. The mice-stalking foxes. And the gulls swinging acrobatically over the descending slopes.

Behind us the mountains rose steeply. There was dust and poison oak and rotten rock which toppled into the road during storms. Two and three thousand feet high, these peaks of the Los Padres were beset with labyrinthine redwood gorges, leprechaun backcountry, bournless wilds of mossy boulders hanging precariously over emerald pools, giant trees felled by age, swathed in layers of shamrock, spanning the shadowy creeks.

Red-tailed hawks volplaned silently amid the ceaseless twilight of ravines, picking up the tremor of motes in handsome light. Mounds of refulgent calcium deposit lay under vermilion rot-wood. Short-eared owls hovered in the tenebrous alcoves of gnarled liana and buggy semi-tropics. The gorges were deep and protected from the wind. The trails which threaded these otherwise impassable heavens, were old Indian pathways, Indians who buried each other naked, unadorned, with palms positioned upright and facing the ocean from atop the beach cliffs.

Of the 10,000 Indians who inhabited the coast in the latter half of the eighteenth century when the Spaniards first explored here, some three hundred of them were of the Esselen tribe. By 1800 they were no more, expunged from the record by Father Junipero Serra and his priestly henchmen who enslaved them, raped them, and murdered them. A Mission in Carmel today commemorates this holy father. A few ranchers, the kind protrayed in Robinson Jeffers' *Cawdor*, settled here. And wealthy urbanites who bought up large parcels of land and built elaborate, isolated estates.

The road came during the Depression. Roosevelt had a secret hideaway in these umber hills, a lofty meditation hutch 2,000 feet above the Pacific. Artists and beatniks and outlaws permeated the scant perches, erecting their comely bastions with the hidden fervor of San Francisco or Boston money. Tourists flooded the scene, hoping to espy Henry Miller's Partington Ridge-top abode, or a nude beach. Then came the Coastal Commission, and with it the National Park Service, to vie with landed gentry for control of the seventy miles of God's country. And Washington was talking offshore drilling.

I'll never forget the Big Sur nights. After the fog had lifted dramatically from the gorges, the stars would emerge in a disturbing firmament. Hipparchus had first mapped such nights. I would slip into trance, rummaging naked through our garth, faint cinnamon and pinion breeze lolling nostrils, and hemp, and ferns urging my genitals. The grass was deep, wet like fuchsia. I knew that quail were tensed and hiding in the coyote bush. I loved to pee in an arc over the hill of morning glories, cold earth under my bare feet. It was warm-blooded reverence. With a gold harvest moon above, splattered in pink and sandy craters. And the undulating eddies of moonlit sea below, tens of thousands of restless hectares reflected in the taupe-blue *Nada*.

The mornings were alive with aerial mists evaporating, with fog horns, dissipating in the air like yawns of a behemoth along the horizon. Harbor seals would come to bark all day. And gliding on their smooth backs, flipping into the arc of waves, the frolicking otters knew how to ingeniously open abalone against their breastbones with a paw-sized stone. All day the clicking would continue. The tide pools were crab infested. In winter, several hundred yards out, the grey whales would come and go on their round-trip mating calls from the Arctic to Baja, and back. Occasionally they would breach, lurching in slow motion. Their hides were battled, covered with barnacles; their immense tails cut the water scythe-like in lusty swipes. Ten spouts might erupt at once in a circus of ejecta, gauzy veils of spray twenty-five feet high.

The sea, with its pelicans and the indelible mirages of cloud and haze on its far edge. Never to be understood. It was *understanding* that I was after in my life. My priorities were unclear. I was full of schemes. I awaited the postman who brought the Wall Street Journal daily. I dragged New York with me even in my accent. There were letters to write. A paradise to ensure.

No outpost was remote enough to elude my cancer of introspection. The burden of excess self-awareness, in the environment of Big Sur, constituted a perversion, an adverse paradox. The pressure to make sense of sea wilds was, in essence, the inability to enjoy myself. I was tangled in backtrack, cultivating opposites, eager to enlarge prospects, not knowing how to live. I eked out a meager livelihood. But money had nothing to do with it. Boredom did. Sometimes nature bored me to death. My aesthetic sense cringed on those days, fearful it should cease altogether.

There was constant duality. Each time I used our chemical toilet. Whenever a helicopter flew overhead. When we had to drive to town. I couldn't get it out of my head, that duality. It was a contradiction in terms. Wilderness. What the hell was it? Thoreau said it had to be inside you. Well was it serenity? Or boredom? I didn't know. I imagine it was this confusion which forged my friendship with Balladeur. Ghisela had all the health and certainty. With Ghisela I was something of a sibling, our lovemaking accentuated by the incest of it. Balladeur, conversely, urged me into dialectics, where higher, fiercer resolves might accrue; where life had more pitfalls, stakes, the pleasure of contradiction.

Ghisela distrusted paradox, accused me (not unwisely) of deliberateness. She had a basic, inflexible stability that granted her amicability, sunrise after sunset. What I didn't know about yet were her untested margins. Later, after bearing disturbed witness to her overthrow, I knew to walk around such a Woman before judging her. She confounded me, fostered destiny, touched my dry Male brow with liberation and the faint, glassy pulse of willows rustling in a bower. This was Big Sur, of course. Ghisela came after Eden, where life had to be dealth with. That was her unique gift to me—the hereafter. Big Sur embodied her, and she embodied Big Sur. Sometimes, from afar, I'd just watch her at pease in our garden. She knew how to become a plant, the very wind, while I thought squeamishly on pedestals self-improvised, dreamt after glories, deferred the life until it was too late, the petals having all wilted.

CHAPTER FOUR

I'd come hiking up from the cliffs, the sun on my back, the sea deliriously below. The letter was on the bed. From abroad. Torn. Stained. And taped. Apparently opened and resealed. I could only guess the vagaries of its odyssey. The postmark was unreadable, the stamps, Indian.

"Who is it from?" Ghisela remarked.

I spread open the scrap of Urdu newsprint. Clumsily written over a chaos of advertisements:

I have met a man. He is over 100 years old.
Still climbs like a mountain goat. He has told me
something of importance. You Must Come! To Ladakh.
We'll need a full rack. Ropes. Dried foods. Film.
Recorder. Cable: Houseboat Logos, Srinagar,
Kashmir. Balladeur.

A great stillness flooded over me. Hilarity mixed with fear, compounded by the force of a seduction I'd now come to expect from Allain during the past four years since New York. A year before he called in the middle of the night from Bucharest. Again he insisted I come. Something about rare rugs in a village on the Russian border. He was later caught smuggling national treasures—embroidered dresses—out of the country. A serious offense. Bu's mother set up the commerce.But he was clever enough to have provisioned his car with a tennis racket and started rambling on about his *friend* Nastase, a sure hero to the Rumanian border guards. In exchange for his racket they let him keep some dresses. He went on to sell them to a museum curator in Germany.

Another time he called wanting me to accompany him to the Jidda fair. He'd buy several new cars in Europe, have them driven to Saudi Arabia in March and then exchange them for horses—white Arabians—which in turn he'd have shipped to Oakland. Friends of his owned a ranch in Mendocino.

But his real mania was race-car driving. He'd had three serious accidents. He once went off a track in Denmark and his Lotus exploded, igniting an acre of sprinkled hay. The papers had incredible photos of Allain running through a field of flames.

I lingered on the bed, staring out at the viscous sea world, hazy and wind-lashed, fog accumulating on the horizon. I was scared. Fingering the letter. An attractive synergy. I needed Balladeur's eccentricity just then. A catastrophe.

I'd been to India on two other climbs. The Himalayas meant diarrhea, loss of weight, pain, and $2000. I had no illusions of any mystery. India had already satisfied my Romantic masochism. Granted, there *was* an eroticism about Asia. A philosophical sadism, part tease, part victimization. As tormenting as it was titillating. Mirages. A Maya of cuisine for the intellect. Dead babies on the street barbing the spirit. And the amusing mediation of minimal technology—old jeeps that didn't work, fifty-year-old telephones that had to be cranked, a general dilapidation. Amusing because it was obvious that the Indians could do well without any of the assumptions of modernity. Better than we could. There was the ambiguity of India, a mighty symbol of inner longing for the past, for a more meaningful lifestyle, a simplicity. And the splendor of the mountains. But a halo tensed over the infinity of sadness for "a wounded civilization." And the allure of a real friendship that had, mysteriously, been cut off.

Allain, with his abrupt egotism, his brilliance, his unpredictability. His communication haunted me. I needed his design, to be the source of events, at the vortex of some chain reaction.

Everything had flowed too precisely. I'd gotten into graduate school by telling one of the many glowering professors that my grandmother was related to Michael Romanoff. In turn he told the department chairman I'd surely lend color to the program. And I learned nothing. My dissertation, in a rather sly way, argued that there was in fact *nothing* to learn. I obtained the Ph.D. in one year, then migrated to Big Sur, where I remained, New York having been finally exorcised.

I didn't know what I wanted. I wanted to climb. Yes.

We studied an old map reprinted in Calcutta in 1925. I'd purchased it from a clothier in the Katmandu Bazaar two years before. The man's father had been hunting for giant panda bears at the turn of the century and possessed illegal maps of all the Transhimalaya.

I knew that the Indians and Chinese had fought in 1962 over Ladakh. A Cold War if ever there was one. The United Nations had helped India build a defense road from Srinagar over three high passes to Leh, the Ladakhi capital, a small town surrounded by glacial cirques.

Westerners started going in during the 1950s. Then the region closed for a decade. Now it was open again. And I was reading posh trip billings in the *New Yorker*. Filmmakers had gone in. *National Geographic* was there. Busloads of tourists. I doubted the likelihood of the region escaping the scathing impact of foreigners. I'd seen it happen elsewhere in the Himalayas. The Spanish Everest Expedition, in an irreverent publicity stunt, sent motorcyclists along the rock-strewn trail to the mountain. A confused lama, not knowing what to do, blessed the vehicles. And all the Sherpa young were given a new vision of the outside world. While ecologists were busy denouncing the action in San Francisco, those Sherpa were busy wondering how they could buy their own, and when their government would build roads on which they could drive them. Sell out. Pawn religious goods. Move to Katmandu. Chewing gum and the Polaroid camera had replaced centuries-old values from the Aleutians to Micronesia.

I telegramed Balladeur, agreeing to his proposal. He responded with quick diligence.

I was happy to be setting off on an expedition. Whatever Allain's motivation, there would be first ascents to forge. A chance to start anew. The total pleasantness of my avant garde solitude there on the Coast had begun to afflict me. I needed invigoration. And though I'd matured beyond the need to flirt with amoebic dysentery, I was dizzy for the salvation of a remote climb.

We found ourselves swamped with details. We went to Berkeley to purchase air tickets, secure visas, and load up on supplies: all of the climbing paraphernalia, medical gear, food provisions. While the Shiptons and Tillmans might have done it on the back of a postcard, it is no easy matter outfitting an expedition in a few days. Ice screws, ropes, snow wedges, jumars (rope ascending gadgets), pitons, rucksacks, doubleboots, down gear, tent, containers, woolen socks, crampons . . .

And all the ill-boding medicaments: injectable lassex for high-altitude pulmonary edema, potassium tablets, lomotile, antibiotics, creams, splints, bandages, iodine. It seemed ridiculous to carry so much on one's back. I thought of John Muir hiking down to the Gulf Coast from Wisconsin through the Appalachian outback, carrying a toothbrush and a book and nothing else.

I like to think of myself as largely free of provisions. Bernardine de St. Pierre's theory, shared by the Yoruba, by Robin H. Tenison, by Wilfred Thesiger, that we can live simply and happily on sunlight and ice water, was appallingly appealing to me. I'd tried it out one summer in the French Alps, or nearly. I ate only chocolate and Cherry Gourmandise, drank from feisty water slips, absorbed UV spectra, and battled ants, laying siege to inveterate mandibles, and squirming indignatly at night as they overpowered me. My provisions, to be sure, were few. And I was fine until the rains came, and the tent floated away, and there was no more cheese. With my down bag water-weeping, ants sticking to my cheek, no hope for a brighter future—and no climbing to be done—I sought out a hot shower, and was glad I did, until the sun eventually came out. Then I was ready to have a go all over again at Man's Incessant Futility.

CHAPTER FIVE

Kashmir

A hideous flight. Thunder and rain aching to shatter the windows. The 707, dwarfed in the high Himalayan blackness, reeling like a Titanic across a gyroscopic nightmare of bad air pressure. For an hour I gripped Ghisela. The Srinagar airport, like many others in India, has no radar facility so it's up to the pilot.

We found our gear in order. Past the tiring tempo of other arriving families, tourists, U.N. officials, and an underground complex of Hindus and Moslems who all seemed to be eager brothers-in-business, we went to place a call. I'd never been to Kashmir. Gazing outdoors at the sultry flat world of dust and wind and pre-drizzle—no mountains, no body of water—I had a hard time imagining a houseboat.

"Yes?" the distant voice answered.

"Logos?"

"Yes!" The voice was screaming into the phone. And I remembered that endearing quality about India. One always screamed into phones.

"This is Balladeur's friend. We're at the airport!"

A pause. "Ohh...! Mr. Michael! Yes. The American mountain climber!" I was surprised. The voice. It was not the characteristic British-Hindi dialect I'd already grown attuned to. "Mr. Allain has been expecting you. We have your letter but you see, he is gone. To Pahalgam. Shall I send a car?"

"Where's Pahalgam? When's he coming back?"

"He was to have returned today to meet you. Perhaps with the weather you know. Delays are common in India."

"OK. Send a car. I'm tall. Big backpack."

We waded the throng and browsed through pamphlets at a book counter in the airport. There were sweet pictures of Dal and Nagin Lake, Indian tourists waterskiing on the Adriatic-like waters. An Asian Sausalito. Fancily carved teakwood boats, containing all the amenities of a fine London hotel, with the added dimension of blue kingfishers and lotuses in the canals. Picturesque boatmen, colorful children, flower vendors, old Nepalese-like homes and watery jungle. It was a luscious, Venetian Siam, with snowy peaks on all sides. But where? Kashmir had probably enjoyed more plugs in the *New York Times* travel section than any resort on earth.

The driver found us easily, as if we'd met before. We piled our gear in his old taxi and tore off into the center of town, over the swollen Jellum River, and out towards a docking. Sure enough, there was a lake. And numerous shikaras, the famed Kashmiri gondola, with embroidered pillows and canopies, named in fancy gaudy paints according to the houseboat they served. There was Houseboat Aristotle, in blue and vomit ochre, Houseboat Cairo, Quicksilver, American Star, Mississippi Queen, and, of course, Houseboat Holiday Inn. And there was Logos. With two young boatmen no less western. They knew their English alright—a traveler's Esperanto of *Le Monde* aphorisms, Italian cuss words, Japanese numbers, American military slang and Swedish phrases for getting dope and girls. But I was afraid to recline comfortably on the pillows for fear of lice. We were paddled quietly on our serene palanquin across the blue-green waters towards the long shanty of houseboats. Passing merchants veered up alongside with displays of goods to bargain.

"Good day madame. Gold? Come on. Look at my finest collection."

Gullible Ghisela. "How old?"

"Ohh, very old. Look here. My great grandfather wore this piece."

"No thanks."

"What about silver. This Turkish yataghan. Very rare. I make you fantastic price. You want rugs? Best rugs in Kashmir. My brother owns factory."

"No thanks. We're tired," I said angrily.

"How about you, sir. A nice massage. Mescaline? Tetracycline? Sealed. Government assured. Come on try some beer. You need saffron? Shoe wax?"

We pulled up to the boat. It was elaborately hand-carved. Worth $30,000 in Indian currency I later learned. Enough to keep a dozen generations fed. The mustachioed boat owner and his son were on hand to greet us. "Welcome to Kashmir. You are Mr. Michael?"

"Yes," stepping carefully from the boat, my camera bag over my shoulder. "And you?"

"I am Lhasa Soma. And this is my son, Tenzing. A mountaineer like yourself."

Lhasa was not clad in the tattered pajamas all the shikara drivers wore, but in newly pressed Indian jeans and a white cotton shirt. A regular Buddhist Danny Thomas. "We are the only Tibetan houseboat owners on the lake. I must be very frank with you. It is very difficult for most Tibetans. They cannot keep bank accounts. None of us are trusted. We are second class citizens in India. But *they* are the ones you must not trust. Just for your own knowledge."

The front room was exquisite. A mixture of colonial pastiche, an Edwardian chiffonier, more recent Americana. There were decade-old *Time* magazines,

Harold Robbins, *Zazie*, a social history of England, poems by Ungaretti, post-cards, and on the wall, above a comfortable old couch, a framed black and white photo of the Dalai Lama greeting a physician at the palace in Dharmsala. Tenzing had excused himself to help bring in the luggage.

Lhasa reentered the room bearing a rich platter of biscuits, sweets, toast and tea, served with a pot covered in an embroidered muslin server. His cheekbones were pronounced, dark and sturdy; he had a brushy crop of black hair. His teeth were straight and white, his hands worn, virile, coffee-colored, with the veins of a West Virginia miner. His son was also tall, for a Tibetan. Slender, fairer skinned, a flawless complexion. His hair was done up in the traditional braided manner tied across the forehead. He looked like a young Stein Erickson. And I could see by his walk as he left the room that he was possessed of that vigor characteristic of other mountain people, like the Gurung shepherds I came to know in Nepal.

Tenzing's family, we learned, got out of Gyantse in 1957. They took two yaks and made their way anxiously across the Rongbuk glacier, through Solo Khumbu in the shadows of Everest down to Katmandu. Later, over a period of three years, they journeyed across to Dharmsala and up to Srinagar. They could not get used to the heat and the low altitude, and the stifling political prejudice. "To this day," he told me, "my lungs are cramped. Too much air. No space for really breathing!" It was an interesting notion and I recalled my own conversations, once, with Sherpa Tenzing Norgey, who told me that the higher above 23,000 feet he went, the easier it was for him to breathe. It was one of the mysteries of the mountains. Scientists had assured the first American Everest Expedition in 1963 that no one, unassisted by an oxygen mask, could live more than ten minutes on the summit of that mountain. And then four climbers—Unsoeld, Bishop, Hornbein and Jerstad—were forced to bivouac all night, without oxygen, just under the top. Some of them got frostbite but they all made it.

While Tenzing lived in Katmandu, he went out first as a porter, and then as a Sherpa with numerous climbing expeditions. His pay was fifteen rupees a day to haul sixty-pound packs up ropes. Many of his friends had been killed. Out of a total Sherpa population of some 2200, about a hundred have been killed over the past ten years in the service of mountaineering expeditions. Still he was eager to climb with us. Foolish man.

I asked him about Ladakh. He wanted very much to move to Leh. But with the houseboat business, he had to help his father. The Somas were, by Tibetan standards, rich. Lhasa was no dummy. He had studied in a monastery for ten years as a young man before marrying. And when they were forced into exile in Katmandu, he studied English and business part-time at the City College. It paid off. Tenzing's mother had died of cancer three years ago. And Lhasa was now raising his two boys to be good businessmen. He hoped to purchase a second land-rover and start a trekking business and so was especially eager to assist our effort.

We walked through the narrow passageway by the large dining room. There were three large back rooms, each with two double beds. The hot water was ready, engineered by the burning of logs behind the boat. And an electric fan. We were soaking wet with sweat. As we rid ourselves of the dead-weights on our feet, sitting down in the dark, gloomy room, the first faint thunder echoed off the forested peaks behind Dal Lake, above the Moghul Gardens we'd seen elaborately pictured in the reading material at the airport. Ghisela took her bath as I lay down, to the squeaking of springs underneath, dozing off to the fresh pattering of rain. A balmy zephyr blew open the muslin curtains. And somewhere in the far back I heard an infant's wailing, a mother's tropical rash of Hindi. Running water, running footsteps, the opening of the sky and a hurling shower through the overcast darkness.

I had returned to the thick, quaking earth; the hearth of heavy breathing civilization; mucilaginous air carrying sentience from all times, through every ling, into every plant and animal. The air was India's unique legacy—hot, hallowed, stamped with the unlikely nervousness of myths still airborn, ready to be breathed.

CHAPTER SIX

Evening. It was still raining lightly. I remembered a similar night, years before, a whimsical kind of depression: Empty-headed, sitting for mute hours. Staring at the trees, the traffic, and listening. Each moment passed with accumulating intensity as my life lost more and more of its importance, its resistance to nothingness. I could have dissected rain drops and the trees quivered violently in my skull, with a vibrancy, a *sforzando* I'd never experienced. The sensation after an hour was acute and through the glistening medium of downpour I felt rapturous, Ethiopic, sucure in Nature's involate nexus.

As a child I frequently lapsed into such trances—in a treehouse, my feet dangling for an afternoon. Or on the road, my father at the wheel, my mother talking. Half-asleep in the back of the car. Endlessly. Through Nevada. Or home late from Friday night services at Synagogue. A pre-conscious power, pre-natal, secured to the throbbing studs of the snow tires, and the mechanics of a deep, dependable outside. Or whenever I'd stare into a mirror, my eyes fixing upon themselves narcotically, until was born against my will the inextricable idea of myself. As separate. Immortal. Destined.

The overhead bulb bore through the tenebrous cast of the room, illuminating the dusty decor of Indian and Tibetan curios. That child was no longer crying. Ghisela was awake, writing a letter. And there was noise coming from the direction of the dining room. I was in a cold sweat. Malaria.

"They've made more hot water," she said.

"Allain come in?"

"Nope."

"You OK?"

"Entranced."

"It'll take you a few days to get over."

"I feel so safe!"

"You are, that is unless you drink unboiled water."

"I'm going to look around."

I sank into the tub. A malignant aura, part discomfort, part habituation, and part exhilaration was taking hold of me, like a drug, a whore's embrace. The rickshaws, oxen in the streets, naked babies, chickens and those colorful hordes, from out of Alexander's world, infesting the mud-gutted streets we'd seen on our drive from the airport. I felt a pang of homesickness. A panic. When I realized, in the sudden cultural strangulation of Asia, that I was not in my world, but in the Middle Ages. Yes, there was *Time Magazine*. And mescaline vendors. And the black market where I could get five-to-one on my dollars. But India had never moved forward culturally. The mystique, that refuge, where the sick, the worn out, the spiritually impoverished came to be nourished back to life, was India. Not the new India of independence, of nuclear reactors and applauded government sterilization, but the India of Calcutta street life, of illiteracy and plague. I'd seen great poverty that afternoon. The kind which is swept off the streets in Kiev or Bern. Or minimally hidden in Detroit. But the context of such poverty in India is more poverty, so that the mores of the gutter are socialized, and acceptable. Sixty percent of all Indians earn less than seventy-five dollars a year: Poverty neutralized in an environment of sanctioned similitude. Such is the community. The family. Strengthened by the castes which in essence delineate and fortify a prolix endurance within the ancient hegemonies of the slum.

We lack strengthening contexts like that in the West. The individual is neither encouraged to express his biologic nor his imaginative needs. The urgencies of his existence are statistical, not visible. He has minimal family ties in most instances, and neighbors who are hidden behind gates of their own. If a man gets desperate, the State deals with him, brutally. Capitalism, and the pressures of social success or failure—in all their entangled ramifications—thwart one's selfness, objectifying everything: democracy, intelligence, inspiration, and money. All are equally charged in the corporate ideal of which the opposite is any kind of home life. And India is the extreme hospice. A stagnant pool of a nation in which everyone can see his own reflection. Sympathy is credible in India, where 3,000 years of eroticism, multi lingual chaos, stultifying mannerisms and neighboring gods have settled to the bottom in a stifling ambience of suffering and the sharing of meager foodstuffs and cloth. In India, man and nature have ceased competing. Even the imagination has been dulled over by greater, messianic urgencies. Natural selection has not singled Man out.

I knew of the Jains, with their Mahavira cult and bug-adoring fanatics in Bombay and Gujarat; the Buddhists, gasoline jerry cans in hand; the Sikh military exemplars from the Northwest with their Golden Temple at Amritsar; and that proud Hindu possessor of the most ancient of worlds, in the *Upanishads*, and the *Mahabharata*. What was meaningful to me about this abundant variation on a theme, was not the differences, but the necessary similarities. That casual, hierarchical, day-to-day impulse, on the four sacred rivers, against the backdrop of the highest peaks on earth and in the mosquito-ridden rice paddies of hundreds of generations, to be saved. To survive eternity in the guise of common rationalism. To know oneself, to have children, and to plant enough seeds to feed one's parents in their old age. Above all, not to fight the inevitable. Not even to imagine it. The Hindus and the Jews, the fifth caste in India—Anjuvar-nar—were the oldest two groups in the country, and they had unities between them. The Jews had come to India during the time of Christ, settling around Kerala in the southern state of Cochin. A King had given them land at Parur, and like the other Dravidians of the area, the Jews had evolved a blue-black skin. I remembered how James Michener had marvelously summed up his history of the Jews by stating that "life wasn't meant to be easy, but to be life," and that "no religion defended so tenaciously the ordinary dignity of living as did Judaism." The Jews had Hillel and Akiba, wise men who made babies, learned to read only in middle age, and went on to see universal principles in bread, in the woman's menstrual flow, in a neighbor's cow, in the Sabbath, and in song. The Hindus had their own theoreticians; Nagarjuna, the grammarian Pantanjali, and the scholar Sankara. But more importantly, the Hindu had his daily life to hold on to, his sacred Ganges to die in, his festering streets, his funeral pyres, and an ambiguous reverence for animals. I remembered those cows on the Delhi airstrip. Moseying as lethargically as the air officials. India reminded me of the Bible ethos, the deep-etched patriarchal faces of the man-in-the-gutter. The same hard innocence, a palimpsest quality graven in the eyes, on the smooth stone steps of courtyards, in the onerous air of marketplaces. It was a historical premonition at once invigorating. At least to a vacationing westerner able to overlook, consumed more by the scent of Frangipani blossoms than by loose excrement all about.

I'd experienced markedly different responses during my first Indian excursion a few years before. After months in the mountains, I'd come down into the Plains, the Duars. From Bhutan to Bangladesh.

I have had a bloated belly but once, for a few days in the grip of an intestinal bug. It felt like nails scratching at my anus, soup jars worth of vomit smothering my interiors, cramping the veins, and squeezing my bowels. Until the fever in the heart, the throat, the porous jingling in the appendages surpassed even the uncontrollable electricity in the head and face. Enough for me to comprehend a small portion of the incomparable agony those Bengali children were experiencing. Were they benumbed to it?

How else could they continue to run after me with sticks and grinning shouts, their stomachs bouncing like old, unbrassiered breasts. A New Zealand family there to deliver technical aid services drove me out to one of the camps. They would not join me, waiting instead along the road. They strongly discouraged my taking pictures and gave me thirty minutes after which they would go for help.

I walked slowly through the labyrinth of dirt lanes, between sagging, dusty tents there in Tongee. Faceless, bloodshot cataracts glowing with lassitude and atavistic malice up from the squalor, followed primitively the shadow of my dumbfounded passage, wreathed in the evincing penumbra of slow death. I doubt if they could focus on me entirely. Thousands of heavily breathing victims of life, survived off the meager trickling influx of foreign foodstuffs, a majority of which never reached them, having first been sold out to border guards and high-ranking officials who could then command their own price for such items as milk and bread.* On the outer fringe of the camp, a Dutch missionary was passing out milk and biscuits, the sole sustenance, once a day, for most of these people. There was not enough for all of them. I joined in with the distributing of the meager rations, to some 5,000 bodies by the end of the evening. I managed to photograph many hundreds of people in the food line, until their chaos of diseases and disfigurement, in the zoom lens of purgatory, dissolved, a singular blur, soft magnetism of the vague, remaining in the rectangular irreality of my camera and senses.

They were a people whom famine had crippled over millennia, each century adding to the toll its hapless children whose brains and bellies, from the outset of their existence, were inflamed, smote with ruin. Young mothers slumped helplessly in the decay of tortured uteri, their whole sense of family, of dignity, diluting lethargically each passing day and each generation with the bitter sting of intractable death. Young men and women too far gone to notice each other, to respond to the genital longings otherwise necessary to perpetuate their race. Though with 84 million inhabitants squeezed into a country the size of Wisconsin, perhaps nature was straining to equalize herself.

The photographs I brought back are difficult to assess. Infants struggling at sallow breasts, old amber necklaces dangling atop their lice-ravaged crania. Dark sturdy males shouting angrily for the canisters of water buffalo milk to be punctured open, grey meal cards in hand. A woman's face clawed from smallpox, veins stricken with the humidity of tropics; brown-checkered teeth defining easily in dental chaos the deeper confusion in her heart. A deadly skeletal veil, mediaeval white, concealing her expiring infant.

A molested carcass of a man, his offal in a puddle of dilution on a street in central Dacca two blocks from the Intercontinental Hotel; another man rushing by indifferently, sheltered in the surplice of biological habitation. There is no one to pick up such bodies, corpses which are legion. Flea-infested rib cages. Dogs snooping around the carnage which droops over mud gutters, children, naked beggars, stepping over the entrails. Behind the hotels—crows pecking at the meat prepared in the kitchens.

Figures can't capture the impossible smiles, the contradictions accompanying such ultimate disgrace. One million were starved in Leningrad, countless more throughout the period of the Pogroms, the concentration camps, the decades of plague and drought throughout millennia in Algeria, Ethiopia, Biafra, in Joseph's Egypt—in all parts of the little planet, in all times.

*Economists of famine cover this erratic dispensation with the term 'relative value.'

Famine is our greatest scourge. As unthinkable before, as after. There is no greater horror, no fuller madness than to die slowly of hunger with the fading knowledge that others are eating regularly, and living, and unconcerned. Which is why people told me it was dangerous to go wandering around Bangladesh. The refugees had nothing to lose and so could not be trusted to act *rationally*. Such desperation can kill 'simply' for a loaf of bread. Or stampede to obtain some rice, as during the Calcutta riots many years ago.

Confronted with such harsh reality, and given the option to completely ignore it, photography risks a convenient, if crucial service. Those who see the pictures will not do anything because they cannot change the world. But they will remember the world rightly, perhaps.

Descending from Bhutan into Bangladesh invokes what must be the greatest cultural and topographical contrast to be had in the world. The lowlanders suspect highlanders of being cannibals. Such superstitions stem from a healthy respect for the mountains themselves, I imagine. And conversely, high people suspect lowlanders of being crude, filthy, indolent, living atop their own excrement, breeding idiots whose brains and mettle have softened from excess oxygen down there in the windless damp. Where dogs scratch themselves and the villages are overrun by rats. Where the old women stare vacantly, lumbago-ridden. Where scorpions abound, black mombas, elephantiasis, leprosy, amoebic cysts, rain, rain and more rain; storms which blow down the shanties of stilt. It adds up—whether Asian, or Polynesian, or Latin American—to enervation, mosquito throb nights, submissive lassitude days.

The jungle and its moist, blood-letting effect on the psyche comes to us through works like Melville's *Mardi*, Fawcett's *Lost Trails, Lost Cities*, Gauguin's *Noa Noa*, Jean-Pierre Hallet's *Pygmy Kitabu*, and David Niven sweating it out along the Kwai. Or Thor Heyerdahl ridden with complaints on Fatu Hiva. Our orientation invariably follows a protagonist's valiant or pathetic range of winces, in chemistry with tawny centipedes and sweet, infested humus; tracks his movements as they jerk over suckling lianas, through interminable, sun-excluding densities. Such jungle is an endless, dreaded Amazon of tapirs, rubber trees, curare arrows. Goaded on by grants, or David Livingstone's missionary zeal (or, in rare cases, like that of the Boas brothers, by paradoxical promptings to channel the ineluctable plight of assimilation confronting the last men), anthropologists shuttle film crews and kilos of paper, sugar, Dial soap and gifts of teflon tea servers or brass hatchets back and forth through steamy mazes in dugout canoes, cockatoos raining cacophanous screeches and turds down upon their shrewd shows. Gangly scholars in bermuda shorts, swatting at no-seeums, type with rotting Olivettis their findings on endogamous sodomy. Where Bogart, Hepburn, and Taylor made their debuts.

We think of the Scotsman, Mungo Park, setting out his last fated time to seek the termination of the Niger, or Henry Stanley, half-consumed by fever struggling down the Congo. The jungle ethos is Robinson Crusoe's legacy. We know that the Thai go crazy in their undergrowth, that the Indians poach their tigers in Assam. We read of the extinction of tropical rain forests, and of cultures, like the Dani of West Irian, living beneath the only tropical glaciers on earth, wearing long penis sheaths which they remove once in nine months. Into such innocent havens, the David Rockefellers beware.

One would think that all jungle lowlanders would hightail it up the first hill they could find. But no! Those fools like it in their armpit domiciles. So say the Bhutanese.

Bengalis are largely unaware of the Bhutanese. There is Bangladesh, all famine and carnage and horizontality. The livid, tubercular mists which sap its depressing uniformities arise at the juncture with the Bhutanese Himalaya, two hundred miles north. The Bengalis are among the poorest, most underfed people on the planet—Bengali Bhiaris particularly so. The Drukpa—Dragon People in the northern mountains—have everything: invigorating air, white water, fruit and vegetables in abundance. Aesthetically, no sultry draft through wilting bananas can stir or pucker the pores like an alpine sirocco. Over Bhutan's narrow inaccessible passes, insects whirr at high speed from one valley down to another. These narrow chutes are mythic, swimming in breezy incense, alive with the spitfire zest of hurtling bugs.* The Bhutanese pasture their yaks at 17,000 feet where thick grasses sway like Kansas wheat, on hillsides. Nietzsche believed that our thoughts should sway like that. Heavenly spurts of flute resound from nowhere—shenai flutes that commingle the essence of bagpipe with tin whistle. Giant panda, snow leopards, wild ibex, and wolves traverse the outer sanctum, timeless in a biology that has no equal the world over. The entire country shimmers on the lambent brink of perfection—ecologically, aesthetically, spiritually. Bangladesh, by contrast, could be any flatland steaming mire.

While plains are everywhere the same, writes Jorge Borges, no two hills are alike.

The lowlander, as Eckerman complained to Goethe in reference to his own earlier, mournful carriage bout on a high alpine pass route, gets sick at the very thought of mountains. In Crete, on the other hand, the inhabitants of the White Mountains don't believe that the plains dwellers even have souls.

I was shivering, pulled on muggy jeans, tennis shoes, and rejoined Ghisela. Her rouge cheeks still glowed by the sporadic twenty-five-watt limit of Kashmiri electricity. We went out into the darkness to embrace the scents. Like moths

---

*Insects are innately driven towards summits of mountains for the purpose of mating, where, in the relative isolation, their connubia are assured, as is the resulting stabilization of gene pools. Of course some of the insects—various Hymenoptera and Lepidoptera, for example—are carried in the allure of winds, only to perish in the nival cold of higher up, or dropped to ground stunned, where they are eagerly consumed by resident creatures. See Larry Price's *Mountains and Man: A Study of Process and Environment*, page 459, U.C. Berkeley Press, 1981.

sucked into light, we found ourselves lured to festivities taking place at the far end of the lake.

"I want to dance," Ghisela sang.

I solicited a boatman. We slipped through murky ripples towards Nehru Park.

A wedding was in progress. Strangers off the lake, like ourselves, had joined in. Men dressed up as female prostitutes cajoled spectators. Chillums rich with musty hashish circulated. Urdu invocations inundated the canvas tent. The bride and groom sat facing one another while the families cavorted, haggled, indulged.

A lean, tenacious dervish of a man grasped Ghisela's wrist, flinging her into a tumult of arms, bangles and sinuosity. Her smile infected me. "Come on!"

I entered the maelstrom, and laughed for the first time in weeks. That's when I realized how seriously my body took India.

Another woman emerged, blonde, Finnish. Her nipples pressed against a violet blouse like crunchy water chestnuts. A veteran hippie took her from behind as our eyes first met.

"She's taken," Ghisela warned from behind, before whirling away into the circle of dancers.

The girl's companion nodded to me. We exchanged compliance, exited, shared the usual pleasantries. Something intrigued me about the two of them.

Hedda and LeBon were their names.

"From Brussels," he said.

"You're Belgian? But I'm waiting for my friend who's Belgian."

"Not Allain?"

They'd met him in New Delhi weeks before, at the Oxford Book Company.

"Tell him I found the Saivite swami. Apparently there are no squares in nature, least not in *Kashmiri nature*. Only Chinese boxes."

"I don't understand?"

"He will."

Ghisela came out, was introduced, and the four of us walked together for an hour, then parted. But in that hour we covered nearly everything.

LeBon was a disturbing young eccentric, a highly articulate and demented European who had come to India seeking the perverse.

It turns out that he used to round up beggar children in Delhi, five taxis following him down the Old City alleyways collecting maimed children. Some grappled confusedly into the taxis from off of roller-boards upon which they were accustomed to dragging their legless bodies around town. Others with permanently distorted faces and fingers, inflamed mouths, heads hairless and overrun with oozing sores, crawled in the doors.

Speeding off, horns honking, into the heart of the city, the taxis would then deposit this unusual bevy of passengers at the finest hotel-restaurant, where he would lead the kids slowly past the reception desk, along the red carpeting, through the lobbies into the ballroom, accompanied by shudders, protests and a variety of Brahmanical paroxysms. Handing out one-hundred-rupee notes, he and the children would be served the finest wines and meats, pastries, creams, casseroles and soups available. They gobbled down their abundant portions, making desperate noises between mouthfuls, physically unable to eat as rapidly as their emaciated tongues and bellies craved. Most of them would vomit back the mousse and soufflé, the meatballs and liqueur.

The strange scene must have been a disturbing one to those who looked on. More so for the children who would shortly be redeposited in their respective gutters.

In Calcutta he preferred to drive his own taxi, he related. For six weeks he studied the whorehouses in that erotic capital. Noting the suppleness of brown, blue, and black women who would mouth genitals all night for a meal of rice and a few paisas. He took thousands of photographs detailing the Indian vagina in every possible contortion. These pictures he in turn sold to an anatomy department of a leading Danish university.

He fought in Rhodesia, sold typewriters from a department store in Port Clinton, spent six months digging trenches on the Suez Canal. He logged, designed dresses, killed people, wrote literary reviews, and remembered once to take out a life insurance policy in a Vienna train station late at night, on his way to Le Havre to be married.

Margaux Hemingway, he said, was not so beautiful. And thanks to Harold Bloom, he decided not to read Robert Lowell. He felt a little sorry for Kissinger.

He told me all of this in a period of twenty minutes. I've since come to see the western experience of India as characterized by that man.

CHAPTER SEVEN

Haze cusped in dark lake hollows. Iridescent dawn. Sweaty bluster in the air. Slowing everything down. Kashmir gets no monsoon. But it has thunder-showers in the summer and fall, and cold snowy winters. The lakes have been known to freeze. But in summer the large bodies of water only accentuate the balminess. The gnats linger over the imperial water lilies, breeding in the suc-culent solitary flowers of the crocus, on the water buffalo dung, and in the open-air kitchens and markets. After our morning iodine-tea (we added our two drops to nearly everything, even the bristles of our toothbrushes) we went out for a tour of the waters.

The Kotwal and Mahadiv peaks rose spectacularly beyond the Kashmiri Valley in both directions. Some were nearly 15,000 feet high. They were snow-covered, the foothills alive with gentia and columbine. Hawks, vultures and crows swept with vocal assertions through rust chenar trees. We went out into the center of the lake, Dorji rowing, some twenty miles around, through reedy canals, on to Nagin Lake, amidst the geese and ducks quacking, the tender splashes of the diving, neon-blue kingfisher, the cotton-garbed harijans doing their laundry over the water's edge, young undulent men bathing and drinking in it, and the far away odor of aliche, betel, rising amid smoke from the poorer houseboats. Merchants lazily sold their wares. I could see that life on these marshy blue thoroughfares probably hadn't changed from the time when the ancient capital of Avantipura, fifteen miles southeast of town, was a thriving commercial center on the trading route from Tibet.

But a new reality gripped this northernmost state of India, discernible in the heavy military entrenchment at the airport, and in certain gestures. The U.N. partition with Pakistan nearly thirty years ago, giving Kashmir to India, engendered a tensity which has not lifted entirely. A predominantly Muslim state, the inhabitants seem to dream their own *next year in Pakistan*. As for Lhasa, his homeland is gone. Vanished in the windswept hegemony of Maoism.

We slowly doddled through the hot light of this ephemeral, steamy splendor, conversing with the diffident Dorji, ignoring the occasional tourists who slipped by—fat American families, lounging legs propped up on the seedy pillows, gorging themselves routinely on the vendors; then the picturesque plants, and then the clever vendors once more.

We were back by noon. Allain had not yet arrived. I stole away to his room: a bedlam, riddled with books, maps, climbing gear, rolled pictures, rucksacks, and a notebook. An outpost of academia.

There must have been thirty books, neat markers throughout each one. An outspread map lay in a shambled corner. I knelt down to examine it. Detailed aeronautical contours of the Ladakh Range with Allain's own marginalia. I recognized his Romanesque extravagance. A sprawl of words in Devanagiri script.

Giuseppe Tucci's three-volume *Tibetan Painted Scrolls, Riddle of the Tsangpo Gorges*, P.G. Tangrède's *Hommes, cimes et dieux: les grandes mythologies*, back issues of the British *Mountain Magazine*, Hume's translation of the principal *Upanishads*, René Daumal's *Mount Analogue*. And little scraps of paper with notes to himself. Everywhere. On the floor, some hand-painted rice papers of mountains and gods.

I sifted through his notebook. A maze of references, and imponderabilia, of Christ, vulgate exegesis, the Minotaur, and river ablutions at the mouth of the Ganges. An essay dealing with *ideal triangles*, comparative masochisms, excurses on Vishnu, Rama and Krishna, the Essene Community, Kukai's Fūji, Dōgen's "Mountains and Rivers Sutra."

There existed an appreciable bias in the climbing world against the written word, and philosophy in general. It was taken to signify a corruption of the sport, of its purity. Climbing was a private affair. A delectable obscurity. The same disappointment I felt in the frenzied wake of tourists to the wilderness encompassed my agitation with literary exploitation—guidebooks, ethical disputes, and the troublesome belaboring of reasons. How often that question had been posed: Why men climb mountains. And how often mountaineers skirted the issue. Ineffable, all.

Few athletes have ever ventured outside the domain of the inexpressible. Inca runners vented no rhetoric. Kalahari hunters, Rastafarian swimmers, Inupiaq sages, all kept quiet about their physiques. Pythagoras alone stands out as one whose wrestling and mathematical inquiry were unified into something approaching a poetics. Yet he never directly applied his theories of the universe, of the polis, the atom, to the pleasures obtained in physical adventure. What would be the point? And how? The body is our one certainty. No paradox there. It is the fulcrum by which our other concerns derive their modus operandi.

And all art could simply be seen as the intelligence, the will, to mold that physical revelation into shapely analogues, from terza rima to skyscrapers. It was the body that the Greeks, the Etruscans, held preeminently sacrosanct. The body, and Nature, the greater body.

We joined Lhasa for lunch. There was no electricity. No fan. No refrigerator.

We nibbled on fetid viands, onion and tomatoes fried into greasy dollops, and downed waxy soda water, gurrim pani, with dyee, roti, mamlet and cherdot.

I dreaded all contact with my mouth in this country, fearing for intestinal upheaval. Germs came from the money, handshakes, from off anything. The Delhi-belly outclassed Puerto Vallarta or Leningrad giardiasis. Asian amoebas—one could just breathe them—presented formidable hardship, capable of permanently gouging out cubic inches of anatomy. Whole expeditions had been halted, not by avalanches or cold, but by the ice cream unconsciously assaulted on the feverish trek in. It comes suddenly, with a turn of the head, over the course of a sleepless night. And by the hard breathing stumbling morning, after twenty runs, an airplane home means salvation.

I was curious about a particular reference in Allain's notebook, "Christ—Rozaball. Srinagar." And something about yogic training.

"Christ is called Yousa-Asaf here," Lhasa grinned. "Some say he is buried there, behind Khanyar Street. They also say he studied in Ladakh."

"Studied?"

"From the disciples of Śiva. They'll say anything here. The Kashmiri are blessed with fertile soil, beautiful women, lots of water. Lazy people and lazy gods. When a man has food in his stomach, what need he care whether it be one god or another who is looking after him?"

CHAPTER EIGHT

A room. Of plaster crumbling in the vortices. A bed whose blankets itch the skin. And springs which groan. With broken drapery. A spider piercing a corner. Gnats dragging themselves along the worn and seedy carpet. A cracked mirror near the door. Fuzz in the window. A chair and nothing more.

Outside, the incessant ache of voices, crows and horns. Of words which nothing mean. A baby crying two days now.

It is 108 degrees. No electricity for the fan. Eight by twenty feet the room provides for two bodies on the bed. Ghisela and myself. Waiting for Balladeur to call. Wet with waiting. The stomachs are heavy with waiting. And with the perspiration leaking into pools wherein our listless fingers dangle from impatience. Desire that dare not desire.

In the prostration every gland is enflamed. Each motion condensing more and more the dread of one more night. Until religious be our necessary submission.

Our heads are dizzy on the pillows. Upright legs stretched to the end and pressing against the footboard. Legs spread naked under eyes which days now have sunk into a binge of lassitude, pacing the void.

No touch is too soft but inflicts an added queasiness. A breathing so heavy, so charged with moisture. Eight times the houseboy at the door is fondling the handle. He wants to see us making it.

Until one day it alights. From the outside it has come, to itch its legs upon her lip. Or on my knee. Then on her foot. Aside my cheek. And over her eye. Until caught, nearly deliberately, in my hair. Which naturally prompts my first and only purpose in the room, amidst the confused buzzing.

She stares at it. And I in turn will gaze upon the two of them. With near jealousy I watch as it tickles her elusively. Its legs and purple brain a grotesque machination, wonderful curiosity, as it moves from angle to angle amidst fine blonde hairs, disappearing finally in her sweaty cleavage.

Until darkness faintly comes again and with it other ones. She gets up to piss. To brush her hair. To eat an old, hardened apple. And sitting before the mirror. With a fly on her shoulder. I try to sleep.

There was an impatient rapping at the door. It was dusk.

"Yeah?" I muttered sleepily.

"Michael!"

"Allain? *Allain!* Damn it's fine—fine!—to see you! Where the fuck have you been?"

"Road was flooded out at Pahalgam. I'm sorry. You look excellent. And who's that!" He laughed boisterously.

Ghisela grinned boyishly, sitting up in bed with the blanket draped about herself.

"It took them a day and a half to clear ten feet of mud. One never tires of the Indian military. Did you hear the latest: shambala. In the Kun-Lun. Italian archaeologists slipped the news to the *Far Eastern Economic Review* in Hong Kong. I mean you both look *good!*"

"You've been over here too long." I couldn't take my eyes off him. There were changes. Salient, mysterious transformations like he'd had a disease, or a revelation.

He'd aged. His skin was not so smooth as I'd remembered. Dark and skinny. A more mature virility.

His blue eyes were eager to share the four years' lapse of time. "How long you been out here?"

"Six months."

"Homesick?"

"No."

"Are you still writing?" Ghisela asked.

"Researching," he said. He looked with a devilish wry candor at Ghisela. "You like to languish. It's in your complexion, your eyes, even in the way your hair hangs."

"God, he's a regular shaman. You're right. Sleep 'till the crack of noon."

"You've a lovely looking woman."

"All right. All right," I blustered. "You *have* been out too long."

He stuttered, which I'd never heard him do. There was something going on. The way a temporal lobe epileptic—fringe electricity—can give you the odd sensation that something's quite wrong. But you're never sure. Blake, Heine, Samuel Johnson: Balladeur, I flashed.

"Traveling alone?"

"More or less. Alone, but not lonely. Not in Asia. There's always some little kid or someone tagging along. Lots of wayfarers, itinerant folks, climbers. Everyone seems to be here, soaking up the sun and each other."

He was forty, and possessed of an etherium, a waif-like visage; hearty, with a background mirth as sure and constant as guitar renditions of Bach. An indecipherable exuberance. But it seemed more dangerous than before. We looked with quick timidity.

"I met your LeBon."

"LeBon?"

"Belgian longhair. Said he met you in New Delhi. To tell you he found some swami."

"And?"

" 'I'm afraid there are no squares, just boxes, Chinese boxes,' he said. I guess the lacquer kind."

Allain was silent. Thinking.

"So what's the story," I prompted.

"Hell of a lot to go over. Where to begin!"

"You dealing in lacquer, Allain?"

"It was a vague hope. This holy man outside of town. That's all he said?"

"Yep."

The sunset was folding heavily through the thinly drawn curtains, the air dense with outside garbled speech, Oriental cadences, far-off cries of the lake vendors. I was relieved at his arrival. Our waiting around had become obscenely uncomfortable.

There was, beneath our small talk, a pressing hiatus. Ever since his first cryptic communication with us in Big Sur, I'd been hoping for something. Like an unwanted lover hanging on, I'd come to Asia with only the murkiest reasons for so doing. There were details to be launched, and Balladeur seemed to be holding out on the trajectory. I emphasized my discomfort over dinner, affecting prolonged silence, catering to no one, pregnant with the first suspicions that I'd come like a fool.

Lhasa passed the traditional chillum around after dinner. I wheezed asthmatically.

Balladeur opened a book. "Did you notice the small Hindu shrine on the hill above the lake?"

"With all the radio antennas?"

"Yes. It's one of Shankaracharya's. An ancient sage king. To unite India he had pilgrim sites built all over the subcontinent, from Kashmir to Cape Comorin where the three ancient seas meet. Look at this." A lavish monograph by Sir John Marshall, *The Monuments of Sanchi*. Its appendix described a Mohenjodaro seal, showing a three-headed figure, horned, with a headdress, crosslegged, on a rocky pedestal. The figure's penis was erect and the man-creature was surrounded by other wild beasts.

"This is the ancient prototype of Śiva. In his *pasupati* aspect. A yogi, the ultimate yogi."

I knew nothing really about yoga. Every bookstore and laundromat bulletin board overflowed with poetry and meditation retreat advertisements in California. I'd smeared T.M., Rajneesh, Muktananda, est, all the other trips, into one big useless bundle. It was pathetic shit—soybean gruel—for which I had no patience. None of it had anything to do with the East. Simply that new narcissism. And though I was prepared to allow for degrees and distinctions of crap, you'd never convince me that because it worked it *wasn't* garbage. I thought of all the screams coming from the various Gestalt encounters on the West Coast—psychic theaters where dimestore psychoanalysis and subsequent confession were on tap, and where thinly veiled voices and bodies caroused all night in a group exhibitionism of the emotions. Anxiety hard-ons! Hate hard-ons, divorce-guilt hard-ons . . . and everyone screaming ME! Personal salvation for ME!

I recalled my mother making Esalen Institute history by having the solid dignity and chutzpah to wear a bathing suit in the communal hot baths. I was proud of her generation. They stopped Hitler at great sacrifice, and said what they felt. I'm not conservative, just impatient with my peers.

"So?"

"Śiva is a mountain god. The patron saint of Indian asceticism. This three-headed image is everywhere. In the erotic embossments of Khajuraho, the Trimurti statue carved in the sixth century at the Island of Elephanta in Bombay Harbor, at Kaitasa on the walls of Ellora. You read *Passage to India*? Forster used the symbol, and was constantly referring to the cave and the mountain as archetypal images of Indian prehistory, typologies of landscape meditation. You've seen the sāddhus?"

"Sickies."

"Well, some of them anyway. Those that the Mohammedans call fakirs or charlatans, with rubies up their sleeves. But of the five million or so ascetics in India, there are a few hundred legitimate holy men."

"How do you define a holy man?"

"I don't. But you've seen some of them. A white string across the bare chest. Open saffron skirt. Horizontal white lines, the tilaka, painted on the forehead announcing which sect they belong to. Ashes besmeared all over their bodies. Their hair matted, rolled around bark, hanging down their back. They wander, chanting the one thousand one Sanskrit names for god, in an effort to break through Maya, illusion. Sometimes their faces are painted green. They gather in large *melas* on the sacred rivers. Some of them carry a coconut gourd, others make an alms bowl of their own hands. They carry a rosary of beads from the Rudraksha tree. And they have four drinks: cow urine, water soiled by hand, drink heated by sunshine, and the water which drips from rocks. Have you read the *Vedas*?"

"It's been awhile," I admitted.

"Well, it is in the *Rgveda*, where the practice of *tapas*, asceticism, is first described. A *muni* like the Buddha, called Sākyamuni, is an ascetic. Tapas also means heat, the fire of austerity, and thus the prescription to wear yellow soiled clothes. The ascetic, from early times, was said to follow the wind, thereby attaining the status of gods. With the wind as his girdle an ascetic could actually fly. They are often described as Kesin—one with long locks—and their rituals are said to immerse them in the ecstasy of a sacred drink which the Vedic Aryan priests knew of.

"In Hindu tradition the full-fledged ascetic, the *bhiksu* or *sannyasa* yogi, a wandering mendicant, actively renounced both life and death. He is one who dresses and acts like a child, a ghost, a madman. He is often portrayed as a naked wild man. Naked in expression as well."

"What do you mean, naked in expression?" Ghisela queried in advance of my own rising impatience, which she was alert to.

"Without inhibition in the broadest sense. He does not mediate experience with his intelligence. There is no mental interlocution. But spontaneity. And because of the immediacy of his being, he is often misunderstood, or silent. He sees paradox as complementary colors."

"What about Śiva?" I interjected.

"Well, as I said, he is a mountain god. But he is supposedly incarnate. Each ascetic is an avatar. And there are thousands of sacred peaks in India. Wherever a pilgrimage has somehow become a legendary fact. The Hindus make more treks to sacred shrines than any other people. They are walkers. Their religion is a holy stride, a physical tempo, a cultural foot-race towards extinction, which they hold synonymous with paradise."

"Jesus, Allain, there an Adidas distributor in this country?" Ghisela jabbed me.

"Have you ever heard of Mount Kailasha?" he asked.

"The holy mountain?"

"The most sacred mountain in all of Asia. It's forty miles into China, north of the western Indo-Nepalese border. It's known as Kailas, Dí Se in Tibetan, and Su-Meru in Buddhist cosmology. About 22,000 feet high. Pilgrims to the mountain circumambulate it on all fours, an ordeal requiring two months. They place skins on their palms and knees. Indo-European tribes once moved across the Kailasha region passing by the sacred Lake Manasrarovar wherefrom the River Brahmaputra issues. Emperor Ashóka, the great Maurya King of the third century B.C., who put forth his famous Rock Edicts, built a hermitage in the area and the Tibetan Saint Milarepa triumphed over a Bön priest by flying to the peak's summit before him, bringing Buddhism once and for all to Tibet. The peak is as sacred to Hindus as it is to Buddhists. It is the god-mountain, their center of the universe. And in the Hindu cosmos it sits in the shape of a square, the Kingdom of Brahma on top, at the heavenly rear of several ever-growing chains of semi-symbolic mountains."

Ghisela, I could see, was in some awe of Balladeur, about whom she'd heard such exotica. She sat on the wooden floorboards picking flea bites on her ankles.

"Semi-symbolic?" she asked, looking up at the quixotic Belgian.

"Well, the Himalayas are in this scheme. They are not only the real mountains, but the metaphorical ones. They are visible to us as easily as the higher, symbolic ones behind them are invisible to us. These ranges are cerebral escarpments, glaciated paradigms of ascetical solitude. Su-Meru is equivalent to the tip of the skull where a thought reaches its ultimate nonplus in a geology of introspection, a psychology of ascent that is divining the holy summit, the Nirvana."

The man was mad, an academic imperialist. His eyes had caught fire, his breath adolescent, and his neck leaned to and fro across the thick of his discourse.

Allain was busy referring to Joyce, Yeats' *Vision*, Milton, and a host of other disparate characters whom he'd consumed in a raging quest to decipher paradise.

"So what does *Finnegans Wake* have to do with Śiva?" I had labored to attain my doctorate, a form of necrophilia, while Allain had always shunned education. He didn't need it. While I was struggling to think up an original anarchy about which to write a dissertation, all my anemic friends developing hunchbacks at their whittled desks, Allain had already written a provocative study of African colonization, four collections of verse, some fifty short stories, translations, in addition to all his nefarious enterprises.

Allain continued: "Anna Livia Plurabelle, the river Liffey in Joyce's epic, flows from the Wicklow Mountains southwest of Dublin. You've seen the illustration Michael—two overlapping circles forming a triangle and its negative image? With three points which Joyce calls alpha, lambda, pi—ALP. It's the geometrical shape of his epic, the ecological cycle if you will. He borrowed the image idea from Vico's *Scienza nuova* which in turn relies on Indian mythology outlined in the *Vishnu Purana*. Śiva is the naked yogi-ascetic, figured as sitting on the summit of Kailasha, meditating on the opposite summit, the symbolic one at the other pole."

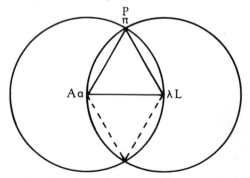

ALP—Anna Livia Plurabelle
(See *Finnegans Wake*,
Viking paperback edition, 1959,
page 293.)

Ghisela showed some restlessness. Balladeur tended to carry on oblivious to our attentiveness. He was savage in this, exorcising demons. No, he was plotting, would come down to earth, re-enlist our sympathies, then race off again.

"Su-Meru or Kailasha?" Ghisela asked with academic acumen.

"Both," Allain replied, nodding, in sure manipulation of the conversation. "The Himalayas are revered by both religions and Śiva is the tangential Prometheus. In the *Ṛgveda* the mountains are called the *Abode of the Glaciers*. They are preeminently divine in the literature of the ancient Hindu, realms of the dead, of all mighty creatures, of immortal saints and ascetics who drink of the life-giving waters the way Finnegan took his resuscitating schnaps. The Himalayas are the *Father of the Ganges* and of Parvati, the *most beautiful woman in the world*, Śiva's consort. The two of them sit copulating in the wind, an eternal, day-to-day contemplation in the high thin air of Kailasha's summit."

"Sounds sort of irreverent. Or X-rated," Ghisela warmed.

"The iconography of the image is complex. Numerous interpretations. But what is incredible, and no surprise to any climber, is the simple fact that it is the mountain realm which links Buddhism with Hinduism, just as Mt. Sinai is as sacred to the Christians, who went there to see St. Catherine's Monastery all through Renaissance history, as it is to the Jews, and Moslems. And in China, the mountain is the source of union between the Buddhists, the Taoists and the Shinto. Despite the diverse traditions of art and poetry in Japan and China, it is the alpine world which acts as an undifferentiated catalyst."

"And what do the Buddhists say about Kailasha?" I asked.

"They've enacted a spectacular assimilation of Hindu mythology. The Mahayana Buddhists adopted a corresponding succession of psycho-physical affixations. A spatial meaning is given to each level of meditation. In the second treatise of the *Abhidharma*, the Buddhist metaphysics, the mountain is symbolically 160,000 miles high. Surrounded by seven concentric ranges. There is complete unification of the devotee's consciousness with these symbolized landforms. And the product of their combination charges one's spiritual posture with a new possibility for pilgrimage. It is a remarkable contemplation. A sophisticated labyrinth of linguistic lemmings, paradox annihilation and the internalization of physical object."

"You've changed preoccupations," I said to him. "What about Williamsburg?"

"Something happened," he sobered.

"What?"

"As you know, I've been to the sacred cave called Amarnath. It's the most sacred Hindu grotto in India. It takes one ball-bust day to get there from a military post in the upper Sonamarg Valley, or three less-exacting days from the village of Pahalgam. The cave is just under 15,000 feet high on a cliff in a narrow snow-locked gorge. It's large, with an arching roof where white doves nest. Some thirty sāddhus live in the cold shadows of its recess. They're pneumonial. One of them does a trick for pilgrims. He is able to wrap his penis around a stick three times. I saw him do it. One woman who'd come on donkey-back, a tourist from Vaduz, fainted when she saw it. He's somehow managed to stretch the tissue. In the back of the cave are two sections of ice. One is curved, with a bell fixed by an old rusty piton. The other is a stalagmite, perfectly smooth, and phallus-like, twenty feet high. They consider it the lingam of Śiva, or one of his many, in other words. And the cave represents the Yoni, or vagina of Parvati. This cosmic prick waxes and wanes according to the moon. In August, when all the thousands of pilgrims come, most of the ice has melted and it's a mere dribble of icicled semen.

"When I got down to Sonamarg after my first trip to the cave, I met an old *lalarogam*, the man who tends the horses. It was snowing and I was eager to get back to Srinagar. But he told me a story that triggered my imagination. I had asked him about the cave, for in his business of packing in tourists, he'd been up there dozens of times. He related the legendary history of the place. How a shepherd looking for his lost horses had discovered it and heard great vibrations coming from within. The shepherd scrambled up to the entrance to see what no one had seen—Śiva and Parvati making love right there. Most interesting, the gods took no notice of the man. He ran down to Pahalgam and told the other villagers. The elders came back up, canes in their hands and barefoot, through the snow, over the boulder fields and past the giant *demon* glacier known as Panchtarni. Secretly, they crawled up to the mouth of the cave. The palpitating HUM burst upon them. Śiva and Parvati were mutely enjoined—immense god eyes shaking in the high lair, now staring angrily at the intrepid villagers, whose rude intrusion had interrupted the ancient coitus. The two gods vanished. The villagers offered prayer, coins and flowers to the cave; a year passed, and in the second winter the ice penis grew up from the granite floor. The vibrations of their meeting can still be felt. The horseman informed me—and he said he was telling me this in confidence for it was a *military secret*—that in fact there was another cave, utterly inaccessible, which he and some other shepherds had seen from a distance with the one pair of binoculars in the area, loaned to them by a hotel owner. This other cave was much smaller, in the very middle of a wall on the higher backside of the Amarnath mountain. Nearly 16,000 feet high. It was seriously believed that Siva and Parvati, irritated by the spectators, had retreated to this reverse conjugal point. And that the hum, still faintly to be felt in the popular cavern, was in fact coming *through* the mountain.

"I asked the horseman if the sāddhus all knew about this but he didn't think so.

"I set off by public bus for Srinagar. Returned three days later with some fresh supplies. It's a mere two-and-a-half-hour trip from here. I sought out the horseman and told him what I wanted to do. He refused to come. An avalanche had spilled over the trail leading up the steep canyon from Balta. Fortunately, I'd brought cross-country skis.

"I took the river, which was deep in snow. It took me ten hours to reach the notch where the trail turns up toward the snowfields under the big cave. The peak was intricate and I could not see how to get around to the backside. I put up a tent there. And left all my gear. I set off for a brief reconnaissance, managed to climb to the ridge, and was able to see why the cave was inaccessible. There was a miraculous amphitheater, closed in on all four sides. I was looking down 3,000 feet to a truncated glacier. Steep walls and alpine faces rose up. I saw no cave through the late afternoon clouds but fixed in my mind where it must be and then descended for the night.

"In the morning I moved my tent and supplies up to a flat section on the ridge. It was unprotected and probably 15,000 feet high. By noon I'd reclimbed the talus slope. The weather had cleared. With my binoculars I studied the face on the backside of the mountain. And there it was. As the shepherd had most likely also seen it from that ridge. A black hole. Curved shadow and rock wall, hanging over bergschrund a good thousand feet below. It was incredible. I studied the possibility of climbing to it.

"I took two ropes and many pitons, downclimbing over third class verglas. Within a few hours I was upon the glacier. I could see my tent blowing furiously up on the ridge. The glacier was old. No crevasses. And no wind! The snow was soft. This *valley*, of sorts, was dead silent. Completely protected from the weather. The four sides enclosed the space and the sun burned down. I was being watched."

"What?"

"I sloshed toward the cliff whose angle had slackened some thirty degrees from that perspective yielded on the ridge. I could only see the formation of a ledge high up on the face from down below. I got to the small bergschrund, bouldered it with great care and kicked steps up a snow chute leading to a deep chimney. It was wet, and long, but not vertical. Nor was it so difficult. I would never have soloed such a thing anywhere else. You know me, Michael. But as I said, I had this feeling about the place. As if I were the first person ever to be there. With a mountaineer's narcosis, I kept climbing. I was my own nerve ending, feeling, feeling so completely where I was. I was drenched. It was early afternoon. I didn't give a thought to downclimbing.

"And then a chockstone. My reveries ended. I stared at half my gear which I'd left on the outside of the schrund nearly a thousand feet down. I got sick. Fast. I had one rope which I had coiled tightly around my chest so as not to get tangled. And a few pins and slings. In that position there was no way to get out the rope. It was either downclimb unprotected or jam around the iced chock. I stood there, my knee wedged tenuously in the chimney. I made a fist and jammed it high in the crack. And then ascended by instinct. Mantling on to the low pebbly ledge which was dripping directly above. I was burning inside with innateness. Craving, insurrecting with a passion I had never known. As if my past had been sheared clean through and I was the result, a trajection of novelty, or renascence. I was alone. I closed my eyes, trying to think above the humming. It was loud! Like a generator in my brain putting out high voltage. I knew I could get down with the rope. And I opened my eyes.

"I was stunned! He was slouched naked, his mouth wide open, his body skeletal and blue. I was staring into the blazing eyes of a sāddhu. His fingers were poised in a mudra I'd never seen, his penis erect and bristling. His face was almost platinum. And his hair encircled his waist. There was deep lichen growing all around him, even between his toes. Mineral water trickling from the rock over his thighs. He was rupestrine. Behind him, sheer wall. It would have to be bolted. And above that, the small cave. I could not look in his face. I, too, was catching on fire. There was no ice on the ledge. And I felt a flowing, a warmth all around him. There was nothing to say. I was sure this sāddhu was dead, mineralized. Probably frozen years before in the posture of sāmadhi, the divine meditation. I was flustered, tried to touch his skin, then backed off. I began to cry, I think. It was too much. Turning back around, I hammered two pitons, fixed the rope to rap off over the chockstone, and stood up. The rope was attached through my rappel system and I started to move off the ledge when he spoke. I thought I'd die.

"In impeccable English he said unexcitedly, *You are leaving so soon?* And his whole face assumed a nearly comical mien. He was a child, an old man. And he began to smile. Then there was a hard silence. I could say nothing. We eyed one another. I was about to speak when he said, *Touch my penis!* I was faint. *Touch it!*

he commanded. I beseeched him, but his eyes were burning into me. My hands were cramped. I was terrified. My muscles quivering, the altitude, the exposure, his penetrating gaze. I stretched out my hand, undecided, in bewilderment, and suddenly, his mouth contorting viciously, he seized my arm. It was death itself. My body collapsed into numbness. Hot death. He pulled my arm towards him. He wanted me and my hand opened. Saliva came out of his mouth drenching his animal cock. Ten inches long it was. I was shaking, throbbing, I pleaded. But he jacked himself off using my hand. I wanted to leap off. His grip was iron. I couldn't move. The rappel was in place but I was frozen in his burning. And in less than a minute, my hand being forced urgently up and down, in the mechanical torch of his lust, he came. For over a minute he came, Michael! A liter of semen, like a jugular emission, spraying into the void, a rainbow of sticky seed. Never, I've never heard, seen, experienced anything like it. He was in ecstasy, unabashed delirium. Such an ejaculation was a physiological miracle. And during his come, all humming ceased. Only my groans of forced submission.

"I shook, dazed. I didn't know what to do. He let go. There was a silence between us. I sat there for a good hour. I knew what I, too, wanted. He had created the want. I took off my harness. And rolled down my pants to the ankles so as to be able to spread my legs. A mess of saliva in my mouth, I took his waiting hand and felt the source of his spirit rush into my genitals. I drooled onto myself and he slowly massaged me into the most amazing orgasm I've ever had. I can only describe it as heat, steam. It was something like death.

"I spent the night with him. And I remained warm. He said nothing. It snowed hard that night yet it was the most perfect bivouac of my life. There was warmth abundant. And a quiet I can't describe. Like being alone in the depth of the night, on a desert. He was a deity. Can you understand? There was such a stillness. All civilization, all knowledge. European history, calculus —*everything*, he possessed everything! And made that night a miracle for me. He never touched me again.

"In the morning the weather had cleared. The sāddhu knew I was leaving. And he wanted me to leave. What struck me was his English. It was absurd. It was perfect. It was the inflection of someone who'd been to Cambridge. Calm, brilliant, lighthearted. It was impossible. There! 1,000 feet up a cliff behind Amarnath! And it was real. I didn't know how to *clinch* my own breakthrough. To maximize it forever. I'd been traumatized sufficiently. I had tried to fling it off, to remain *me*. But he was the more powerful. And I fell into him as into a new mother, against her nipple, my rutted consciousness no longer *mine*. A secret, an easy domain had been opened to my ego. As if I'd been punctured and in a second had entered a new perspective, but so lofty, so transforming . . . how to explain?

"I peered up at the cave. *Śiva?* I asked. He nodded. *You have seen them? Only Śiva*, he said. *Never Parvati*. And then I had an idea. *How old are you?* And I had understood. He broke out laughing, good and hard. Hysterically. *Three hundred years old*, he cranked. And then I asked him where he had learned such English. And he in turn responded with a question, *Where had I learned to climb?* I could not penetrate the irony he was forcing. It was a radiance. A shield that was only accessible if I, too, let myself become vulnerable. I giggled. And he giggled and I felt the first urgings of an uncanny affection. And I was loved, completely, in return. We touched and he told me his name. I told him mine.

"I stood up to rappel and he looked softly at me. *You don't need the rope,* he shook his head happily. But I knew better. There was an awkward incapacity between us. And then he said, *A garden. Where the trident looks to the moon. Therein. Go to him.* His face flushed wide and for a sliver of eternity, in the wrinkle of his left eye, I saw the atavistic iris hover faintly. Ageless. The eye of a wild beast, untamed, undimmed.

"I rappelled off. The rope kept jamming up and I had to reclimb. And I wondered, as he said, if I really *did* need the rope.

"I got to the glacier and it was dark. But it was clear and I knew exactly where to go. By flickering starlight I trudged back through the fresh sparkling snow. And then up, all night, the 3,000 feet of shale. I was breathing hard but I was also warm. And just before sunrise I collapsed on the ridge into my sleeping bag, engulfed in a cold gale.

"Later in the morning I roused myself. I downclimbed the other side of the ridge in sunshine and skied the gorge, oblivious to the midmorning heat. I should have waited until the night to do it. I dodged slab avalanches all the way down, some of them hundreds of yards, powder clouds rising above the very mountains. But these avalanches became a game to me. Any one of them could have buried me. But I slipped through. And by the time I walked out the twelve miles into Sonamarg, I was laughing.

"I got back to Srinagar. Started searching for books. And found just a few references that were pertinent. That's when I wrote to you."

He showed us the references. There was an article written by a German in 1940 that dealt with *siddha ashrams*; a passage from an old and dusty British encyclopedia of ethics; and doubtful anecdotes in some books by Miguel Serrano.

"Serrano was the Chilean Ambassador to India for many years. He tried to get to Kailasha too late. The Chinese had already closed off the pilgrim route in 1962. You might know his work on Jung and Hesse?"

"No."

"He compiled letters between them, and now lives in Hesse's house in Montagnola. He advised me to visit Almora and sent me a copy of his book, inscribed 'from the Andes and Himalayas' but then we fell out of contact, when Allende was butchered." He caught his breath, then: "I think we are looking at some vast underground physiology, a sect, spanning innumerable centuries and cultures. Do you remember the Biblical Methuselah, in Genesis, said to have lived nine hundred sixty-nine years? And there were many others. In Ireland.

Norway. The Easter Islands. China. Serrano is a scholar, a serious man. He, too, seems to believe that the síddha ashrams exist. And don't you see. Think of it. These men have all been guessing where the secret monasteries might be, relying on data—religious, artistic, philosophical speculation. But we have directions. From a síddha himself. I mean you heard my story. The trident. Here. Look at the maps. The choices are limited. Leh, we'll go there leisurely, two days. Tenzing will drive. He's been twice. Leh is 10,400 feet in elevation. Good acclimation time. That's Kang Lacha. And it might very well be our mountain. My map shows it at 20,080 feet. I ran into some British climbers in Srinagar on their way out. They made the peak last year."

"What did you find out?" I was rising to his own clamoring heat.

"Well, no one called it a trident. Though the fellow I spoke with, Martin, said it sort of resembled a trident. Apparently the Hindus call many of their unnamed peaks Trident. It's after the three-pronged staff, representing the three forms of Siva. They said the approach was miraculous. Six easy hours from Leh through a secretive system of deep river chasms. All desert up there but for the lombardy poplars which cling to the loamy river beds. They put Camp I at 15,000 feet. Moved it up to 17,500 the following day, on a ridge at the foot of the East Face, and climbed it over the course of the next week, moving usually at night when the ice was hard. They rated it hard. A rockband at the top, after 2,500 feet of steep ice. No one else has ever climbed it apparently. The Indian military *did* climb Sasur Kangri a couple years ago. It's well north of Leh and the second highest peak in India. Another American group went up Mulkila 6 in Lahaul some time back. And you probably know of the many ascents on Nun and Kun. Italians. Japanese. French. Last summer an American. For a while I thought the ashram must be in the Zaskar Range. A Frenchman named Peissel's been back in there writing a book. It's near Nun-Kun. A week's trek behind the Tibetan-Pakistani town of Kargil, which is our first night on the way in.

"Ladakh you see just opened a year or so ago. The military had it all sealed before. And there were still reported skirmishes until just recently along the frontier with China. It's a very sensitive area. Tenzing says it is crawling with military vehicles. Most climbing is forbidden and many of the monasteries are off limits, but there is no way to check the overflow of tourists. Over a thousand camera flashers went to the dance festivals last June. It's desert. A Tibetan wild west. We'll talk to Tenzing. He says the place is overrun with westerners, tour groups, a boom town above timberline."

"So you think Kang Lacha-Stok Kangri is the peak? Right there above Leh? Then where's your monastery? It's probably playing host to Indian Greyhound throngs at this very minute!"

"It's worrisome. To a degree. Here's the catch. Just as the backside of Amarnath is enclosed in an impenetrable square of walls, I think the monastery is as well.

"This guy Martin was plenty sick. Just sitting there sort of dazed. Had the shits bad. And he warned me about the cholera out there. Apparently, after climbing Stok, they set off on a traverse the next day to an adjoining peak. Martin said it had to be a first, though they didn't complete it. Weather came in and the snow conditions deteriorated. They attained a niche on the peak and opted to give it up. This Martin belayed the rest down. And just as he himself was fixing to rappel off he caught a glimpse of the other side. And sunnofabitch if he didn't mention an incredibly closed in glacier, square-like, two miles straight down. Clouds came in, he descended to his friends, and never bothered mentioning it to anybody."

"Did he see a monastery?"

"No."

I remembered something. The magic square of the Esselen. We lived on it.

"The Indians who inhabited the Big Sur Coast evidently worshiped four points of a religious square formation in the landscape," I told Allain.

"I'm not surprised. There are myriad references to such a square. In the *Egyptian Book of the Dead* the universe was conceived as a square atop pillars, at the far edge of the desert. Though there's never any comment on the possibility of actually climbing those pillars. And along comes this book published in Calcutta about asceticism in ancient India. It mentions the ritual of *fasting in the form of a square* on the summit of Kailasha which is also said to be square shaped."

"It's strange, though. I would have felt the circle to be more spiritually intoxicating."

"Yes, but have you ever seen a mountain valley, an enclosure of granite walls, in the form of a circle? It doesn't happen in nature. The square is a refuge. And just as every town has a center, a village square, there is, I'm sure, such a place, exposed, in the geologic life of the Himalayas. A center."

CHAPTER NINE

We'd need chocolate, for Ghisela, who was as much addicted to her newly discovered Indian Milky Ways as was Allain hooked on his beloved Coca-Colas. And a spare jerry can. Some jeep tools. Cordage. Containers. White kodas, scarfs for giving to lamas. Five kilos of rice.

Tenzing, Ghisela and Allain took off for town. Allain left me his notebook to browse through. I lay in his bed, surrounded by manuscripts.

I slept, tossing for an hour. India had given me insomnia. I'd never experienced it before. But then this heat! I'd take six cold showers in the afternoons. How I looked forward to a glacial stream, to the blue vitriol insides of a crevasse. This transitory world of the houseboat. I needed a nerveblast, a puzzle. And it looked like I'd gotten one. A four-man expedition. A first ascent at 20,000 feet was attractive. Either by fear, or lack of charisma, I'd never been on a major climb. I'd been accepted for an American K2 expedition in 1973 but everything had collapsed that summer before when the leader and co-leader fell from the top of the north face of the Matterhorn, roped together. I'd climbed all over Europe and had spent nearly a decade on the cliffs and peaks of California and Colorado. And two past climbing trips to Asia. One with Ghisela and two guys from Lake Tahoe.

We made some interesting first ascents in Western Nepal over a period of two and a half months. And one morning, while ascending a scree slope, we all saw a creature on a distant ridge. We argued all night over what it might have been. Tall, dark, it stopped as we shouted hellos to it. It was motionless there on a sun-drenched rib of seracs—then ran off taking enormous leaps along the jumbled amassments of the ice fall, before vanishing over an edge. I preferred to think of it as a yak herder who wasn't right in the head. But yeti or no yeti, it left no tracks. And this we were never able to figure out.

I opened Allain's large notebook which, by now, had come to represent a sort of ledger-book of the arcane. Several doctoral theses in one.

There was much more material on Śiva and the seven Saivite sects. References from the *Śiva Skanda* and *Linga Puranas*, and the word *Digambara* meaning "skyclad." Unkempt hair, a body smeared in ash.

These yogin paid special veneration to the Natha, or serpent-guardian-spirits of the Himalayas, modeling their discipline after the eighty-four Siddhas, or "perfect ones" whose practice of yoga had taken them into a dimension of "non-practice." Some of them were said to be living still within the mountains. They disregarded caste, dress, drink, and they ate as they pleased. No abstinence whatsoever. They were said to have transcended time and all spatial limitations. Salmon-colored, henna and red arsenic paste adorning their long hair, their bodies, in a text known as the *Laws of Manu*, were described as the color of lightning, tawny.

Allain had juxtaposed some quotations from Colin Turnbull's *The Mountain People* to emphasize the intrinsic relationship between these ascetics and their mountain *destinies*.

"The Ik, without their mountains, would no longer be the Ik, and similarly they say, the mountains, without the Ik would no longer be the same mountains, if indeed they continued to exist at all."

An astonishing diversity of notions and eras had been subsumed in this fever to unravel a mountain vision. A rage characteristic of Balladeur's style and tempo. When he did something, he did it completely. The ascetic's role in all this seemed diametrically opposed to my own Apollonian-Dionysian enamorment. The Greeks never allowed themselves the luxury, the intonation of the immortality metaphor. Take Paeonius's "Floating Victory," the metope, even the pediments of the Temple of Zeus, at Olympia, the works of Praxiteles, and the bronze women: Aphrodite of Cyrene, of Cnidus, the Venus de Milo—glowing motionlessness, a sovereign immunity to the other world figured in serene metal. The poise itself might be interpreted as eternal, but only to the aesthetic imagination. There was no catechism of heaven, no prescriptions for escape. Nothing that even intimated of some other, higher reality. No desire whatsoever to leave *this* world, with its laurel-scented shepherdesses and olive oil and open air. And its islands in the blue sea. There was the splendor implicit in the "David" that permeated the Greek vision of mortality.

These ascetics on the other hand were waiting spectres hanging heavily over their own transfigurations. Yet the idea of their mountain-center, a sort of British Museum reading room of nature, was appealing.

Nikos Kazantzakis had said at the beginning of his autobiography, *Report To Greco*, that "ascent" was the most important word in his life. He had climbed Mt. Sinai, had lived at Mount Athos, and had fashioned, from the Nietszchean prototype, an Odysseus who would sail alone—sāddhu-like—to the Antarctic, live with island denizens for a winter, then set off on a fated journey to a towering iceberg, seal hatchet in hand, and climb the overhanging wall from out of the polar sea. The sun would consume his old, but vigorous body. A marionette of fiction, in transcendental wriggling. One of Allain's *semi-symbols*.

I took the notebook and went up to the rooftop. There was an umbrella to keep out the intense afternoon sun. I sat back on a bamboo deck chair, propped up my feet and settled into a relaxed few hours gazing out over the rippling lotus-infested waters. The life of Dal Lake was intriguing. Metaphysical laziness. Oars slipping through the ancient liquid. A word spoken, or giggled, or chewed up in a moment's anger over centuries. The same daily tasks, the same love affairs under infinite moons, and the resonant incense of Himalayan India. The Muslim women wore polka-dot pajamas. Squatting in their open shikaras, slapping worn articles of clothing, rubbing them with soapstone in the same water that their community drank, and had shitted in for a thousand years. The men were bare-backed, with their gangly sons, out hustling in the markets, predacious, selling nuts, black bananas, cloth, trinkets. Or in the marshes dredging up roof insulation. And there was a class of wealthy Kashmiri, some Hindu, some Muslim. The businessmen who owned the rug factories, the embroidery shops, the walnut packaging houses and antique stores. Men who knew only business and could cite Gumps, Bloomingdale's, and half a dozen stores on Bond Street as customers.

In the ninth month of Ramadan, these same men would take their food and drink only in darkness. They were fanatical Muslims, would never touch alcohol. And the Hindus were equally conservative, pro-Gandhian. They had immense families. A process that was commenced painfully early in a boy's life. There were grandfathers thrice over still out in the streets kicking rabid dogs. But these Hindus and Moslems seemed to get along marvelously, despite the greater Indian-Pakistani rivalries. Kashmir had always been the favored retreat of Kings. It was called *paradise on earth*. And the modern-day inhabitants recognized that communal heritage. So had the British, who built their large Victorian manors on islands in the lagoons, and a ski resort at Gulmarg south of Srinagar.

I looked out at the old fortress above the commercial district, and to the tenderly cared for rose gardens of the Shalimar. Acres of hanging garlands, a Babylon of lilies, against the blue steeps of fir tree and deodar. And along the 12,000-foot-high mountain crests, snow and rock walls. Kashmir was a sacred square in its own right, and said to be the birthplace of humanity in early nineteenth century British literature.

My directions were utterly disoriented. We were near China. K2. Nanga Parbat. Even a corner of Russia. And only fifty or so miles from Pakistan. But I was lost, in the soft, compassless enclosure of mountains.

I waded through Allain's notes on asceticism. He'd computed motifs in both the Eastern and Western traditions that promulged a meditation in which the medium was the body. *Vocational asceticism* involved the landscape. Aaron, David, Elijah, Paul, Muhammad, Buddha, and Moses were all called into the wilderness. Similarly, Mt. Su-Meru, Kailasha, had its attractive counterparts, summits which compelled pilgrims: Adam's Peak in Sri Lanka, the four mountain shrines of Omishan in Japan, and Mount Colzim at the eastern end of the mountain chain known as Gebel-el-Galaza, adjoining the Red Sea. It was there that Anthony drew the graphic parallel between material ascent and spiritual elevation. And it was this tradition which drew St. John Climacus to Mount Sinai.

Allain had secured photographs of numerous cliff monasteries from throughout the Sinai Peninsula, from Thessalonike and the Pyrenees, from Chile, Switzerland, Bhutan and the Urals. Taktsang Monastery above Paro, Bhutan, was certainly the most austere and magnificent of these, hanging in the mid center of a sheer 2,000-foot granite wall; St. John, the seventh-century Abbot of St. Catherine's Monastery beneath Mount Sinai, had adopted the most literal of ascetical-mountaineering lifestyles. His book *The Heavenly Ladder* outlined the discipline of attaining not Christian Heaven so much as the heights in general. By the ninth century, copies of this enchiridion manual existed in Greek, Arabic, Russian and Spanish. The Spanish edition, *Escala Spiritual de San Juan Climaco,* was translated into English in the mid-nineteenth century, and was one of the first books printed in North America. St. John apparently spent some forty years writing, praying and climbing. To ascend Mount Sinai, he said, was to ascend to heaven. An icon, painted by a disciple at St. Catherine's Monastery, depicts St. John guiding his fellow monks up a thirty-rung ladder. Those who lose their grip plunge into a mire inhabited by devils.

A Princeton Codex, dated 1081, provides a series of illuminations which Allain had xeroxed and attached to his notebook. One in particular revealed a cave, high on Sinai. A weary monk was lowering a rope down from his aerial habitation to obtain food from his friends. This image of being isolated *on high* was characteristic of the early pillar cults.

The famous Symeon Stylites had chained himself atop a column forty cubits high for thirty-seven years. He was considered *the most holy martyr in the air* and when at last he died, hundreds of fellow saints, all enclosed in suspended cages, sitting on elevated pylons, standing on erect pillars, paid tribute to their master.

Allain cited similar cults which the Paleo-Tibetologist Wojkowitz had un-covered in his study of the iconography of Tibetan protective deities.

I was intrigued by the obsessive references, the runic mysteries. I could easily see the relationship to Himalayan mountain climbing, to Allain's experience at Amarnath. But I didn't care. I did not want to think about climbing. Only to climb. And I was certainly not enamored of these ascetics. Saints always seemed to me to be the anemic misfits who snickered in the shadows of their cloisters. I could not believe that the history of the Church, Vatican bureaucracy, or the Talmud, for that matter, could have anything to do with mountains. Granted, Moses hiked up a mountain to receive the Ten Commandments. But as I re-called Charlton Heston's portrayal, Moses was no religious figure, but a muscular hedonist victimized by a wrathful god.

CHAPTER TEN

By six a.m. we were lifting our packs into shikaras, then the land-rover. In India, it is good manners, good survival tactic, to honk at all other vehicles. Parents have been known to throw infants into the way of a passing car. The maimed child thereby solicits greater empathy in its capacity as beggar. A remote road takes on a city's cacophany. A mountain Forty-second Street. We forged eastward through Kashmiri outback. Dense tropics. People in banana cluster densities. Children guiding water buffalos with staves through banyan. Wide bouldery riverbeds. High deodar trees. A brown and bloodied mongoose flattened on the side of the road, its bellicose jaw grimacing Guernica-like. Old wobbly diesel buses loaded beyond capacity, men hanging out the sides, engines groaning up hills, then roaring out of control down rutted gravel steeps.

We were quickly surrounded by high mountains. We passed farm communities with large communal threshing houses. The road had suddenly deteriorated after the last village into a narrow obstacle course. Crews of loin-clothed migrants were chopping the limestones to even out the muddied furrows. Down below flowed a tumultuous river, milky white, which I knew to be glacial runoff. We had gone up to 9,000 feet and suddenly, rearing majestically behind two high sequestered slopes of pine, brilliant for just an instant, I caught sight of a hanging glacier.

We drove through the village of Sonamarg, a single dirt road cleaving rows of tents, a guesthouse and several dilapidated tea and cracker stalls. Off in the distance against the northern slope of the Sind Valley was nestled another enclave of thatched roofs and scaffolding, terraced plots and cascades. Nearly tropical. And above, the glaciers. Six lateral ice fields, topped by rock walls, 16,000-foot-high arêtes and leaning pinnacles. We went through the first military checkpost on the edge of town. Tenzing hopped out with our passports. One official eyed us carefully and then the crude pole was lifted by a manila rope pulley system from the road. From here we started up the Zoji-la, an 11,000-foot pass which looked down on Balta.

"That's the gorge I skied. And at the top, out of view, the snow fields leading to Amarnath," Allain narrated. We looked down into the clouds which hovered there. We were above them now, skirting the tenuous edge of rockwall. It was rugged terrain alright. There were immense avalanche chutes and dangerously steep slopes of mud and talus. The river of the gorge had begun to show through. Huge seracs, like icebergs, had ruptured into perfect rectangles and were hanging pell-mell over snow bridges. Remains of wide runaway slope scarred the chunky sides where ice had accumulated one hundred feet high in places.

The road narrowed. We traveled ten kilometers an hour up the spectacular path still thawing from a snow-gutted spring. There was a dead horse, frozen and scattered in a bleached medley of thick bone. The scene was truly Oriental in the way elongated mists clung to the thinning trees, embroiling both sides of the converging gorge. Above us, more glaciers and granite skylines. At one point we had to get out and lay rocks across a section of deep slush. Heaving, the wheels burning into the bottom mud, the land-rover spun out over the alluvium and Tenzing, laughing, a mere two feet from the unrimmed edge of a 2,000-foot plunge, expertly swung the vehicle steady, racing into the cleared section above. We passed the great ice pinnacle, Machoi, leaving the Kashmiri side of the pass. Above us, across a grassy slope, a dozen vultures were picking off a shepherd's youngest sheep, curled talons pincing the soft napes into the air and flying off, great guttural groans of satisfaction disappearing in the mountains. The poor lad was crying, chasing his flock downhill. But the vultures were crafty, staying fast to the animals, eyes on the choicest victuals.

Below, to the east, lay the Tibetan Plateau, *byang thang*. A high altitude desert extending clear to Mongolia. We descended 1,000 feet, wending laboriously around sharp turn after turn through high meadows, cultivated between sand, surrounded by the grey world of rock and wind. Shards of boulders, fractured convulsively in forces of ongoing creation, lay in shambled, austere wrecks about the freezing turf.

There was little humidity up here. We reached the dismal town of Dras in mid-afternoon. There were some Chinese faces. Numerous military caravans gassing up.

"We must hurry to stay ahead of the convoys. They have the right-of-way," Tenzing exhorted, his right hand gripping the violently shaking gear shift with youthful ardor. As we sped off, I counted, plastered on the white adobe barracks, notices of reward for reporting cases of smallpox. This was not only considered one of the coldest towns in the world, but about the last spot on earth where that disease had not been contained. And I was to witness its workings in the badly pockmarked faces of many men and women in Leh.

We moved on the first straightaway that day, through a narrow canyon. The sun was setting and poplars were ablaze in a dusty splendor where a small clump of life—perhaps a dozen hamlets—stretched peacefully in their inaccessibility along the gorge bottom.

Shaken from the bumps all day, and car sick from the smell of gas escaping somewhere, we reached Kargil, a large town of several thousand. Faces from everywhere—Nurhistan, Burma, China—timeless welted expressions, glowing eyes. Suffusions of lame creatures, with cataracts, maimed legs; a dog, dying unobserved in the street, a pink bloodied bone protruding from its ruptured back, a young baby throwing stones at the tortured animal. And the baby not looking too good himself.

Hard-working Muslims. And the first apparition of the Tibetan Buddhist world. Kargil was at the crossroads of Pahari (Indo-Aryan-speaking Hindus), Bhotiya (Tibetan-speaking Buddhists of the higher altitudes), and Moslems. A hangout for nomads from throughout Central Asia. We drove up to the government guesthouse in darkness. A mob. Two busloads of high school girls with their armed escorts were staying there that night. No more room. In the turn-out, we were greeted by five young hippies from Luxembourg cooking dinner on camping stoves in their open van. Pidogs were snooping around the garbage which was strewn lavishly about the place. Tenzing knew of another spot. We drove back into town, to the river embankment. It was grassy and though scattered with multi-species' turds (a fact of life in India) it proved far more appetizing.

It was a clear, cold evening. We were 9,500 feet high. What a delectation after sweltering Srinagar. There was far-off singing across the rushing river in Pakistan. We opened dried stroganoff, from Ski Hut in Berkeley. The first of our provisions. Sizzling the delicacy in pots over MSR stoves. Two small boys wandering home along the river watched us from a short distance. The starlight was luminous.

I felt snug in a time warp. Like some Asian farmer 10,000 years ago with his village friends. There was nothing to do. I looked at Ghisela: bountiful pulchritude embosomed in a $300 sleeping bag. Balladeur and I shared looks glaring across the years between us. I'd once felt close. Now I was unsure. But I felt close enough. Was it ironic that a man bred so completely on European luxury and richness of experience should immerse himself in the lore of ascetic annals? I didn't know. But it was safer than fast cars, and cleaner than that flat he kept in New York. How strange this man was. Bored with riches. Tragic family life. His real mother had sent him away to private Catholic schools in the beginning. His only true friends were the Jesuit fathers who taught him his Latin and mediaeval geography. He'd been married once, to a lion trainer from Uganda—Peggy, of Dutch lineage. Bizarre's the word. But then that was Allain.

Allain had sired no offspring.

The early morning struck the anvil desert beyond Kargil like an orange hammer. Resplendent cloud. A warm wind. A loom of silky light discovering each rock, remarking upon each distant, unreal peak of snow and sand. The whole plateau, beckoning barrenness, was on fire before us. Somewhere behind: the Zaskar Range, Ringdom Monastery and Nun-Kun.

We cleared camp. Tenzing had already been to market to purchase fresh eggs that we fried. We doused ourselves in the icy water. The real journey was just beginning.

Through another checkpost and we were gone, into a white Asian Hoggar. The road was now paved, as we passed by two unnamed giants, tridents of ice, and by ten a.m. had come into the poor village of Mulbeck surrounded by prayer flags.

"It's Buddhist," Allain marked. "And look!" Across the arid wasteland, on the side of a snowbound precipice rested a cliff monastery. Painted brilliantly white, like a Greek Oracle on Olympus. Hanging in a line with the sheer sun. Ghisela had the binoculars.

There was a rope, and cutout footsteps descending from a crest above. And higher, split spectacularly against the wind-battered expanse of hard blue, an 18,000-foot section of ice. Part of the Zaskar. Horizontal strata, basalt, eerie. Some villagers were coming down the road. Dressed in long woolen coats. Painted goatskin boots. And crazy hats.

"Peiraks," Tenzing called them.

"Jeelai, jeelai," two middle-aged women cheered as they ambled by offering succulent cherries from the paper sacks they were carrying. The prayer flags were tattered red, yellow, white and purple, with Tibetan printed roughly on them.

At the edge of town we stopped before a ninety-foot statue carved in rock. It was the Maitriya, future Buddha. The ninth incarnation of the historical Gautama.

The second pass commenced from Mulbeck. Up the Namki-la, 13,500 feet, where we were well above the snowline. It was an awesome seclusion. Bitter silence. On the exposed sand dunes of a mesa, the grinding land-rover crawled on. Buffeted, leaning into the gusts, their faces red in the freezing air, two old men, rosaries in their hands, shoes worn through, in rent layers of washed-out habiliment, stood motionless along the winding road, holding their beads, their wizened faces emitting faint smiles at the passing phantom of ourselves. The wind flung tatters of their raiment into their faces, and like animals, their heads slowly turned with the upwards meandering of our vehicle. There was no hamlet, no tent in sight, anywhere on the horizon. Only the spiraling declivities of ice and steep desolation.

Their youngsters shiver compulsively from habitual cold and chilblains; the women are beautiful but sickly, their Pashmina goats skinny and agile, cowled fleece which belies mange. These goats, these yaks, and vague herdsmen come and go. During migrations in Bhutan, throughout the Hindu Kush. And without much belaboring of basics they live on, propagate, and vanish.

I had a tendency to thrill before such thoughts; to see the flickering candle leap before blacking out and know it to be our life, the life which is so ignored, which swells magnificently on the Asian steppes, where the light and the wind brace so comfortably the human spirit.

We descended into a Cappadocian-like fortification of caves and mudflats and barley fields, then back up the side of the third and wildest of the three passes, the Fatu-la.

On the back side of it, we had our first real glimpse of the Ladakh Range and of one of the oldest monasteries in Southwestern Tibet. Lamayuru. A pedestal of ugly sacredness. Mute in the morass of tired silence. White chortens (pronounced chod-rten in Tibetan) in row after row of adobe commemoration, fanned out over the salty cliffs upon which hung the massive grey tenement. The chortens contain the ashes of select lamas. Deep down in the ravine under the cliff monastery were cultivated fields. As wild and unlikely an apparition as the timeless mountains themselves. With binoculars, we could see red-robed monks on their hands and knees tilling the soil with their slow fingers. Tenzing informed us that there were some one hundred monks living here. It was a ghastly place. Frightening from up on the intruding road where a few old toothless ex-monks (I supposed) were pawning fake gold amulets and prayer articles. Seeing our stopped party, one old guy came huffing up the loose trail, ten minutes of urgency in the cold air, to try and sell us twenty cents worth of butter. He was barefoot, with pearl earrings and grey hair cropped short. His teeth were chattering. He was begging, with dignity. Clouds were moving in behind the ridge over the monastery. We had a long way to go. I gave him a rupee and took the butter.

The descent from Lamayuru was dangerous. An engineering feat. The road turned back on itself perhaps thirty times. Without embankments. Sand and stone kept sliding down. The road had just opened for the summer and would close again in early November. After that, if one were still around, there would be no way out. The Indian Military maintained an emergency airstrip in Leh but it was unsafe and for top-dogs only.* We saw the strewn remains of an aircraft that had crashed in the early 60s on a far slope.

*In 1979 the Leh airstrip was opened to twice-weekly Indian Airways commercial flights out of Sringar, thus insuring ever more tourism and the erosion of Ladakhi culture.

At the bottom we met the Indus River swiftly flowing in a gorge which we drove along into the village of Saspool. Adjoining it, an hour's trek through the desert, were two very old monasteries, Likkhir and Alchi. The village was all Buddhist. No military in sight. And it was here that I got my first real look at the Tibetan women. We stopped for tea and I appreciated the usefulness of Tenzing's Tibetan. We were invited into a farmhouse to warm up and chat. On the bottom floor yaks and goats fed from a hay pile. Up a thick carved-out log ladder into a small courtyard, we were greeted by the father of a large family. His wife and mother were boiling cauldrons of chang (Tibetan beer) in the dark interior. We entered. What struck me were the woman's necklaces of coral and turquoise and their equipoise. We received drinks in old stone mugs. Allain was admiring a thangka on the wall. The father shook his finger.

"He says not for sale," Tenzing admonished him. There had been hordes of tourists through here last summer. No doubt we were some of the first this season. In another month we'd never have been invited up. A naked baby was playing with the tie string of Allain's parka. Snot drooled from its nose.

"Tenzing, isn't the baby cold?" asked Ghisela. The mother shook her head, humored by her concern. Ghisela took up the baby in her arms and sang to it. The Tibetan women were delighted. The mother left the room and came back with a very old piece of green Chinese turquoise, in a polished brass setting, for Ghisela.

Overcome, she gave them everything on her person in return. Amazing, Levi-Straussian, how distance separating people decreases at the juncture of gift giving.

"How long have they lived here?" Ghisela asked.

A brief interchange, then, "Since always."

Ghisela and the youngest of the Tibetan women were fixed in a reciprocal grin. "She's beautiful!" The women chirped, then posed a query through Tenzing.

"They asked if you are married?"

"Tell them no. But I live with my man. Maybe marry later."

This elicited nods of approval.

"They ask if you have children."

"Tell them soon," she said.

"Tell them *after* soon," said I.

This brought forth guffaws. I encircled Ghisela with my arms. She tended light lip nudges along the veins in my forearms.

We all drank Tibetan beer until there was creeping irrationality in the heavy smoke-entrenched space around me.

"Is there sex before marriage in Saspool?" Ghisela asked, reclining comfortably.

Unabashed, they exuberantly nodded. Affirmative. "Definitely so," said Tenzing. "Every place in Tibet, loving good thing!"

"I think they're more attuned than women in the West," Ghisela went on.

"How so?" I asked.

"Look at their certainty about themselves."

"Certainty?"

"Don't you recognize how adjusted they seem to be?"

Allain, "You mean natural in their environment?"

"Yes," she continued.

"What's natural?" I said.

"Don't go getting philosophical. Look at their hair, the eyes, the narrative brow. They're fantastic!"

I stared fleetingly, surveying the household. A pang shot through me. Ghisela picked up on it. I wanted something that these Tibetans had. In all their ephemerality, they seemed to be *complete*, whereas I was wandering the planet, incomplete.

"They do look good," I said. They looked better than good.

It was late. We descended the log and headed for the land-rover. Suddenly, several children accosted us, hurtling their dark, scrawny bodies up the dirt road after us, a dozen mutts in hot pursuit.

"Chewing gum, chewing gum!" they shouted, clapping their hands. Allain did the honors. Their mouths were going a mile a minute as they ran off, consummated in their well-learned exchange with westerners.

We passed the strange cliff-dwellings of Nimu by a pink sunset, went up the Nimu-la, and entered a straightaway. Thirty fast-going kilometers through a desert at 12,000 feet; with the high snowy Ladakh Range, magenta in the waning sun, directly before us, we'd come four hundred kilometers from Srinagar.

We overtook a small military convoy, Allain now driving exuberantly, passing a dirt road-head that went up to Phyang Monastery whose walls and gardens we could barely make out high up in the vortex of three peaks. We descended through the desolate military complex on the outskirts of Leh.

Nightfall had come, and with it the most brilliant display of galaxies I had ever seen. The sprawling town was set back against an amphitheater of snow-glittering ridges. In the blue darkness, rearing high above the rippling eddies of the Indus River, we made out the faint, ghostly image of our mountain.

The Dalai Lama had built his summer residence across the river some six kilometers east of town. Tenzing knew of a fine spot not far from it, adjoining a Buddhist orphanage. We parked the land-rover up on the road, unboarded the night's essentials, and made for the grassy stream edge, down a sandy embankment.

That evening, as I lay dozing beneath firmament, fingers nestled lightly about Ghisela, my thoughts were troubled by the ease of our entry into Ladakh. A road. Before 1962, the only way in was by foot, ski, or caravan. We had been cheated out of a special need. Mankind was laying such roads across the last acres of wilderness, accelerating the pace of extinction for land and animals. Why, *why*? Greed? Fear? Certainly not out of love for anything. The artist, the visionary, the sensitive recluse in our society was falling back, further and further afield, like the Naga, as technocracies continued to usurp. People who had any conscience at all were on the run, digging trenches. And before 1962, Ladakh had been one of the places to make for.

I lay under the stars, weak, unavoidably stymied, in all my misgivings. A mere tourist.

"What are you thinking?" Ghisela whispered.

"We don't belong here."

"Huh?"

"We're out of rhythm. We're exploiting, somehow."

"That's what I meant about those women," she said, turning over, propping herself up on her elbows so that her cross-eyed breasts hung pendacled outside her blue quilted sleeping bag. "*They* belong here. We don't belong *anywhere*."

"You feel too much."

"And you *think* too much."

"Any remedies for two space cases?"

"You haven't made love with me in days. Why?"

"Tired."

"No."

"Alright, I just don't want to."

Pause. "What's wrong?"

"Apprehensive."

"About?"

"I need to know, what's natural. I mean, what *is* it?"

"What is *what?*" she asked.

"How do you define nature?" I went on.

"Why are you changing the subject? I'm asking why we haven't made love and you're getting philosophical."

"First give me your definition of nature, then we'll make love, then I want to know what the hell's wrong with being goddammed philosophical, serious, anti-comical."

"Right. Nature." She pondered with that Plato-holding-the-bust-of-Aristotle look. "That which flows, is process, unimpeded, free to grow."

"Hmm."

"Well, what do you think."

"They say there used to be ten million Tibetans in the Middle Ages. They apparently deforested the whole plateau for firewood. Now the population's down to just over a million. The balance would appear illusive."

"We're able to love, as a species," she said. "And when we do, we're in balance with Nature."

I stared vacantly...frugal, sacred. Perhaps this was only entropy at work. A last ditch stabilization of culture.....Because of an unusually short growing season, the Tibetan society had been kept from the awkward growth occasioned in the West. Was this merely luck, or true totemic, deep ecology? I wondered...

The Tibetans had their own indigenous constraints—heart disease, stomach carcinoma—but they compensated these distractions with added bone marrow, enlarged lungs, a lower shivering threshold (a naked Caucasian begins to shiver at 80.6°F). Because of an unusually short growing season, the Tibetan society had been kept from the awkward growth occasioned in the West. As a result, his culture conversed fluently with its environment. If the stunted birth rates of the seventeenth-century Spanish conquistadors at Potosi, Peru, are reliable indicators, it will be many decades before the Chinese communists incur the true assimilation of Tibet they're after (it took fifty-three years for a Spanish infant to be born in highland Peru, and no imported livestock survived there).

If in fact the *selfish mind* in the West had haplessly, rationally, tragically, replaced environment with culture, and falsely augmented the carrying capacity of exploited ecosystems with technology, what then? *Pejoristic thinking* was a start; the recognition that this earth was perfect to begin with in its scintillating prolixity; beauty that was no accident. And which commended our preventing its greedy dissolution over our erratic evangelical callings to improve upon it. Following such disabuse, one fought cunningly, swiftly, to defend the zoösphere, to begin at grass-self, and work intimately with people, to prepare a good heart, as the Hopis say.

Platitudes, I feared. I was, after all, doing nothing; repeating adages, exercising my mind. The subject was too large to tackle.

"We have hands. So we're materialists," Ghisela jarred me.

"Is there no moderation?"

She was a hard woman: "You've got to get beyond this rugged individualism crap of yours. *That's* the terror in Romanticism, Ecology, Democracy. That Aristotle and Jefferson could justify the keeping of slaves."

"One trigger-happy fool at NORAD will serve that function."

"No alternatives?" I gloomed.

"I do believe that ecologists are impotent!" Ghisela harassed.

I went deep, fathoms into her. We clamored for air in the thin heights of the desert plateau.

It was good. She came quietly. And cried.

That night I had a dream. It was one of those sleeping apparitions which tries so hard to convey clarity and falls frustratingly short of the mark. I woke up and by candlelight noted the dream in my journal:

The body refuses to let go, waywardly continuing in its course towards the top.

Like a maddened dog, with a thorn in its behind, dashing, stopping to lick, lunging forward again, I race from the congested ice couloir back to my tent, breathing like a man who has just declared bankruptcy to his adoring daughters. Staring at some facsimile reproduction of a map that traces Balboa's journeys, in the only book I have brought along.

Slight traffic out-of-doors, alpine crows in the flowery boulevards below. Cherry blossoms scenting the springtime breeze up from the approach march in. Nothing, nothing that needs to be done or remembered. A bitter blue sky overhead. A meal, for which I have dreamt all day. A pulse rate twice its normal speed. I fix all my attention on a single cloud, a snow plume, gazing dumbly for an hour until it is no more.

Standing immobilized on the steps of a trolley car, or in a phone booth near the headquarters of a Trotsky sect chewing licorice stick, thumbing absentmindedly through a Paris directory.

Until purposeless days mounting one atop the other have ended abruptly. The skin of my fingers has shriveled. The chest is tighter. My face has taken on a bluish, dark appeal. Staring down into the mirroring sunglasses. Or across a hundred miles of unrecognizable glare. In both instances, the same horizon-worth of confusion, other dim hopes, a variety of names and stubborn fears. The ineffectual belaboring of rationale, now lost, for starting anew. This tedious omniscience, that there is no other choice. In the flurry of snow that has nearly eaten me away with boredom. Choice? But to go down all over again. From the summit? A cairn in the wind. As empty an emblem as the old moraines beneath so much solitary labor. And in the shadows, under some loose stones in the frost, an image of Olga Korbut twitching upside down.

Last details to subsume, along with cream to keep the face from breaking. No glories to mention. As if everything had been vacuumed up in the unfruitful scuttle for more air. The somber or jubilant halo-worth of ideas scattered in the fresh snow. The arc of sky rendered intolerably wide by the expenditure required even to look up at it while breathing.

A dismal rattling. Inescapable aches and drives. Retreat an even greater burden to think about. For the legs, overwrought to begin with, to ponder.

A bus ride out of there. Bernard Berenson discussing the universal applicability of Sanskrit. A baby pees on the floor beside me. Fortunately I am wearing Swiss double-boots. Pushing the infant away with a muddied ice ax. Long hours back to where I came from. Hardly aware anymore of having done something in the rain and the snow for six onerous days. The first ascent of a big mountain, rarely visible, whose name the bundled shepherds and glacier beggars eking miserable sustenance beneath it insist has absolutely no meaning.

CHAPTER ELEVEN

It was immense. A revelation in our face. Oddly pyramidal. Deep white, with a windy snowplume glancing off its summit pyramid. Striped in the gold and lavendar of dawn. The mountain.

I had my directions and knew that we were looking at the East Face which had been climbed. Its ridge was spectacularly long, heavily corniced and marked by a spasm of sheer ice at the top. We studied the vast cirque, tracing in our own minds the route previously forged. It was more intimidating than any of us had conceived. And the approach, that supposed six-hour jaunt, was nowhere to be seen. Only hard steep desert, ugly grey gorges of frozen dirt, before which, emblazoned in stone and fields of maize, lay the imperial village of Stok.

We boiled water for tea, made freeze-dried bacon chips and eggs, set up the two tents, carried our sleeping bags to the vehicle and sped off to Leh. We'd decided to spend three days relaxing, visiting monasteries and acclimatizing before we started up. And Allain, with his Sanskrit, and Tenzing with his Tibetan, hoped to get all the information they could regarding the back of the mountain.

We drove into the crowded town past a long series of chortens, all of them encircled by engraved *mani* stones. The villagers carve these prayers in memory of their own particular lamas. Leh was on the ancient caravan route to Yarkand and Lhasa.*

We parked the rover and hiked through town to the Potala (seven-tiered) Palace, not to be confused with the Royal Palace in Stok. This monastery sat high on an eroded slope. Monstrous adobe walls grew out of dusty, dalmation granite. It was closed up, the thick teak torsi entrance swathed in rancid prayer flags, the wooden beams decomposing and bolted. A trail circumvented the square-block fortress, leading upwards to another imposing religious battlement, a high tower half-sunk in the sandy incline. We climbed behind it, to the top of the 12,000-foot peak from which our view of the Trident was unobstructed. The Indus Valley spread out in three directions, yielding a view of adamantine desert embracing exiguous cultivated fields. The Ladakhis eat baked barley flour (sattu), wheat cakes, turnip-pea broth, numerous summer vegetables, and occasional fruits—apples, cherries, grapes and delicious apricots. They are rigorous and healthy, beset with no obvious maladies.

The eye of a cyclone, a rose in the dust bowl, Leh was swelling with buttercups and columbine, bold summer witness to a natural balance between heaven and hell. The centuries-old erosive furiousness of the land is everywhere conspiring around the village to engulf it. Still the community thrives, teeming with the animated, if weathered, residue—families and their animals. And it is apparent by this arid gallery of human expression and by the thickness of their garb, that the winters must be exacting.

The sun was blistering against the fierce talus which stretched endlessly beyond the Indus. Flies were squirming irritatingly on my arms, nourished by an unrelenting stench of excrement in the air. I was breathing pretty hard. Feeling the altitude. In all the monochromatic space of the desert, my eyes floundered, searching to seize upon form, structure which might appease their restlessness. Only the Trident offered resolution. Blazing nearly two miles above and across the broad valley.

The tower we'd climbed to was a monastery known as Tsumo. It looked like a lighthouse, a beacon for some Himalayan Agamemnon. It, too, was locked up that morning.

"A shame," sighed Tenzing. "The largest Tibetan Buddha is in there!"

*Borax, jade, velvet, silk, wool, silver, gold and coral were exchanged from the north for opium, plumes, pepper, pearls, honey and tobacco in the south. In the 1830s the Maharaja of Jammu annexed all of Kashmir, including Ladakh, and Alexander Cunningham went in shortly thereafter for a year, subsequently publishing a comprehensive study of the area which is still considered the definitive text. The early exploratory history of Ladakh, and its immediate environs, is the history of England's presence in India, and her efforts to balance power with the Russians. It is a record of conundrums, ill-fated adventures, and strange heroism.

Allain was off climbing the brick side of a wall towards a small nook still partially exposed beneath a corrugated aluminum sheet.

We all buildered the thirty feet to the perch after him, up the tower. Tenzing
climbed effortlessly. One at a time we were able to move our heads under the
aluminum and stare directly across at the serene eyes of Buddha, sixty feet high,
sitting peacefully in his dark sanctuary.

"I don't like that guy's look," Ghisela confessed.

We descended the loose scree slope into town. Ghisela was eager to go
shopping for a thick Tibetan yak-wool sweater, while Allain and Tenzing were
off to another monastery behind town known as Shankar Gumpa. We were all
to meet up by late afternoon at the land-rover. I was mostly interested in being
alone with my camera.

I went into the heart of the village. To where all the women were sitting. Some
were still coming up the road for their day of bartering. An old woman with
pointed felt boots, carrying a bucket in hand, a staff in the other. Trundling on
her back a tremendous load of grass, a precious commodity in this desert, which
she would probably trade for cooking oil or talcum powder. She was arched,
permanently I imagined, down to half her normal stature. Her face was as
wrinkled as the velvet dress she wore. A mop of dust around her approach. Blue
eyes, an ancient goddess.

Throughout Tibet—and to a remarkable degree among the Lepcha of Sik-
kim—sexuality is a free and easy pastime. Tibetan women are engaged in frater-
nal polygynandry, usually managing a family of several husbands who are
generally brothers. The exception to this is called the *magpa system* which takes
effect when no son exists to inherit land. Then a likely son-in-law is sought by
the father to marry his eldest daughter, taking the daughter's family name and
taking all the girl's sisters as wives as well. Divorce is an easy matter. One simply
walks out of the house and never returns to it.

The woman is autonomous, riding stalwart and nobly in her lamé yak saddle.
In charge. She chooses her mates. If she is homely, she feigns conversion to
Islam, becoming polygamous and conjoining with many other women to a
single male. Either way she gets what she needs.

Goatskins and tallit-like embroidered shawls fanning out in white-haired
dangling trails behind them, long brown or black velvet dresses dragging in the
dirt, the women were strolling alone and in large groups giggling. Their teeth
were white, straight. Two thick black braids entwined in colored silk extended
characteristically beneath their carousing waists. Around their necks dangled
rusty filigree pendants of silver, delicately suspended by necklaces of cat's eye,
ox-red coral and Tibetan black matrixed turquoise. They are said to never wash
during their entire lifetime.

Their inviolate visage was Navaho or Cherokee. Bright burgundy faces. Of
tall skinny Madonnas in the Italian Quattrocento, of adoring slender sylphides

in the Indian miniatures produced under Moghul rule. There are some 50,000 of these Ladakhi women. They marry usually at age seventeen and have very few children, for there is minimal food to go around. One of the many husbands will usually care for the child while the mother is busy at the Leh Bazaar, day after day, from morning until night trying to make a few rupees off her vegetables: barley, mustard, turnip, potatoes, beans for fodder (one seed of barley in Ladakhi sand will yield twenty barley corns). The mustard is traditionally mixed with blood and monkshod, coated on lances, and used to poison musk deer or to hunt yeti.

She sits in a large group, sometimes with her daughters, drinking brick tea from *phor ba* wooden bowls. And sometimes the young girls are there on their own.

Muslim merchants, Mongolian caravanserai of Bactrian camels, Indo-Tibetan uniformed police, Sikh military, German, and Texan tourists, Turkestani, Kashmiri swindlers, Hindu quatro-runes, Chinese, red and yellow-robed Buddhist monks, an albino Englishman's child happily frolicking with boisterous Ladakhi children, World War II jeeps, asses, huge yaks, dees and zhos (cow-yak mixtures), roosters, mastiffs, vultures and crows, filthy flowing gutter water, goitered monsters from Hunza and the Hindu Kush, Afghanistani and Nepali traders, Sherpas in exile, hippie adventurers, Khampas (the tall, good-looking protectors of the Dalai Lama who fought the Chinese for years with CIA backing), goats, mamo (adult female sheep), diesel-spilling government transport vehicles splattered with Urdu graffiti and warnings of smallpox—the chaos of color, odor and physiognomy which infests any Central Asian town seemed vividly augmented on the circuitous, mangled streets of the Leh Bazaar where I was loping.

Dramatically singled out amid this atrocious medley are those smokey-eyed Tibetan women, smiling exuberantly, chattering away with each other, selling beer in gasoline jerry cans, trading in tomatoes, half-eyeing the Tibetan men and westerners. Though in general, with such well-groomed exceptions as Lhasa's family, the male Tibetan did not seem much to look at. Sharp, dangling whiskers, long unkempt braids pinned atop his head, dung-infested shoes and dusty untailored pants, he hardly complements the woman he enjoins. His face at age thirty is a burned-out image of the desert and glaciers surrounding him; of the eight months of deep snowfall a year, the one hundred-degree temperature inversions during a day in January, the constant gusts and zero percent humidity, of the sparse diet and the incessant primal boredom. A Himalayan Sahara embraces his wrinkled little plot of face.

Gold and amber earrings, a turquoise pierced nostril, burning skin, aquiline nose, a maroon scarf, her intestinally long braids in her squatting lap, I noticed a particular young woman dusting off her cauliflower in the center of the market. She couldn't have been more than sixteen. Sitting beside perhaps a dozen other women, this one alone was watching me coyly. I was sitting across the road under a row of poplars taking it all in, changing lenses, wiping dirt from my jeans.

Her tongue was sliding over her tight parched lips, fingers slowly fidgeting with her produce, casting glances and nervous good-afternoons at this and that passing friend, but always coming back and fixing her uneasy gaze in my direction. It's what I'd been dreaming about ever since Allain mentioned his amphicillin provision.

My reverie was bolstered. A yak and dee, five yards from my side, in a sloppy massive commingling began to hump each other like bulls in combat, thick white fluffy tails sweeping up the many inches of dust from the road. The spectacle broadened as they turned semicircles, no Klimpt-like lassitude; merchants running to the side, the yak on its hindlegs aching with a perilous love muscle forcing forth its awkward knees up into the screeching mate's muscle. Their skewed horns shone in the splay of sunlight, traffic avoiding them, laughter from the stalls, a frenzy of stones thrown, chickens running to all sides in typically terrified manner; and the women squat in their pow-wows before the scene, russet hands upon mouths. The younger girls watched wide-eyed, as the yak discharged its missile, erratically catching the frayed sleeve of a merchant lingering near.

My eyes were pressing home toward the servine girl. With magical conviction, I finished putting all my camera gear away, got up and moved around the two beasts who were now exhausted and supine on the side of the road, their legs propped in the air, the yak gently biting on the ear of the dee. I went directly to her, through the throng of others in the road.

"Jeelai," I said.

Beaming, she quickly gathered her vegetables in a canvass sack, placed the sack in her head-suspended basket and nodded. Through an ascending ghettoed jumble of alleyways, over millennia of caked filth, past prayer gumpas, we moved abruptly away from the market until we reached a small teak doorway adjacent to a potato field, at the rear of a choked passageway.

A grandmother was there with two infants and a sheep. The girl, a hint of tension, turned to me, named the old woman who respondingly opened her mucousy mouth and shouted chirpily, *"jeelai."* The Ladakhi *shalom.*

The girl widened her astonishingly blue eyes, took my hand roughly with a giggle and stooped to usher me into the dark interior of a room which evidently was the family's kitchen, bedroom and animal shelter. A silver tea kettle was steaming. Grease lined the stones which supported a bed whose tattered blankets were woven in the Tibetan design of a snow leopard, teeming with lice, and smelling dubious. Growing more accustomed to the darkness, I watched the girl latch the door and turn, uncertain of herself for the first time. I sat on the hard floor, she above, letting out her braids. I couldn't think. Softly I caressed her cold ankles.

Moaning in a dialect I doubt has changed in 2,000 years, she pulled me onto the bed. Tibetan women are infamous for the elaborate variety of venereal diseases they transport. All across Asia. They have more energy for lovemaking than any other woman. Leh is 10,400 feet in elevation but many Ladakhi women live as high as 16,000. High altitude intercourse requires less aggression, and slower breathing. Or so one would imagine. Tibetan syphilis inching up to me, her mouth watering, her bed-length hair now draped about us both, in the incensed eerie darkness we began to expose one another.

I removed each garment hesitantly, as if there were dynamite. She kept one hand on my shoulder, and with the other she rubbed herself, index finger smeared in dee butter. Soon the darkness was lambent with her nakedness. I was dazed. She waited. Breathless. Smothering her giggling in my vest. Her hands still smelling of uncooked kholrabi, she grappled for me. The first scent of accumulated fecula about her anus. I wrenched frantically in the nerve spot. Hairs hot with friction. Her arcane hugging grip in the haloed dark bringing forth my liquid elicitations. Spit on her hand, pulling me urgently, her naïve soul flinging itself into the fantastic, inflicting mindlessness, cold dirt against my testicles, fingers slimy with her behind, my mouth rapturous with clitoris, and blood-red lips devouring in the air their frenetic pulse; pursuing nothingness with contingent ease, frenzy in the pure river of touches; by braille in the primeval fluidity. Until the vacancy, the explosive upwards gasp, onto my fingertips, then down, rolling, mushing into her, penetrating muscle with flat muscle, backwards in the frigid rent, spiraling in seed of myself, in blackout, until the fresco of our secretions dribbled out their exasperated orifices; until our eyes—hers like bright marbles, exaggerated swallows, gasping, fingers oily and sliding to the enunciations of unabashed Tibetan flatus, odoriferous rhubarb gas—until our eyes had finished gorging on the inner vista, slime plastered on our tongues, on every appendaged edge, until her vagina was fully softened in the cream of her becoming. To sink away, rootless, rooted, paroxysms still squirting from the jugular of emission, red boundaries broken open, infant pulsations, meteor-like, dissolving in the furthest reaches of our intoxication.

It went this way, our legs entwined like liana, my mouth erupting over hers with taste-enrapturing lunges, my hands upon her rough-hewn mountain nipples, for hours, until her mouth swished its last slaver. She bore into my Caucasian flesh, asking for my world.

She was a child. Had only recently come into menarche. We lingered. I stared upon her shadowed body whose limbs and decorative form was like a clod of unmoulded earth, damp, of willow brooks, given to the hereafter. I held her in my look. Shyly, she hid her face.

Soon she was in velvet again. We decamped. A tear on her cheek. The old woman was still standing by. Her look penetrated my own. The girl turned her head and reclined. I bent over and kissed the both of them. She sat motionless. Staring at the sheep that the baby held by a ribbon. In their eternally same back alley.

I left for the market, not wanting to turn around, but as I moved under an archway that verged with mingling rot-wall, I knew I had to see her again, to fix permanently that Asian Aphrodite's face in my mind. But she was gone.

That evening Tenzing volunteered to fashion delectables while the three of us went for some bouldering across the road on a mountain of jumbled granite. Like the terrain of the Lone Ranger's Alabama Hills.

We approached a smooth, twenty-foot overhang. There were finger lieback holds up its slanting edge. Ghisela went first, her feet swinging onto the rock. She pulled up, and lunged for the next higher steppe, coming off without recourse. Allain then tried and managed to get nearer the top in an inelegant but nonetheless impressive foray, followed by a leap.

We moved from boulder to boulder in the warm crepuscular dusk. It was invigorating at this altitude. I'd always felt a special reverence for the *art* of bouldering. It possessed none of the dangers of regular climbing for it was in theory practiced on small rock faces; ten, twenty feet off the ground.

Mysticism in microcosm, an accumulating of keen breathing, centeredness, and strength, bouldering is devoid of the paraphernalia which hoists the spectacle of more complex mountaineering assaults. Axiomatic to bouldering is the sensual privacy. Risk-free, uncompetitive, not to be exploited, extreme in its necessary regimen, bouldering had its real inception among alpine shepherds tracking their flocks over rugged terrain, or Paleolithic artisans climbing into the penitralia of deep caves to affix their ochres to the cold stone. I've always wondered who cracked the first joke in ancient times, and over what. More so I try to imagine the first instance of vertigo.

In contemporary climbing circles, on Flagstaff Mountain above Boulder, Colorado, in Camp 4 at Yosemite, and elsewhere, boulderers have formed their own hermetic societies. Traditions have grown, and legends. Of aerial aesthetics, and philosophies of the musculature, after Yukio Mishima. It is dance, vertical ballet. Some climbers *only* boulder. And they have established an intricate rating system of difficulties. The Colorado master of bouldering, John Gill, a mathematics professor, does one-fingertip pullups on overhangs. He has fixed B3 as the limit of what's possible—and has done such moves. How does one *know* a limit? The body knows. One can risk imagination, can afford the fullest physical extensions when only five, ten feet off the ground. And this is the seduction of such an artform. Bouldering moves are Gordian knots more difficult than anything ever tackled on a high mountain. Of course danger means difficulty. Or so most climbers assume. And so the high mountains, which kill, they say, six percent of all climbers, are considered *real* while bouldering is still laughed at by the European old-timers, in their hob-nailed boots.

I'd spend whole days working on some problems and had come to feel a secure, nearly religious familiarity with rock. The original form of Zen was called *wall meditation*. Similarly, Japanese *Yamabushies*, religious ascetics, were known to practice on cliffs.

Boulderers were wont to emphasize the fact that such endeavors came close, if not altogether, to resolving the mind-body dialectics of lore. How did they know? We felt it to be so.

We crossed the road and joined Tenzing by the small fire he'd created. Wood was extremely precious in the desert but Tenzing was clever. Fried wontons and vegetables, tomato soup with croutons, chocolate pudding with mandarin orange slices.

"Tenzing, you're brilliant!" Allain gloated.

We chugged the Indian beer that had been cooling in the river. Spidery nebulai were coming out all across the sky.

Life in the mountains was regulated according to this most basic of rhythms: movement during daytime, sleep with darkness. Unlike the desert, the animal life of a mountain was neither nocturnal nor even *willing* to venture out in the cold glaze of evening. Only wind picking on the stones, molesting freely through the radiant blackness.

There were some one thousand species of hearty plant throughout the Himalaya. Blown low, colors sophisticated, muted, more ephemeral. All the world's arctic and alpine plants came from the Himalayan. Pleistocene refugium; flowers pollinated not by Tibetan bees, but by insects with glycerol (anti-freeze) in their vascular heat exchangers to raise their air-to-body gradients. They may never have heard of Allen's, or Bergmann's or Gloger's Rules, of high altitude, but they made excellent sport of marching out onto glaciers in the morning to pre-heat their flying muscles, while snow worms fed off aeolian debris, Collembola and glacier fleas hopped clumsily about, and Ursus thibetanus rummaged for Carabid, dark-spotted ladybug and cave beetles nestled in metallic ice grottoes. On endless high heaths the voles and shrews were racing about seedy soil, while yak (Bos grunniens) meandered across heaven, mites to their imperial napes.

It was a full world, that gave me the most satisfying dreams I've ever had, night after night. There was a powerful ecological clue to that catalyst. Whenever I thought about where I was, and all the subtle things happening out there, why I simply fell back bewildered. To do more than twice a day defined paradise, heartstop, god.

CHAPTER TWELVE

Balladeur had been to Shankar monastery and learned of a very famous lama living in near-total seclusion at Hemis. We decided to go there the next day and chance a meeting.

The road was gravel; it required three hours to make the twenty-mile trip. Feng Peak reared its high snowfields in the dark rabblement of clouds above. Against the mountains lay waste and dunes, gutted with barrenness, lonely chortens.

We drove across the Indus, past a small checkpost and up a winding dirt road through the sweltering midmorning, to the 12,000-foot-high poplar orchards of the remote monastery. It was an extensive complex. Courtyard within court-yard. Coming up from one of the many gardens was a ludicrous figure astride a white ass, both of them frowning. He sported a dunce cap, red cloak, and gruesome solemnity.

"Chhagzot," Tenzing whispered. "He collects *sakhral*, land tax."

"Tax?" I asked, puzzled. "From the monks?"

"No. From the people. Land doesn't die the way yak and sheep do."

We parked the land-rover near a footbridge, took a tape recorder and cameras and set off up a trail in the shadow of the cool arbor glen. It was a strange quiet world. Exceedingly isolated, even from Leh. Above it was a steep mountain, deeply clad in acid rock. I recognized a thin path.

The *konya*, the monastery's traditional guardian, was nowhere to be found. We entered a maze of muddied passageways, stooping, stepping over collapsed beams. Carved and wobbly whitewashed walls had been eaten through with age. There was dust and cobwebs atop mud and old excrement in the corners. A tangle of unused poles. A pile of mildewy cloth. Thick boles of teak, wrapped in forty-foot-long prayer flags stood like totems in a courtyard we descended to. They hung over the entrance to a large shrine. Surrounding the courtyard were hundreds of chipped and cracking frescoes of poor quality.

Allain and Ghisela went over to examine them. Tenzing and I took off our shoes as is customary before going in. A ceremony was in progress.

Allain had recognized a fresco of the sixteenth-century Ladakhi mendicant

Tsaluka, a man ostracized from his community for sleeping so much. Legend relates that a certain yogi told him to meditate on an ocean, and to conceive of his own consciousness as a duck floating in the waves. Tsaluka had never seen an ocean, did not know what waves were. But the yogi, who presumably had, described it as wet sky on the ground. Tsaluka dreamed the infinite and attained Nirvana asleep. The fresco at Hemis pictures him peacefully snoring on a rug, his dog snoring next to him.

The four of us entered the altar room. Sitting crouched on beaten rugs forming two parallel troughs were a good thirty monks. Tapestries hanging over the altar were woven in patterns of chrome yellow, royal blue, vermilion, and the top of the sanctuary, known as the Lhakhang, was lost in the dark meniscus over one hundred-fifty feet above, where the cross-eyed porcelain statue of Buddha—Shakya Thubba—was soberly scrutinizing us. There were numerous photographs, butter lamps, brass censers and coin trays at the silk-draperied table up front. On all the wooden posts hung thangkas and along the shadowed peripheries were other effulgent frescoes, their adobe backings crumbling to the floor. I felt buoyant with high nervousness.

They were deadly serious. Bloated on their bellowy readings. An aura of soot, pantheon of sculptured gods, monsters, hung dolorously over the chamber. The buckling greasy floor was cold and hard. Such a religious chanting service, Tenzing told us, was generally performed three times a day. In unceasing monotone, portions of the *Do* and *Vinaya* were recited in a dizzying elevation of song. Not unobserved, the four of us sat down in the corner near the entrance.

Suddenly, like the trajectory of a roman candle, the monks broke out their instruments. Pipes, hand drums, trumpets fashioned from human thigh bones, 10-foot brass horns, shenai flutes and shattering cymbals sprayed the air with a fireworks of incantation. A Buddhist Bartok of delirium, like harmony oxidized in the rush of vibrations bursting over us, these high-altitude symphonics got into the gut, the nostrils, burned the eyes.

And as suddenly, the prolix chorale had dissolved into a hard-moving rhythm of more chanting, great baritone velocity, cantors on the lowest rung of the voice digging melismatic trenches in the air, all sparks and incense.

The monks were wearing a variety of heavy woolen robes; kilt of patchwork, known as the *sanghati*, and vests of silk. Hemis was Mahayana and the monks' red cloaks represented the oldest monastic color in India. The Dalai Lama on the other hand (Gyalba Rinpoche, in Tibetan), belonged to the Gelukpa, yellow-robe or *virtuous* sect, originated by Tsong-kha-pa in the fourteenth century. The vast majority of Tibetans still follow this sect.

Buddha renounced Nirvana at age twenty-nine. He also got rid of his estate—two palaces, four pools filled with vari-colored lotus flowers—at the same time. Sitting under the pipal tree in Buddh Gaya, he saw an old man, legless, dragging himself along. The realization of suffering, that something—albeit something painful—happened in the world must have been thrilling for him. He sat under that tree waiting. He was lucky. It took a single night. By sunrise he was clear. One needed to *feel* for that man. To feel . . . And six other young men heard about this Prince who went around *feeling* things. Buddha's sayings were written down in the *Sutras*, compiled in the *Dhammapada*. Some of his teachings were redescribed and compiled in the *Tripitaka*.

Fixed in my mind was the murmuring night's snowfall and solicitous embrace aboard that inviolate cliff. I sought answers from Balladeur, whose own cynicism had softened to the point of believing. There was contagion in that. I always trusted his instincts.

"What are they saying?" Ghisela whispered to Tenzing.

"Praying to do good things."

"What things?"

Tenzing thought, then: "Grow juicy turnips."

So that was Buddhism. And why not.

"You're disappointed," Allain averred, seeing her discomfort.

"No, just pragmatic."

"What's practical?"

"Eating, sleeping, lovemaking."

"OK, and then?"

"And then, raise a couple of brats, aspire after heaven."

"Fine, fine. There's the extent of your pragmatism. Now you've got most of your life to live in the interstices. And that's where metaphysics has a place."

"I can *see* what Gandhi, Mao, Mother Teresa, have done. But turnips?" Ghisela couldn't contain herself. She laughed—so hard I had to tackle her and get her out of there before the monks turned on us.

"I'm sorry," she gasped, tears coming from her eyes as she bowled over in delirium. "But turnips?"

We'd come to Hemis to find the *skushok,* the spiritual head. With Tenzing we went looking. Allain had a hunch. The lama at Shankar had eyed him suspiciously when he first inquired about *the garden*. And then led him to the Head Lama there who in turn suggested that we seek out the Hemis Head Lama.

We passed a monk, who slowly slouched to his Jerusalem, prayer-wheel in hand. His mani-chhos-khor, a metal cylinder three inches high, was filled with scraps of prayer. It was fastened to his robe by a chain and by merely turning it he was satisfying his daily quota, generating a continuum of good tiding. In some Tibetan villages, a turn-wheel is suspended from a stone hut, over a runnel. The water turns the apparatus which is tied at the top with prayer flags. I've seen Sherpa put prayers on their jeep tires in Solo-Khumbu.

"Where is skushok?" Tenzing asked the monk, who motioned we should come. We followed him back to the courtyard. Off with the shoes. Into the sanctuary. The chanting had ceased. Two young boys, maybe six years old, were awkwardly struggling with steaming Tibetan samovars, trundling them from one monk to the next. Some of the monks were rapping them *compassionately* across the back with sticks. The boys were in tears. An old man passed around lentils in a large wooden bowl. I watched some of the monks taking extra portions and sneaking it into bags under their wood-block psalters. They were rapacious, eating rabidly with their fingers. One had a yellow pencil which, in conjunction with a poplar twig, he was wielding as chopsticks.

The monk motioned us. We were left standing before a grey-haired old fart.

"Labrang?" Tenzing inquired politely.

"On the mountain," the monk garbled as he crowded his foodstuff. "Gotsang Gompa at top of mountain. But you cannot go!" Tempting us. Adamant. Mean-looking.

"Why?" Tenzing pressed, translating for us.

"Because! Nobody go!" He gave us to understand that we were not wanted here, mumbling indictments, sixty eyes following us.

We took the direct route up the talus so no one could possibly see us on the long, exposed trail. I don't know what we were afraid of, actually.

It was precipitous, angling into an obscured area of rocks about an hour above the poplars. Tenzing and I were both in jeans. Ghisela and Allain were in cooler dhotis. A black Himalayan eagle, common in these parts, swooped circles over us, screeching in its falsetto curiousness. Its beak was large, sharp and brilliant against the cerulean sky. The four of us continued stealthily to the ridge, lost now amidst spooky clusters of boulder. *Om Mani Padme Hum* had been engraved copiously all along the trail, in stone. Tenzing offered us the Ladakhi translation of this infamous aleph, the Tibetan *Sadakshapa.*

"I invoke the path of truth and experience of universality so that the jeweline luminosity of immortal mind be unfolded within the depths of lotus-centered consciousness and I be wafted by the ecstasy of breaking through all bonds and horizons . . . . " He'd recited it to other tourists.

We were in ankle-deep snow. The ultraviolet rays were coming up into our eyes and I could picture us all, snow-blind, slipping like idiots into the rancid cloister of angered hermits.

We came to the top of the rocks. From here, due west some twenty miles, we could see what looked like the east ridge of the Trident. It was three p.m. We sat down on a flat granite boulder. I yawned. We giggled.

Suddenly, the air was hot with throaty rends, crashing, menacing on top of us. What sounded like cymbals echoing off the rocks. The screams were rebounding, heart-stopping, coming from the other side. I lunged for the ground, covering my head as a torrent of objects shot towards us.

"Tenzing! What is it?"

"Don't know sab!" he cried. I crawled around the rock.

Suddenly there was total silence. We waited, then approached a closer boulder. And whoof! Another rain of screams and little objects. I picked one up. Wax? A square of waxy butter inserted in brass. This was crazy. There was the banging again. Unmistakable cymbals now. And screams, larded with coughing and ridiculous wailing. Allain and I looked at each other. "OK?" I said.

"Let's do it!" he nodded.

We ran for the edge. And sure enough. There was a stone hut, with an unprecedented view of the Ladakhi Himalaya on four sides. The hut clung to the mountain's backside. And sitting there comfortably in a chair, with cymbals in his hands, a bellow mouthpiece around his neck and a box of the soft little butter candles beneath him, was the lama, the *wizard of Hemis.*

"I'll get Tenzing," I whispered to Allain. I ran back.

"Ahh . . . skushok?" Allain called. "We're friends!"

"So!" the lama roared back through the bellows.

"Michael!" Allain yelled to me. "He speaks English." We all stood there before him. The skushok took one look at Ghisela, who was mad, dropped his cymbals and ran into his hut. He was a midget. I held my laughter. Tenzing pleaded in Tibetan.

"Skushok, my friends are Buddhists. Scholars from America. They are eager to meet you. They have come a long way."

Silence.

"I think he is shy," Tenzing whispered.

"Skushok," Ghisela yelled with caustic verve, pronouncing it more like *kojak,* "we're coming in!"

"Wait! Please," the lama shouted in perfect English. "Just a minute." We were all bewildered.

"Where do you suppose he learned such English?" And then he stepped out. He'd been busy changing. No more scarlet chasuble, no rosary, no cymbals. But a miniature pair of cotton slacks and an old lambswool sweater.

"You really must excuse me. But there are rivalries here. No need to explain."

"Where did you learn your English?" I asked.

"You may come in. It's small, but sufficient." We entered, Tenzing last. The walls were decorated in thangkas, the Tibetan silk paintings carried traditionally in rolled-up cases on long journeys to ward off evil. Extravagant talismans. Taoists carried mirrors on their back when entering a mountain. Attacking demons would see themselves and flee. Buddhists carried paintings.

"So! You like my thangkas," he said, apprehending our thoughts. "This yellow one is chamba. The Maitreya Buddha. And this one, holding a flaming sword and a lotus, is Jamya Manju-sri. Adjoining him is Chanrazek, our protector Bodhisattva. And the three-eyed one, Vargchak, our male Tantric divinity. His loins are covered with leopard skin. He is a sex maniac. He tramples everyone. They are all painted by a very close friend."

"But they look very old?" Allain said, acknowledging the cracked canvasses and greasy sheen which comes from countless, smoking censers and butter lamps.

"Oh yes, hundreds of years," the skushok smiled.

I quickly caught Allain's bemusement. We all eyed the lama, not knowing what to think. He was no more than four and a half feet tall. I was unable to decipher how old he was. His pupils were incredibly vibrant, but there were faint shadows under the eyes. The skin of his hands was tight, golden. As if he'd had it lifted. But there was the half-inference of progeria working in reverse. A Merlinesque figure. He was Tibetan all right, with a Mongol's mustache. But not his voice. And by then I could have sworn I'd heard that voice before, something I...And then I recognized him! "Balladeur!" We started towards the door.

It slammed. There was no handle. I pushed against the stone in the darkness. Immovable.

"Wait!" the skushok ordered.

"Open the door, Wangdu!" I threatened. And it swung open.

"What?" Ghisela burst.

"Well, sonofabitch!" Balladeur ignited. I was stunned. "Hey!" Tenzing was scared to death, witnessing some frightening replay from his youth, among the lama *heavies* of old Tibet.

"Dr. Wangdu isn't it? Jigme Wangdu?"

Without any surprise in his voice, "That's right."

"Jesus!" Ghisela gaped at me in wonder.

"I sat in on one of your lectures at Harvard many years ago. Intriguing . . . " Wangdu as I recall was there a whole semester teaching in the religions department. That same semester, Timothy Leary and half-a-dozen Babas and Dasses had come through Cambridge; the Chinese year of the ass. They were all driven around in 450 SL's, garlands of flowers thrown to them by doped-out wailing girls without bras. I'd only heard him speak at all because of a lady I was mad about who insisted on going. But we both walked out after five minutes. It was the kind of psychic crap I couldn't stomach.

"That's quite alright," Wangdu said calmly.

"Huh? What's alright?"

"Your disinterest."

I shrank. Allain and Ghisela were mute, confused. I sat down. I must have been hyperventilating.

"What do you lecture about?" Allain asked.

"Allain . . . I wouldn't . . . . "

"Everything!" Wangdu assured him.

With his beady eyes, irksome humpback, and mechanical jaws, he was physically revolting. And there was no way around it. He'd heard my thinking. I wanted to stop. To escape that look. To think, without *overtly* thinking. I became nauseous. A wind had brought clouds from the west. Shadows had swirled onto the ridge. The horizon was immersed in a cyan of cold and rolling glaciers. Illuminated cirques of granite wall and snow. Fantastic.

"You like it!" he preempted, orchestrating the cause and effect of my perturbations.

"Yes," I conceded.

"Good. Now. What is your business this afternoon?" and he ushered us out of the cold wind back into his hermitage, handing us four cups of hot tea. Though I saw no kettle. No water outlet.

"I have read of a manuscript supposed to be near Hemis. Very ancient. And written in part by Christ," Allain started.

Wangdu laughed. "You are Jesus freaks then?"

"No!" Allain retracted, a little indignant. Unsure whether or not to fully expose our expedition's plan. Though by that time he'd doubtlessly done so. "We are looking for some sāddhus."

"Well, then you ought to go to Amarnath," he said paternally, leading Allain on.

"I've been to Amarnath. And that's why I came here."

"Who sent you here?"

"Well, no one really. I mean the lama at Shankar told me about you. But we've come looking for a mountain. There is a sīddha ashram."

"So! That's it!" Wangdu looked enraged. "And you know where it is?"

"We think so."

"Well, then go there!" he said bluntly.

I looked at Ghisela. I felt we'd overstayed our visit.

"Déva has sent me to Ladakh!" Allain stated with final resolve. Wangdu halted, looking hard at us. His glance was like a dam of water ready to burst. Allain looked down. It was the confusion of a Lillian Hellman story. Wangdu turned his head, slowly, bit on his nails. His fingers were Cretan, stubby. He was thinking, deciding.

"We are all Dévas," he then started. "It means nothing."

Allain gazed back at him. Yearning, locked in. I stared at Allain, amused.

"It *could* mean something, it must!" Allain proceeded boldly, having lost his foothold.

"You are young," Wangdu asserted. "Crescit eundo!" he adumbrated with his finger, but it passed us by. "You are young. You possess what you are looking for. If you did not possess it you would not be looking." The door flung open. "See that dog!" And sure enough. There was a mut. "It struggles in circles to lick the mange from its hind leg." The dog was turning, whining with frustration. The wind rushed in and blew out a candle. Wangdu glanced at the door and it shut, reigniting the light.

"How do you do that?" I asked, unnerved.

But he didn't answer. We finished our tea, setting down the cups alongside the narrow bench upon which three of us sat. Tenzing remained standing, on guard. Wangdu was up on a high swivel chair adjoining his desk. A clutter of books and letters there.

"Where do you sleep?" I inquired.

"Wherever I want to," he replied with a tenor of delight.

Allain had had it. "Thanks for the tea." And he started for the closed door.

"I didn't say *that*!" Wangdu chided him, impatient with our ineptitude. "I merely suggested you've been misled." An asphyxiating silence. "You see," he continued, "I too was misled. In the beginning." His face shone against the dwindling light.

"How long have you lived here?" Ghisela asked.

"It's my family's summer estate." And he again began to giggle, a child, his face wrinkling and an ooze of slobber dribbling from his mouth. He brushed it off.

"You go down to Hemis for your food?"

"Occasionally," he replied.

"You *are* a lama?" Allain reacted.

"Only when I have to be!" he said. "A job, like any other. You see, we are many things. And we go many places. Each human being is his own residue of arcane secrets. Every old woman you meet on the road. You can learn a lesson from time. But don't ever believe it. Go with it, but never believe it! Why? Because time changes dimension once you truly know what you're doing, why you're here and where you're going. I think you are hungry."

The door flung open. Wangdu pulled a bronze sword, its razor edge gleaming, from under his desk. A plump chicken ambulated by outside. In a great stride—ten feet through the doorway—he leapt at the pathetic little creature and grabbed it tightly.

"No," Ghisela reared, covering her face. I was sick. I was no vegetarian but this was too much, the one barbarism of India I detested. I well remembered an incident at a Base Camp in Nepal. A Dutch expedition, sharing our same camp-site, had just completed a new route on a nearby peak. They walkie-talkied down from Camp 3 to say they'd made it, were pulling the tents and would be down by dinner. The expedition lead climbers had a special craving for lamb-chops. I was in my tent reading. It was a rest day for us. Getting acclimatized. Their Sherpa cook ran by. I poked my head outside the tent to see what was up. I'd heard the radio static and the two-way shouting.

The Sherpa chased one of their last sheep down to a creek coming from the glacier above, a cutlass in hand. The sheep was rocking, wailing with an agoniz-ing foreknowledge of its fate. There are people who love to kill animals. They know that the animal knows, and this accentuates their sick pleasure. Even the Sherpas, with their Buddhist summits, their endless religious holidays, their *mani rimbdu* drama, can be cruel shitheads.

The sheep tried to lunge across the creek. That sonofabitch cook grabbed it, cajoling it, torturing it. The sheep screamed, writhing under the excruciating fist which pulled its fine white nape. My chest was throbbing. My throat smart. I had to watch, and I took up the binoculars which I kept inside the tent's en-trance.

The Sherpa had picked up the young animal, talking to it, laughing. He walked downstream. The sheep had become totally quiet. Its eyes were closed. The Sherpa was fondling its throat. He set it on the ground and one last time the desperate animal tried to run, lurching, but its skinny legs buckled under as the Sherpa's foot plunged into its belly. I saw the animal's nose burst with foam, its head vibrating. It collapsed. And the small kukri went for the throat. The Sherpa was drunk. He missed, bashing into the animal's chest instead. Blood burst from its neck as the rapier sawed off the head, slowly, in horrid jerks. The belly was zipped open. Two minutes later I saw the leg throb upwards one last time. I buried myself in my sleeping bag. I never wanted to climb again, to eat, to be alive.

With his bronze samurai sword the midget grabbed the chicken's minute neck. Gruesomely taunting us, the chicken's tiny legs running in midair, its muted little sobs choked in aerial strangulation. And my mind raced to another image, a Gregory Bateson/Margaret Mead film dealing with trance rituals in Bali. A man I recall had bitten off the head of a live rooster!

"No!" Ghisela screamed again, running up to Wangdu. "Let go of it!" She slapped him hard across his face. He dropped his sword, and the freed chicken ran frantically, flinging itself under a boulder. I stood petrified. Thank god for her. Wangdu was looking visibly shaken. He bowed.

"I didn't think Buddhists took life," Allain marked sternly.

"But people do!" Wangdu said solemnly, rubbing his cheek where he'd been swatted.

"Allain, it's getting dark. Let's go," I said. We had no parkas and the cold was beginning to penetrate our thin clothing.

"Goodbye then," Wangdu said with sweeping affection. There was a strange tone to his voice. A teasing invitation to suffer paradox, the contradiction of our own beings. He was a bold and ugly asshole, I thought. We started down. Allain looked back one more time. Wangdu was chiarascuroed on the ridge. He called to our descending party in guttural hilarity. "Her name is Kali. Be sure and taste her fruits. And watch out! The ice fall *is* dangerous. Despite what they'll tell you!"

By the time we had reached the poplars, the night was black and we were shivering with cold. Our pants were sopped from glissading. We'd made it down quickly. The high thin cirrus of the afternoon had blown over and a tickling serein was moistening the chilly air. The moon lay low in its quarter phase. The monastery, like a great moth, had closed its wings for the night. By dry white stars we tumbled, worn out chinks, along the stone path which snaked down to the footbridge.

The land-rover was gone! And all our gear with it.

"Damn!" I screamed, hoarse and shrilly. We recognized tire tracks leading downhill. What to do? The four of us took off for the imposing main entrance.

"It's the chhagzot!" Tenzing shouted with the sharp aura of certainty these Tibetans were supposed to breed.

"The archetypal trickster," Allain mused, hugging himself in the freezing night. "It's one of Wangdu's psychic jokes!"

The great beam door was locked from the inside. "I'll climb over," I said. "Give me a boost." I got up on Allain's shoulders. Mantled over the adobe crenelation and swung down on the other side. It was a crude old lock. One of the antique kind which can be purchased for twenty rupees in the Leh Bazaar. "Anyone got a knife?"

Tenzing dug through his pockets. "Khyakpa!" he cursed.

"What is it?"

"I left the keys in the land-rover, boss!"

Ghisela sighed, wan, ready to drop.

"OK, you got the knife?" Tenzing tossed it over. I fiddled with the keyhole. The lock sprung free. And the huge portal was open, our Trojan anger ingressing up the inner enclosure, as we searched out someone to accost. We heard clapping footsteps coming down a wooden stairwell from above. Two monks appeared. Seedy characters, a Tibetan Abbot and Costello. Tenzing fired off at them in a wrangled spasm of Tibetan cuss words. "Who has stolen our landrover? We will go to the military!"

In their high defenseless phonation, the monks said they didn't know. Only the chhagzot would know. And where was the chhagzot?

They led us up steps to a new area of the compound we'd not seen that morning. Here the walls were many feet thick, lodgings in the heavy abbatial decor of the other world. In the rear of this powerful gallery the managerial head of the monastery reclined on his silk pillows. Not about to fight with us.

A flood of sparring obscenities ensued. Tenzing was hot, choleric. Ready to strike and wanting to show us his stuff. The chhagzot became tranquil, resilient, fingering beads of yellow amber. And I could see he was not vexed. He nodded with executive flourish to one of the monks who went out and returned with chai.

"Your vehicle is at the river. Hemis is closed. You should not have come!" He was adamant.

"Where are the keys?" Tenzing cursed enragedly.

"Everything is as it was."

We gulped down the tea. And by then we'd warmed up. The Indus was a good two-hour trek from the monastery.

"You may take two horses," the chhagzot said, seeing our dismay and wet pants.

"Well, that's decent of the prick," I said to Allain.

"Tie them at the same place. I am sorry." There was nothing more to say. He gave swift orders to one of the monks. We were led back out. Two swayback

Tibetan ponies, hardly large enough it seemed to accommodate one man, were offered us in the cold darkness, with a cord for tying them. It made no sense. A stupid inconvenience on both sides.

We mounted the two overworked animals and made our slow departure down towards the Indus Valley. We felt ridiculous all crunched up like that. The animals didn't feel too happy about the situation either. They were better suited to carrying little girls at zoos, and had the forlorn green eyes of Hereford cows, of seals that have come inland to die and respire calmly, propped belly-up on sandstone biers.

By midnight we reached the vehicle. It had been left at the military checkpost. Two lanterns were glowing coldly. A Hindu soldier in a moth-eaten khaki jacket, a ruffled cerise scarf and readied rifle, greeted us wearily.

"You are the owners of the vehicle?" he asked in choppy English.

"That's right," I said. Ghisela and I made a quick check through all our provisions. The Indian shook his head and guided the horses to a post. He sat back down in his dismal canvas tent, waving us off, his head against the din and static of an old radio, his one friend in the harsh and lonely darkness. We crossed the bridge, angling for our tent site twenty miles down river, the landrover lurching through the lunar landscape of sand and tormented ravines. Tibet's many enigmas were beginning to *feel* like khyakpa.

CHAPTER THIRTEEN

We tried to sleep late. But dozens of curious orphans from the lamasery up the road were glued to our tent entrances earnestly distracting us so that we might examine their ear diseases, their throat maladies, and their lice-ridden scalps. We cut up a bag of potatoes, fried them in cooking oil and salt, applied the Indian ketchup and spent a gusty lunch with them. Snow clouds seemed to be accumulating over Stok.

That afternoon we assembled gear. Four packs of fifty pounds apiece. I sat by the river snow-sealing my boots, taping my ice ax, staring up at the silver-grey mountain. Ghisela read Bailey's *No Passport to Tibet*, while Allain was involved in swinging the kids in circles over the sweet grass. Tenzing had gone to town for extra gas. We planned to leave early the next morning, driving as far as the village of Stok, then locking up the land-rover for good.

Hemis had affected me. Or something had. I was feeling a new admiration for Ghisela. Our relationship had been a convenient one up until now. I'd taken her for granted. Our meeting, our sex, our food bills—everything had been emotionless. Even our prior trip to India had been strained. The closeness of living quarters in Big Sur added tension to tenuousness. I lived by extremes. How would I ever learn to live? I craved other women but had little opportunity for finding them in the unpeopled wilds of the Big Sur. That Tibetan girl had torn my loins apart. And I needed a good deal more of it. But the intriguing events of the past week provided a new access to Ghisela. I'd never seen her in such action as with Wangdu. She possessed a clean simplicity that bore down on me with meaning, meaning I could identify with. And which I was beginning to see as sufficient semantic cause for naming. Love. Though I shirked the word. I was still a child. The word could only be a front. Still, it was there. For the grabbing. And Ghisela was the woman in my life.

The three of us spread out together on the banks of the river, ancient mud, glacial eddies of alluvium. I felt good. Beginning now to acclimate. I tackled Ghisela, giggling, goosing her. Allain joined in. The three of us rolled rambunctious, then we stripped and jumped into the fast side currents of the Indus. Across the river, the Dalai Lama's white palominos were grazing. A goatherd wandering near them glanced on undisturbed by our foreign nudity.

Tenzing returned after sunset. We sat out over dinner. An evening breeze, a whirlwind of dust. And somewhere off in the darkness, two dogs fighting. One cried for hours. Then suddenly, hiatus. Tenzing informed us that this was no bitch, no injury, but rather a trick which thieves used. Scaring their victims inside with trained dogs.

The morning broke in furiously. I was up and spitting out toothpaste into the river whorls. The sky was unmarred. We packed up. Then drove down the road, across the loose bridge and up through the dark desert into Stok. The village was deserted at five a.m. On the ridge of a hill, the old palace. The packs were thrust on our backs and the long sludge through town began, stepping through primitive irrigation ditches towards the unknowable gorge in the rear. From here, a crude drawing by the British up to Base Camp at 15,000 feet is all we had to go by.

We had been above 10,000 feet for almost a week and the trek felt good. Usually the first hour of a hard hike would wipe me out. It would require a consistent pace, a hard-driving statement to the body that this was real. There was no backing out. But now from the outset I was moving fluently, without asthmatic churning or back pain. Sweat evaporated in this sere-like atmosphere before it was noticeable. There was a herding trail leading above the village along winding runnels. Skews of tortured poplar, frail contrasts to the desert gorge which engulfed them, clung tenaciously to the waterway's broken edge.

Up ahead three young bare-footed girls in goatskin attire and jewelried necks were moving their small flock with gnarled droving stocks quickly down the mountain. "Jeelai, jeelai," they sang, happily touching fingers to their foreheads.

Following the map, we turned up a right angling side canyon. The river's course was bare and gutted in the debris of old moraines. Bones of rock. For two hours, closed in on all sides by steep ribs of scorched dirt a thousand feet high, we continued, resting every twenty minutes or so, gulping down Gatorade. Our shirts were off. Ghisela's hair was back in a turquoise beaded headband from the Smokey Mountains. Tenzing was wearing a pair of Indian corduroys.

The gorge broadened out into a flat plain of rubble, the progressive incline so subtle we hardly knew we were ascending. At the top, the channel forked, a flume coming swiftly down from the south and the arid steppes rising in a steeper chute to the northwest. At this junction we encountered a home. A goitered idiot sat there. A member of a large family, Tibetan rock troglydites, whose complicated structure of graveled bunkers and mud archways embraced built-up holes leading into the earth. The boy was sitting on a stone file, slobber around his mouth, nettles in his long hair. His hand was under his robe. Turning his head back and forth, groaning. One of his eyes was gone, foul secretions running from sores around his ears. The mother stepped outside the enclave of rock, nodding her head in silent greeting.

"Stok Kangri?" Tenzing asked.

She shook her head. Had never heard of such a mountain. But ahead, ten miles or so, we spied a snow-covered ridge, and high behind it, the flat side-glacier on which Martin's party must have set down their Camp I. Stok itself was obfuscated by the ridge. We set up on the last of the gorges. A poisonous yellow berry spotted the dirt here. A hundred water trickles gurgled through the steep stones, carrying many with them so that all the course land underfoot was alive with pleasant clicking. The trail was no more. Before us rose a grassy series of hills, sepia yaks grazing along the pulpy terraces. On their eskimo necks, far away chimes, a cool zephyr carrying the ringing music down from the mountain upon which they had wandered, mouths to the soggy pasturage for centuries. Children were on the hill amid these fluffy, complacent behemoths.

When they saw us they charged down, howling, like raging Bacchae, amazed by newcomers to their hidden world. They knew where the last expedition had camped and dragged us by our hands, right to the manicured circle where three tents had once stood. Water runoff trenches were eroded through and dandelions had sprung up from the soft grass. It was an ideal Base Camp, protected from behind, with a sharp vantage of the depths. The Indus Valley was discernible beyond the tallest of the gorge walls, and beyond the Indus rose the first layer of peaks north of Leh, 17,000 feet and capped in snow.

By the time we'd set up our tents, the children's father, dressed in a vermilion *bokhu*, had sauntered down from his underground hamlet above. We could see the smoke from the fire which kept going all summer evidently, taking yak dung that they continually were drying for fuel. He offered us a bag of homegrown dee cheese, in exchange for salted sunflower seeds.

"Stok Kangri?" Allain asked, getting into his wool knickers.

"Yes," the young father replied.

"You speak English?" I asked.

"Wintertime. I go school in Leh."

"You're just here in the summer?"

"Yes. For my father. To help the yaks. Yaks not so happy in Leh. Too much warm for them."

Tenzing spoke with him in Tibetan regarding the expedition here the year before. "He remembers there are many avalanches up there, boss. He says not long after the other expedition leaving place, the whole mountain came down to very close here. He says he lost many yak. Very bad place in spring. He say you must no make avalanche."

We fixed up a Darjeeling brew, ate some chocolate, and before the gigantic mountain darkness snuck up on our campside, we hiked the hundred soggy meters up across a steep hill to visit with Pemba's family. They were agropastoral nomads, *so ma brog* in Tibetan.

We were greeted by a Tibetan woman. She was radiant. The same blue eyes, turquoise-coral necklace, in velvet dress, goat-hair rain cape, and felt boots. We stepped down to enter the smoke-engulfed underground adobe. A half-dozen kids, adorable ragamuffins, were sprawled out on rugs covering the earthen floor. A neat, swarthy jumble of animation. Two other women with waist-length black braids were stirring corn soup, millet gruel and steaming some wild cauliflower in large brass pots over yak-dung and rhododendron-chip fire. Basic provender. No polyandry in this household. Proud Pemba was relaxing with his children, his head lodged snugly against a damp sod wall.

"You don't prefer an outdoor tent?" I asked him, smiling.

"No . . . tent too cold!" he said.

"And the smoke doesn't hurt your eyes?"

"Smoke?"

"From the cooking."

"Cooking warm."

The women were giggling. And Pemba too. "What's so funny?" I asked Tenzing, who was also beginning to grin.

"His wives think Ghisela is beautiful."

She blushed. They were all matriarchs, with a language of their own. A vocabulary of skin tone, painted nails, white teeth, rouge, hair pieces, jewelry . . . For thousands of years, while men killed mastadons and each other, the women adorned themselves. Brazilian headhunters proudly brought back the flesh of Frenchmen to their camp cauldrons, but all the women really wanted were those Portuguese combs and ivory buttons.

Ghisela gave one of them a scarf, and another one some lemon-tasting chapstick. Six hands went out, "Chewing gum, chewing gum!" "'No!" Pemba shouted. The women were wide-eyed, intelligent.

They prepared bowls of spiced dol, hot mushy ruffage. And wheatcake, which we dipped in a tangy sauce. We ate with our hands from off the rug. No dishes. I knew this wasn't wise. We drank fermented kumiss, mare's milk, a favored draft in Mongolia and Tibet.

"You go up Stok Kangri?" Pemba asked.

"Yes, tomorrow."

"What is the name of the mountain next to Stok?" Allain asked.

"No name," Pemba answered.

"What is behind Stok?"

"More mountain."

"A valley?"

"I don't know. Have never been." Tenzing spoke Tibetan with him. And then shook his head.

"Do you like the mountains?" I asked.

He smiled full. "Oh, yes! Mountain good place to looking. Good drinking. Good a sleeping."

Pemba went on to warn us of the *mu rgod*—a wild, untamed man, known to the Sherpas as *Yeti*, and to Tibetans by *lung-gum*. He was variously named *gangs-mi*, meaning glacier man, and even *mi bom po*, strong robust man. Pemba said this creature fed off flowers which grew in rich clusters atop high white shaman trees of smoothen bark, trees growing from the ice, their flowers glowing in the dark. This abominable snowman had in fact drifted linguistically from the legendary yak-eating beast, to a harmless rascal of a man, much like Uncle Thompa, the Tibetan grandpa lecher. But there was no doubt about Pemba's belief in the existence of such a one. His children doubly counted on its existence. They seemed to dream of it—from what I could glean of Tenzing's narration—the same way American kids look to unspoiled Alaska; or Smokey the Bear.

And in eastern Nepal, scientists were looking for the last vestiges of Neanderthal hiding out in the backbush. The Chinese are convinced the Yeti exists. The Academy of Sciences in Peking sent an expedition into the Yangtse gorges. Tracks littered the karst caverns, creatures were sighted. So far none have been captured.*

*The Mongolian term for Yeti is *al-mass*; Kazaks call it *ksy-gyik*. The Chinese know it to be *Yeh ren*. There have been over two hundred sightings of the creature in Hubei Province's virgin northwest, and along the 1,200 mile Shen Nong escarpment, a region of overhung cliffs and pockmarked caves, some 3,000 feet deep. Scientists from Wu Han University in Shanghai have found seventeen-inch primate footprints in the area, which in itself controverts the prevailing theory that Asia's giant apes died out in the ice age 500,000 years ago. All sightings of the "wild man" agree on certain elements: it imitates the cries of other animals, claps its hands, even smiles, about six and one-half feet tall, its face resembling a man's, and reddish-brown hair covering its muscular body. See "China has its Yeti too," by Ji Ti, pp. 18-19, International Wildlife, Jan.-Feb., 1981.

In the overcast morning we packed the gear and started up steep sides of a gushing rivulet that was partially concealed beneath the mammoth boulders. It was hard going. At 16,000 feet I could feel the first real pangs in my forehead. The altitude was cutting into me, the pack getting heavier by the minute. I sat down. Breathing fast. Allain was way in the lead, Tenzing and Ghisela behind. Up ahead, the slope was severe. A gulley of grueling scree led up a good 2,000 feet. Snow covered the ground in white patches. Above that, a curving slab of blue ice, bottomed-out, small waterfalls running down its center. The glittering ice against a grey-white sky produced a sensation that the scree was nearly vertical. I watched Allain beginning to struggle with it, his ice ax flailing against the deep sliding detritus.

I entered the battle, every step an agony backwards, each two feet gained accompanied by one foot lost.

By noon we'd reached the ice barrier. With a heavy pack it was as difficult as anything in the world could be. I envied Pemba, surrounded by his subterranean warm-blooded clan, daydreaming with those blue-eyed velveteen women all over him.

I cringed. A loud splintering above. Screams!

We lunged into the small cave of snow abase the ice, as a rash of nevé and pieces of the moraine came rushing over the rim in a crackling volley. The mass crashed into the scree out some fifteen feet from where we huddled, heads pressing into our packs.

We made for the shoulder, ascending delicately over steep layers of shale.

A new gale. New odors. The east face of Stok Kangri, an immense glacial basin, the unnamed peak, all awesome above a salient knife-edged arête that rose elliptically thousands of feet to an apiculate, cobalt seizure of summit. Heavily corniced ridge melded these two fluted edifices. The North Ridge, cleaved by the oppressive rock peak Parchikangri, wound upwards a mile. No pasture.

The remains of avalanche were ubiquitous, of the slab kind, and indicating precipitation. We sensed some immunity along the flat snowy, uncrevassed perimeters, only. And there we set up camp.

The tents were placed to combat a storm which was soon to spill. Another crackling.

Night, hurling snow. The first real mountain weather since I'd come to India.

There is rare abandon in a snowbound tent of darkness. The body is charged with exhaustion and a splendor of nervousness both real and unreal, agoraphobic, vainglorious, and tempered in the island of weary circumstance. It is good, with the wind, snow floss careening into nylon sides, wet globules of hail settling along the edges and drops of water—dolt—condensing on the insides; every effort is laborious, weighted. There is confusion amid so much gear. No possibility for coherence or complete security. The storm might last a week. Might blow down the tent. And only the sleeping bag is real.

When men are close to death they often indulge in a kind of humor, in nervous cracks and grotesque grunts with a semblance of metaphor, a verbal conspiracy with pain and potential fatality. The reason for this Buddhist or inappropriate giddiness is variable, but generally such speech takes place in sagging tents, while blizzards are raging outside, and avalanches and stones are careening down on all sides in the unknowable darkness; or in prison camps on the eve of an escape, upon ships taking in more drawl water than they can hold, in deserts when the eyes can no longer fix steadily, or in jungles which have suddenly boxed one in, macheteless.

Mountaineering is particularly prone to the humor of great risk. For its dangerous moments can be calculated well in advance. It is a macabre courting process which tempts, with a fantastic verbosity of abandon, the terrible coming event and ritualizes, by superstitious placation of the elements, whatever horrid happening has been designed, or, in the case of known routes, precedented.

As on the 6,000-foot Eiger North Face, where many of the sections are named after those who died there: "Death Bivouac," or the "Hinterstoisser Traverse," in memory of the daring young German who crossed the steep rock, only to freeze to death marooned on its far end. Or the numerous *classic* sites on Nanga Parbat's Rakhiot Face, which took thirty lives before the peak was finally ascended. Then there is the infamous Whymper Couloir on the Aiguille Verte, with its dangerously loose snow top perennial ice, or the ice gullies which must be crossed to begin the Bonatti Pillar on the Dru, the South Face of Huandoy, the lower chutes on the West Face of Makalu, the South Face of Aconcagua, the traverse between the two summits of Nanda Devi, the East Ridge of Mt. Deborah, the Matterhorn's North Face, or El Capitan's Sea of Dreams. Routes, in other words, where the hazards are historical ones, and where successive attempts are made precisely for those reasons.

"You're talking to yourself."

"What!"

"You're mumbling," she warned. "I think he's succumbing," Ghisela said to Allain, who sat crunched up in our tent gnawing on a dried salami.

"What if it snows for days and days?" I said.

"Cover the crevasses. Cozy enough in here."

"I don't mind," said Ghisela.

"I hate small talk," I advised.

"You're really nuts," she sighed, drawing in an extra breath to compensate. We were high.

"Yeah."

"Do you two *ever* get along?" Allain inquired.

"Only when neither of us talk," I said.

"We understand one another." She fondled my neck.

"You're lucky," he smiled, a bit saddened, before stepping out into the blizzard.

"We *are* lucky," she went on, repeating a pledge not altogether applicable.

"I suppose." I was unsure. There had been *so* many fluctuations in our relationship.

Allain went into the second tent, where Tenzing lay.

"Tell me something," she sobered. "Why are you afraid of me?"

"What makes you think that?"

"You are. In five years you've never *shared* a look. You're always looking *at* me."

"Because I find you fascinating."

"No."

"Beautiful, then."

"Stop."

"It has always bothered me that you speak with so little confidence."

"You don't help and you're supposed to. You find all problems tedious. We mortals don't fit into your scheme."

"What do you want?"

Pause. "I want you to say you love me and mean it."

"I've lived with you for years."

"Do you want to have a baby with me?"

"No. I don't know."

"You don't, do you?"

"I'm not a bastard, if that's what you're after. I love you. I also have no compulsion to get married any more."

"You did!"

"So did you. Then you severed it. Then you came back. Then I broke it off. Came back. We did Fred Astaires with one another. I think we're sick. You're a few years older. I see a grey hair. You're more desperate than I am. You don't—under any circumstances—want to grow old alone."

"Do you?"

"No."

"Well?"

"I have to tell you. Since you can't walk out on me, not now, anyway."

"Tell me what?"

"When I see another woman, sometimes, a particular kind of woman—thin, tall, long hair, animated expression, good jaw, white, swift-arrayed teeth, tightly embedded, emblazoned crotch, I gain new fervor, want more from life. My thirst . . . well, I pity the poor bastard who can drink his cup dry. Mine's never dry."

"And you don't think it's the same with me?"

"I can't bear to contemplate so disturbing a possibility. Yes, there is—damnit!—a double standard. Just like there's a double helix, a double in literature, duality in every living psyche."

"No!" she roared. "No there isn't."

She got up, put on her boots, her jacket, breathing hard, burdened, and scooted out the tent.

She can't go anywhere, I thought.

I waited.

Ghisela!

I got up, went outside. There was already a fresh foot of powder. I followed her tracks. She'd circled out into the glacier. Not cute.

I found her sitting. Wet.

"Come."

"I hate all of you."

"OK."

I went back to the tent. Within a few minutes she returned.

We lay awake nestling for warmth, feeling bronchial in the cold moisture, and on edge about the morrow. What dangers it would bring. Why I did this to myself; vacillation from great, nervous excitement to downright depression. Only sleep, or the literary can reverse an otherwise pernicious tendency of thought to self-inflict with apprehension.

I recall the words of Li Ho:

> "Then quietly comes the dream
> of an aged woman
> on an ancient mountain."

The vague glimmer of a radiant acacia in the eye of an old woman in the Karakoram one deserted April afternoon in the early twelfth century.

Each utterance is woven into the greater adhesion of a surrounding. Any human being readily grasps a lake, a tree, a high hill.

Imbedded in the logic of millennia, the woman, the glow of the afternoon, her sentiments, we feel akin to. She lives alone, in a village far from anything. Her husband was gored by a buffalo two decades past, and no relatives survive her. A monk brings her food every third day.

Her ideas inhabit her mountains. There is a wildness about her thoughts, despite whatever practical concerns embellish them, a universal wildness which philosophers on all continents will idealize forever, almost nostalgically.

We were restless to get moving. Everything wet. We spent the whole next day drying all our gear, sizing up the route. Straight up an hourglass formation, a dazzling steep ice couloir of at least ten pitches, the lower half-pinned by hanging serac in midcenter face. This two hundred-foot high obstacle might be turned on its right side where a large dugout seemed to exist. Here we could place Camp 2, assuming the lower chutes went smoothly.

The next day broke flawlessly. We were up before the sun placing wands to mark our way across the glacier. The crevasses were all covered with the new snowfall. White parallel chutes were venting furious fusillades of powder but the hourglass alone was quiet, its ice too steep to hold snow. We went to within a hundred feet of the bergschrund, deposited six ropes, and then returned to

Camp 1.

We all felt strong. Allain and I would push for the snowy platform area adjoining the center of the hourglass in the early morning, fixing ropes, while Ghisela and Tenzing rested. Then we would descend and all four of us would jumar-ferry the gear. Normal routine. The weather was good. A big mountain. Beyond was Sasur Kangri, 7,000 meters high, entrenched in a half-dozen granite sentinels that stood out against thick cumuli like swords. And beyond that, China. Unexplored regions of prehistoric drapery left over from the Tibetan ice ages. I was happy. Concerned only with climbing that ice couloir and getting off. To have climbed it. Already craving the relief of getting back to Pemba's cheese, the land-rover. In an instant of homesickness, girded by fear of the face, of being on ice, of being alone. And there was the other side. Where were we going? Into a final night of sleep.

A dream. Sweat, eyes ablaze and loony. Cheyne-Stokes breathing for the interminable night's duration.

CHAPTER FOURTEEN

"Let's do it!" Balladeur's voice rasped through the hard crystalline dawn. In a pause of enervation, a lightning recognition that I was condemned. The heavy burden of frozen boots. Ghisela fast to her deep drowsiness. She and Tenzing would ascend the route later in the day, once ropes were fixed.

Light clouds spotted the ridge. Sasur Kangri simmered in darkness. We trundled two damp rucksacks. Hard snow. The useless glow of dawn steaming off numb cheeks.

I led through the bergschrund, up a chute and onto the lower trench of the face, my ice ax plunged onto tenuous snow; friable stone; windswept sugar powder. Nothing certain. I pulled up the ropes and dangled them, whilst belaying Balladeur. He then set off above onto steep water ice. We could see all too clearly the serac hanging 1,200 feet over us. Our progress slowed down, as ice screws became increasingly recalcitrant. Only the two front points of our crampons could penetrate the armor of the couloir. Breathing was encumbered. We were ascending in a ratio of ten breaths per foot; whereas a Reinhold Messner—superb Tyrolean soloist—apparently travels upwards at three breaths per foot. An unimaginable difference.

Spindrift, bare, delicate, added cold, was sweeping the frozen face where we stood; like snow flurries across an abandoned gas station of the mind, in some outpost of aloneness, northern Wyoming perhaps.

Deep beneath us, beyond the vestal glacier and our tents, spread the Ladakhi Sahara. Embroiled in clouds, a pattering of sunlight inundating dramatic side deltas of the Indus Valley. Two pitches above the schrund. Ten a.m. Steep. Exposure mounting. A feeling of ninety-five degrees. No understanding. Just the irksome feeling. My calves a little cramped. My neck itching under a woolen hat. Cold. My toes numb. Leading. We were going on into a cul-de-sac, unclear, laboring under the plangent throe of cliff, in a gnarl of sweat-giving umbrage, air guttural and causative. I sensed a snare beyond, communicating its ploy. Our very transport was intuitive, alert to magic signs now, afraid, thinking by its own momentum.

There was no stopping. The slope gave nothing. It hardened, becoming aerial, as we wound upwards through Cenozoa, bushwacked beyond into an earth gone flimsy and insecure, passed the final bone of mountain. I sensed antagonism in the air, a secretive recognition of cross-purposes that had been building towards this last bend, where the ice plied a sharp turn. There were dying snowfields caught in the northfacing shadows like immense rafters. High against the wind was more snow, in flumes that bisected cuneatic cloud. Hanging on tight to my hammer, I staggered backwards. It was all rainbow. Where the terrain swung precipitously downward, the sun's striations poured through.

We continued towards the place. It was in the center of all my thoughts, an eclectic piece of desire that madly encompassed many prizes of landscape at once. My wanderings were sheer compulsion. I'd destroy myself if I didn't move, and if I did. This was in my character, and I relished the knowledge of such dilemma, felt the rush of fear, of fabulous culture shock—*wilderness shock*—set in all over again, as it had in hot waves from the beginning. Shot through with sentience, I was surrounded by myself, awkward, misshapen, rank, a dreadful spectre of youth hellbent, feeling better and better.

My body throbbed, had been abused and I was proud. For it was golden, the muscles pronounced like never in my life. Each pain I gave into with something approaching eagerness now. I was craggy, like granite, a bulwark. Hard-stomached, steel-armed, Greek-legged. To be lost, lusting after alpines, near China, or wherever the hell, was to be bronzed over with the eye of cloudless noon, ultravioleted; to be filthy with chaste dirt, dusted by the ebony stream of particle vision. The tidbits of humus, flotsams, of microfauna underneath nails; to be chaffed and fitted and raw and goaded. All lithe with wildness, and the venture of it. To have come down from the mountains, from off the sea, or out from the desert; emerging from gauntlets vengeful, athwart with some untellable mystery. And this look catapulted by the halo of a Rublev Saint, the lackadaisical insouciance of Tuareg whose dark blue desert saunter commands the testimony about which they are so brazenly mute.

Twenty feet above my last ice screw. A dilemma overtaking me. Out of control. Nowhere to move but up, awkwardly stemming, that sure sign of trouble. No say in the matter. The course too clearly defined. The route beckoning, teasing me. A hole in the ice. Close rock underneath. Everything loose. "Watch me!" I cautioned Allain who stood perched, leaning out from the wall against three tubular Salewa ice screws.

The muscle in my right thumb was pressing into the palm. I couldn't flex it open. My front points were barely in. Nothing holding me. And my faith in the system waning rapidly. I slammed my ice hammer high. Nothing. The ice crumbling into my face. My ax wouldn't hold. Something in my eye. I slammed again, this time closer to my left shoulder. How did I get into this? Squirming now. The route was too hard. Sweat coming. Guttural grinding. Something still in my eye. Slam again. No good. Don't even bother to test it. Got to get the ax stable. Get the ax in! My mind flinging frantic demands. I burned. Maddened warnings to myself. Terror encroaching fast. Allain far below. Get it in! I plunged it. Hit it hard. My left arm hanging from the wrist loop, connected to the ice hammer. My mind slow. *Get a screw in!* it said. Change hand positions. Hammer and twist, twist and hammer. Too steep to change positions. Shit! "What?" Allain's faint voice responds. "Watch me!" I yell. Move! A little higher. I see ten feet above a stance where I might be able to belay. I keep moving. Twenty-five feet above the last screw. My arms are nearly gone now. "Watch me!"

The ice was thin. Too thin. I was afraid to kick hard. Yet I had to if I was to connect. I was climbing in a thin layer of fog on the wall. Uncertain now if I would adhere, each step, thrown against the sheer, unrelenting sheen, a question mark of expenditure. It steepened. My body overhung. All on the arms. Aerial. The glacier beneath, four hundred feet. Allain, a mere shade. Stifled in the gleaming contours around him. My arms giving out, pain in the muscles, losing the grip. Squirming, squirming, and all hot. Ropes, yellow, orange, purple . . . drifting under me. Nothing left. The ledge too far away to lunge for. Nothing. Hanging by both . . . "Allain!"

Smack! A flash in my groin. Out! Head out! Flailing, endlessly spinning.

Spitting. Sharpness everywhere. "You got it?" his voice echoed from somewhere. " You OK? Get yourself in. Get into the ice, Michael!"

"What?" I murmured, dazed. Hurt? Voice breaking. Legs shivering. Thirty feet above me, that last ice screw I had placed. Sixty feet below me, the outstretched Allain tightly gripping the rope with both hands in hara-kiri. "You alright?"

"I think so. My balls."

"You alright?" he screamed up again.

"Just hold me, goddamnit!" Kicking my points frantically into the ice. A shrug of convulsed release. If that screw had come out . . . He couldn't lower me. My leg was bleeding. No way to check it under the tied gaiters. And in that situation. I thrashed to reclimb.

Back up to the ice screw. Now slanting downwards. It had bent, nearly popped. I placed a second one high above, fast. Moved up on tension, no more free-climbing, seven feet above, another. In this aid fashion I reached the belay, a friable corner, frozen up against a convergence of near vertical wall above, the steep bulb of the lower hourglass.

"First fall in years," I remarked, as Allain surmounted the ledge.

We undid my pants. A rift on the inside of my left thigh.

I remembered his definition of a sāddhu. One who lives without regrets, who stares into the Abgrund without looking away. And Kazantzakis' stalwart encomium to Mind: it heads fearlessly for the cliff and plunges. All fine and good. But my thigh was punctured, and if that screw had pulled, my crampons would have gone right through Allain's cerebellum. Noon, the sun was softening the ice. We had to move.

Allain led up on aid over the next steep section, a string of thirty-five screws strung across his chest. He made painfully slow progress. My feet were without feeling and I remembered they had been so for the whole morning.

"Hold me!" his voice bellowed, two hours later. "I've got to make a tension traverse. You got me?"

"Yes." Our goshawk yammers out over the glacier interrupted the fast calm of these steeps. The rope was burning through my mittens. Allain had leaned way out and was pulling, walking sideways like a tarantula across the quartzy cragline towards an obscure glint above the headwall.

"OK, slack! More, let it loose!"

He was at a sling belay high on the rampart. No more ledges for a good seven hundred feet. It was the hardest ice gulley I'd ever experienced. I jumared up in waning orange glow. We left two ropes at the cramped belay. Then rappelled the entire bastion through ice rivulets until back down on the glacier, an hour later. We'd climbed a fourth of the wall. Harder than I'd bargained for. Allain was not about to yield. I didn't have to say anything. His face betrayed stubbornness. A jacking-off of inexperience. Back across the glacier. I was limping. Hungering for pillows, hot water, the vestigial hearth. Had human beings ever fashioned a more compelling picture of heaven? With its satin cushions and tenebrous nights and gusts of warm tropical winds across Polynesian havens? Where the eye traces patterns in some future, festive feather bed, a future lit up in the embers of simple destiny?

Ghisela was there for me, all fresh and eager to hear of the climb.

"You look troubled?" Allain disappears in his tent. "What's with him?"

"He's possessed. I'm not."

My head lay lithely on the cold lining of Ghisela's sleeping bag. She scratched my head. The firmament shone disinterested. Primeval silence. Only the far away roar, miners at work in my deepest suspicions, the roar of fear, of falling all over again.

Morning.

Gloam inundating sleeplessness. Everything stiff with frost. My breath swirling around me in the weathershorn tent. Crackles of ice somewhere. A few stars left from the night. Real nausea now. We were going for good up that wall; would have to uproot camp and haul it a glacial mile, then into the sky.

Later, we heard groans from the other tent. Tenzing.

"He's sick," Allain acknowledged.

"No good stomach, boss!" I got into my double-boots and crawled out into the stinging dawn. The amphitheater was ghostly mute, tinged with the icing of sunrise. The walls were foreshortened, gloomy in their darkness. My lungs, blitzed with prickling air, started jerkily.

"Bad stomach, eh?" Within minutes my toes were again numb. My thigh throbbed. I was exhausted from yesterday. "We wait a day?"

"No, no boss. You go. I come."

"What does that mean?"

"I come."

Allain was up. I went back to Ghisela. She too groaned. Her face was burnt. Peeling in the wrinkles of her forehead. Tumid lips. Not a pretty thing. I had vowed not to look at myself. Now I couldn't help staring into my snow goggles. A solar leper. Older-looking than the hoary men of Leh. My skin had been beaten by the sloughs of runoff, the constant pulse of altitude, the incessant touch of cold. In a matter of days I'd become chancred. I tried to groom. But the cold prevailed. My hands were dumb, no reflex.

"Get up!"

I didn't want to go. Allain was out peeing. He looked eager as hell. Saccharin. I *couldn't* go. He turned with that baroque smile, his manner of imputing silence with orthodox suggestiveness. "We take down the tents?"

"Sure," I aired. Shit.

Tenzing was dressed, clumsily maneuvering the stoves, in obvious pain. Nobody said anything. Stok Kangri's east face hung swollen in the air, peppered with brittle arrays of loose ledges, and sheer drop-offs. All attached to nothing: snow, that became ice, that became rock, becoming sky. A delirium of elemental gloss, without a point, an Archimedean reference, where one could definitely decide what was what. And staring from the glacier, our tents rolled up, the rucksacks ready to be hauled towards the bottom spur, I felt an asphyxiating tremor of freedom, sudden nudity. What if falling ice had cut our ropes? We heard it coming down all night. What if Tenzing couldn't haul? What if my leg prevented me from leading? Those clouds. A storm? What ifs . . .

The freedom to turn back, I thought. To go home. Pemba's underground, that steaming hospice of giggles and blue-eyed young ladies. A paradise, by contrast to our bare world of 17,500.

Then, fluttering wings.

I dove down instinctively. We all lunged for cover which didn't exist. A shattering thunder from high on the mountain. A couloir's old fracture line widened slowly. Then burst. The ice was falling. I clung. Watching the slow-descending, pulverizing armageddon of fury from the embryo of myself, dug behind my pack for protection. A fireball of exploding powder ripping the air, or the illusion of air. Cascading, gaining a frenzy of speed, coming out towards us. I remembered Pemba's description of the avalanche. *Jesus!* I moaned. Ghisela's head inside my chest. A plenum of mad clapping, gigantic, hitting the hourglass from the side. An explosion! A section—like railroad cars—three hundred feet of crackling, whiplashed momentum, immense shards of earth whamming into the serac. Another explosion! The huge overhang itself, shuttering, ungluing, breaking off, and detonated in the ruinous flush of lightning tons.

"The ropes!"

Our couloir was now alive with the burning. A cyclone of powder, ice, visible wind bursting down in volatile streamers. Clacking waterfalls dissolving into the atomic rupture of severed space. Collapsing into the bergschrund. Our route herniated, the air of the amphitheater rent in the rumbling after-concussion of shock, of nature. A million pounds of razor, frozen pressure consumed invisibly by the glacier, eaten by a cycle of eons all indistinguishable from each other in the flow of up here.

We stood up, stunned. There were scars, breaches of gutted metamorphite high on the left couloir and down along the ice we'd climbed. Half of the serac was gone, as well as our proposed Camp 2.

A deliverance, Kiplingesque. Allain and I set off. I was relieved. I sucked in the enthusiasm still settling between molecules.

There was little else to say. I hugged Ghisela and took off through deep snow. We were no longer roping up on the glacier. We'd marked it well. Allain moved fast. I was elated. I wouldn't have to climb. No matter the meaning of that. Pemba was the only significance worth considering. Pemba was life. Children. Safety. The fur of yaks. The sward of his hillside nestle. There were still rivulets of snow and ice chinking in the aftermath of the avalanche. the one extendable aluminum six-rung ladder we'd brought along was up against the lowest outside wall of the schrund. Now I could barely climb it, my muscle thick, hard, painfully locked, each step a jolt. Allain disappeared over the last fling of ice. It took me ten minutes to join him at the commencement of our route.

"Rope looks fine," he said indifferently.

I hung on it. Swinging. Did every goddamned thing I could to rip it out.

"I'll go try the next one," he ventured.

"Make sure, when you test it, you're tied into number one." He jumared slowly. The first pitch was so much steeper than it had seemed the day before. Some new rocks were showing through, the ice skinned right off. The blue of his parka and knee-length gaiters, the red of his hood, gave off an upwards dangling effigy of clownhood: vulnerable flesh made ridiculous in the thoughtless passion, for a summit? He reached the belay pedestal.

"Ice screws are in solid. The rope looks untouched!" he yelled down, his tiny figure now wrapped in the impending shroud of the bulb above him. I watched him tie off onto the screws and attach both jumars to the next rope.

"What does Number 2 look like?"

"Fine!" He was hanging on it, bouncing up and down. "No problem!" He unsnapped his binders from the three ice screws and started up. "Come on!" he screamed fanatically.

"I'll wait till you get to Number 3," I shouted back, genuinely fearing he'd come off. And I did not intend to be under him when he died.

Nor could I stand watching Allain tempting those ropes which I knew to have been hit. Our entire lower route had been smashed open, scathed with tons of torrent. I leaned against an ice out-cropping, helpless to stop our presence on the face. The same old unwanted self, reeking of coercion, eluded me. To have just reared up and said it—No!—in the morning.

"OK!" the smeared voice bawled from high up on the wall.

"Fuck you!" I screamed, clamping on my frosted jumars. I'd raise the right leg high and stand, my left leg thereby elevated. I was breathing hard. Scared to death. I saw remnants of the ice fall everywhere. Large pit marks, grainy contusions on a surface which had been fine lustre the day previous.

I reached the first belay, snapped onto the second rope and proceeded with even less confidence. Hanging out over the inferno of the schrund. Mentally choosing a landing place should the rope break. Allain was at the sling belay, gazing down from Number 3. Probing slow, short heaves upwards, feet in midair, standing in awkward stirrups, I plowed through the vertical cold, feeling like an idiot. Up to the second belay. The next pitch, my nemesis overhung at top. I felt a little proud for having climbed it. And stupid.

Now I was unsure why I'd returned. I'd made it. Had even enjoyed it despite, or because of, the fall. Surely as much as any summit. But now the situation was reversed.

It was the summit we seemed to be after. And Allain was psychologically in the lead. This, too, was a big change. I'd taught Balladeur how to climb, talking him into his first three-pitch scramble. He took five falls that day, dangling stubbornly off a facile projection, staunchly refusing to push for it and threatening to suffocate if I didn't let him down. I didn't. Ortsa! I'd cheered him on. *Arriba mas arriba!*

Now I was stricken with dangerous vanity, a refusal to assert what I was really thinking. The fear of getting wiped out in an instant. The face was no longer alluring, with 2,500 feet of ice left to climb. I hung mid-rope, pondering our situation. *The face is too hard!* I'd tell him.

We met at a sling belay, without a word, at 18,000 feet. My breathing was pronounced, painful, seizure-like. He snapped on the last of the fixed ropes. Above us hung the two other ropes we'd left. I crouched to the side as he yanked on them. I was not willing to exchange jumar-leads. Either he risked going first, or I was going down. This angered him. And with cold defiance he was assuming leadership, naïvely. We'd hardly had a talk the whole climb. Ever since the Indus afternoon following the incidents at Hemis. We'd both taken separate inward flights. He, I knew, was absolutely convinced of that ashram. I just wanted to enjoy the mountains. Not Allain. And he was off, edging into space up the wall. Not saying a word, not looking down. Possessed in his incensement. Crampons and ice ax scraping against the downpour of steepness. I wanted off, fast. My knuckles were bloody. We'd already put up a partial first ascent, and that was enough, more than enough for me.

I'd seen markings on the third rope. And more on the fourth. No climber can forget the death of John Harlin. On the Eiger Directissima in the mid-1960s. The rope had held for three men before him. But he was not so lucky. I thought of Ghisela and Tenzing having to jumar up here. Never! I inched up to the fourth belay.

"I'll lead!" Allain stated emphatically.

"Oh, really?" I said, baring my condemnation. "And who's going to belay you?" The route was mangled above. Large blocks, left from the explosion of the serac, ready to come off, five hundred feet above. So precarious, I felt a wave of panic shred my thoughts as the impression of our standing, arguing under it blossomed with malignant vulnerability.

"The bivy is gone, you asshole. We're going down!"

"Why?" he answered crazily.

"What do you mean, *why?* Allain!" Two egos sparring in an aerial hypervacuum, under a guillotine. He was ill. Hallucinating. Something. But he was dreaming out into the air, mindless. I shook him. And shook myself for letting him lead me back up here when it was so obvious.

"Allain, we're going down. Now!" I quickly adjusted the harness on his waist, for he had suddenly gone all numb and helpless. He'd proven something to himself, and it was done. I lowered out the two unused ropes, tying a triple fisherman's knot and running the doubled rappel line through two carabiners off the ice screws to be left.

This time I went first, anxious to get off. Without even looking up at the wall. No regrets whatsoever. I went quickly to Number 3. Allain followed suit. I kept my fingers crossed. The sun had punctured the shadows of the couloir. Down to the second belay. Eleven a.m. I heard shouting. Ghisela. She'd come alone to the base of the climb and was waving. Allain led the last rappel. I hammered in the screws and joined them on the glacier.

"Hurry," she cried. "Tenzing—in a crevasse!"

"How long?"

"Twenty minutes!"

We moved fast, my limp sublimated to greater urgency. The amphitheater of snow burned beneath the bald, exasperating desert sun.

Vomitous, he had dizzied out in the crevassed region, falling off the laden path into virgin ground.

"Tenzing?"

Faint whimperings. He was deep. Mindlessly we set about rigging a pulley over an ice ax. I rappeled down into the ultramarine gape. The temperature dropped precipitously as blackness merged with granular sheen.

He was wedged upright. No visible damage.

"Can you move?"

"Uh."

"Tenzing?" I shook him, maneuvering his feet into stirrups.

"I am sorry," he repeated.

"Shut up. Force your legs. Do it!"

I wrapped him with the parka and mittens I'd brought down. Within moments he was free of the cinch. Together we moved back up the rope on jumars. He had, remarkably, incurred no injuries of any interest. Crap in his pants, mangled knuckles, skin torn all over his thigh, clean gouge on his temple. A little shock. Nothing a rest day in the sun wouldn't remedy.

It was night. Balladeur remained vexed and sullen. Stars swelled the halo of sky. Ghisela's face shone nacreous beneath the sprawling night.

We'd be able to climb the easier face, I thought. And then there was the other side.

Tenzing snored. Talked in his sleep. Like an animal's, his words were deep as estrogen, unfathomable, reaching to some remote, cavernous coziness, a splash of manures, perhaps, and red wolves fighting over the succulent blood of a winter hare.

"Climbing is neat," Ghisela stated with satisfaction.

"Neat?"

"You disapprove of my choice of adjectives?"

"No, I, I tend to agree."

"I want to lead."

"Why?"

"I'm bored with sublimating, always deferring to you."

"I'm bored with it as well."

"Tomorrow?"

Our feet plied awkwardly beneath all the down, straining for reconciliation. Numb love.

CHAPTER FIFTEEN

We followed our same rhumb-by-rhumb route to the bergschrund, collecting all the wands, then traversed the face across the glacier to the lowest angle of wall beneath the col, two thousand feet above. There was no ice. But firm snow. It could be climbed easily. Tenzing vomited in the night, dry heaving. His face was tawny and he was losing weight. But he wouldn't say anything. The three of us conferred and decided to postpone a day. Allain, who had simmered down, would rope Tenzing back across the glacier. He'd go on to Pemba's, carrying his own supplies and a tent, and then continue to the land-rover and the camp on the Indus where we'd meet him in a week or so.

Tenzing balked when we told him. But only by way of an initial reaction. For he was very ill, beyond the fall. I suspected hepatitis.

Allain carried Tenzing's pack for him across the snowbridges to the shoulder and they vanished over the edge. Ghisela and I slept. Allain didn't return for several hours. He had to lower Tenzing down the shale to the scree and bring him across under the ice-tip of the glacier from where Tenzing went down on his own.

We were up in the dark. Sorting gear, dismantling the tents, assembling the packs. By five-thirty a.m. I was leading. Ghisela belayed, standing against the consolidated snowslope, a friction plate on her seat harness through which she let out the rope. I wore my pack with some forty pounds in it.

My boot sank in six inches and held. Like climbing a ladder. This was pleasure. The sun was coming up over Central Tibet, blazing broad prisms towards the sovereign Karakoram. The desert floor was still dark. I thought of Tenzing down with Pemba. And felt glad to be where I was. I'd always wondered about the extreme vacillation of sentiment, of energy on a mountain. Oscillating bravado, cowardice, excitement and abandon. All within an hour. Hundreds of such cycles over the duration of a climb.

I stabbed deep beneath the crust, implanting myself, tying off the rope for Ghisela to jumar ascend. She was up in fifteen minutes and led the next pitch flawlessly while Allain jumared. He then continued up to her belay and led on while I in turn jumared to Ghisela. In this braiding style we moved rapidly. Ten pitches by noon and another seven or eight to go. The angle a little steeper but still easy. The sky was cloudless, bremen, the glacier glittery in emperor whiteness. Across from us on either side, sheer walls, seracs, and the hourglass, mostly concealed in its central toboggan indentation. A grey lammergeyer circled over the ice. I remembered an incredible photograph of a like bird, frozen in its dauntlessness, discovered above 25,000 feet on Everest.

I was eating snow voraciously, for the water bottles were stupidly packed deep in Allain's pack—and he was in the lead. I stood on my snow platform with Ghisela, in a cherished daze. Flakes of snow spun down, powdery buns of sparkling light stuff. The hush, a sphinxian glisten of white polish, engulfed our communion on all sides. Not a sound over Asia.

As the day wore on, my temples throbbed. My energies were waning.

The mark is a temporary one. But of all memories, the labyrinthine mirages of weariness, spasms, salt-mouth, Saharan fatigue, Arabian nights . . . of all memories, exhaustion never forgets itself. It is the impetus of artists, and the impotency of others.

The intense concentration diffused over hours, the consequent thirst, the dust mingling with sweat on a tanned skin and the developing muscle tone all contribute to a heroic visage which will dream of itself at nights, configuring resplendent, cosmic tenors of action, dressing its wounds and hangnails with every vainglory the world has yet conceived to adore itself. Until the flesh is emptied and replenished with the meaning of its own collapse, its abandonment.

Lichen of gold, rust, grey, umber; gold rock, gleaming white glacier; swallows whistling maniacally through the crisp etherium. Seduced into lavish disarray, the climber's rumination hangs suspended over unutterable vastness. Delirium. Dozing at belays, the body hugging itself. Moving in enshrouded, tandem silence with his partner. Conscious of the parody they're formulating up there. Mangled happily in the fear, the race of adrenalin, the self-effacing, self-confronting consciousness.

Small and breathing, undressed and dwarfed, by mildly hallucinogenic response, the climber cuddles the exposure, the whole life of his mind distilled, yet fraught with the living legacy of itself, sprawled out on nubbins, asleep on ledges, autobiographical, and relentless. The rope's shadows bob back and forth. Parka sleeves pulled up, the nose daubed with zinc, muscles on edge. Amidst the nerves and reveries, the bleeding knuckles, disheveled, speck-larded hair, flooded veins, bronze skin, hard lips and cracking eyelets, an evolving mythology. The lambent, sun-splattered noon-time.

An epic burden, like electricity, buffeting the face, parching the throat, hampering blood flow to the toes. It is an eccentric collaboration of space and self, mountain climbing. Yes, it transcends metaphors. It is ineffable. As much as we try to convey it, we are stopped short of our goal. Danger was the original subject matter worth talking about. The forests of the world are nearer our disposition, our genetic calm, than is a cliff. As one walks one loses thoughts, is more relaxedly immersed. The very meaning of woods is this loss, this stunning, gliding serenity of entry by foot. There is no entry on a mountain. One is suddenly there, pinned, or exposed to the volatile impingements. And then comes the aerial anxiousness, the dire weighing of strategem, and that wavering apostasy which transforms subtle possibility into fantastic danger. Similes of risk compound fantasy; the wilderness of the wall assumes a character, an archetypal personality which is fanciful, introspective, but dangerous. Enraged, almost desperate, the quiet ego maims itself with worry; it can no longer see things. It construes them instead, stacking cairns, falls, piton placements, loose flakes, and storm into a lethal perspective which self-aggravates, and dextro-amphetamizes all beauty.

The backpacker can afford to be philosophical. His route does not demand his hands. But the artisan of ascent is committed, often times against his will, his better instincts, to an all-out grappling. The graphic alliteration of air around him, a constant likelihood of falling, procures no grandiose conviction, no better marriages. Nor has there ever been a brilliant book written about mountains, to my knowledge. Climbing courts a pantheon of hapless reactions charged with the overpowering, faultless sense of self-importance. And when alpinists refuse seriousness, they become ludicrously banal instead. Nerve-wracked, even pitiful in middle age. The pleasures to be derived are those of an escaped convict. He is fraught with a paradox which molests him on the condition of movement. His fondest ideals lack substance, in the end, for they are always construed, implanted, or arrested on the edge of the imagination. A purple-shadowed mountain on the horizon all too quickly becomes the tedious, steep and undistinguished talus slope. That hypnotic spire is suddenly a point of rock under one's bottom, like tens of thousands of others. What counts is the world below.

The climb distorts sensation into superstition, while a hike promotes the senses, revealing them in their natural turn. The energies of enjoyment are diverted on a wall, its aesthetics concentrated like a knot of apprehension allowing for no swoon. A hike can be awash with the thought diffusing levity of uncommitment. But inherent in this leisure, the hiker confronts his own shortcoming. He may swoon for trekking duration and still go home empty-handed. Here is the insistence, the Mallory-22, at the essence of the mountaineer's own eternal return. In the vague recesses of his past, the climber remembers something akin to a totality of response, which he finds nowhere else.

Horizontal perception is at ease. It has a composure, an excess of self-awareness. The climber on the other hand experiences something akin to a vertical dark night of the soul. His hyped-up frenzy is like continuous revelation for he sees himself clearly caught between two possibilities and it is up to him to maneuver the outcome. Having trespassed on the no-man's land of himself, he is in a sense freer than the walker, for he has touched the live wire, has tasted the limit. A walker can go forever and never know limits.

Exiting the face we were confronted with a steep ramp that merged some three hundred feet above onto the col. I led up without my pack. The climbing was serious here. We were nearly 20,000 feet high. I dug through wind slab to place an ice screw. All with difficulty. Suddenly I was scared to death. We were high, really high, and the face we'd climbed seemed vertical. Difficult to downclimb. We'd have to do it laboriously facing in, I supposed. And I wondered if Martin's party had had enough bollards to rappel with. I mantled onto the first of several steppes and secured a belay. Ghisela seconded, then continued upwards while Allain joined me. Another steppe, an ice incline. Spread-eagling awkwardly between the ramp and a seventy-degree wall. Up to the frightening zenith of the smooth dihedral. She stemmed onto the ridge. Flat · Wide. A gentle long place. "Off belay!" she retched. I followed, then led on to the summit.

I could not see the direct backside. The ridge curved gradually over the disappearing edge. Large drifts of corn snow had been rubbed hard by the wind into an ebony accent of glaze. From where I sat the magenta mystery of hundreds of miles of glacier and colored talus slope, pinnacles sun-illumined, hanging in vast silence, lay still and shimmering across the breadth of Asia. To all horizons. The western side was on fire with twilight. Details of crevasses, weathered slopes, cliffs were all graphically charged with an aureole. It took my breath away and flung it into the sea of mountains.

The rope pulled taut. Like a fishing line, twitching and shifting for seconds, for minutes, I watched from my erotic stupor. And within twenty minutes Ghisela came over the edge. Her head down, breathing hard.

"You see it?"

"Only the distance," I radiated. She stood above me.

"OK to jumar," I yelled down to Balladeur, my voice winnowed and sucked up in the fresh air. The moon was big, ripe, rearing herself over a continent entire. In the far distance shone Nun and Kun, hues glancing off their summital precipices of ice. Allain emerged over the last mantle-shelf, anxiously sliding his jumars towards us.

"Well?" he cried, out of breath.

"Can't tell yet."

"Keep me on." He climbed down towards the edge, his feet falling through the skin of hard snowcrust.

"Careful, it might be a cornice!"

"Michael!" We belayed each other across and then brought Ghisela over to the perch.

Awe. Hanging over the wintry interior of some forgotten pyramid of the elements. A good seven, maybe eight thousand feet under us in a steep rock-strewn drop-off: the square!

A freakish enclosure. A few thousand feet across and half that wide. Closed off with finality from the surrounding range. Staggering cliffs and couloirs falling off peaks 20,000 feet high. It was the essence of Gloucester's terror, the addiction to blind emptiness beneath one's feet. Another world, lodged in the abyss of geometrical ceasura. Like an empty moment in the ageless time that confected these mountains. It was spellbinding, heaving in steepness, a hesitation in the world, a whispering pause that saddled the second of glacier with barriers for all time, closing it off one ancient day in a mighty holocaust of formation.

And the green! There it was unmistakably, a small convoluted plot right up against the snow. I dug out my 300mm lens. Scanning the impossible cloister.

"It's a goddamned vegetable garden!" I squinted wildly. "The shadows make it difficult. Wait! A waterfall!"

"Give me the camera . . . . "

The glacier slanted east from off a peak. At its far lateral end it stopped abruptly in an overhang of seracs. A channel of swift water poured off this debris, into a large dark pool. The garden adjoined it on the far side. I remembered Keats' poem "On first looking into Chapman's Homer" and felt like Balboa (Cortez), with eagle eyes and wild surmise, staring silently at the unknown Pacific from a peak in Darien, legs tingling.

"What do you suppose the altitude down there is?"

"Has to be low enough to grow things." The Indus Valley was 10,500 feet. But the Ladakhi snowline was nearly 17,000 feet. It didn't make sense. A garden, adjoining a glacier? Fracture lines of ice, thin and sinuous as a shakuhachi, broke pen-and-ink against the rock barriers.

It was haunting. And how to get down. We were on one of those rims. There was no way to ascertain how far the cornice, if any, extended from where we were standing. We moved back to the belay and set about to dig out a flat platform for the night through the blocky snow.

It was the most comfortable place on earth. Soft. Perfectly smooth and well-secured. The wind hit us consistently, but from all sides and the tent was thus neutralized in opposing pressures, swelling with capaciousness. The hot flame of our stove dwarfed in the infinite surrounding cold, we gorged on mashed potatoes, pea soup and gorp. Allain opened up sunflower seeds. We were craving the salt. The moon was our sole company up there. Perched over everything. Like my ocean hamlet. Cast up on the waves of ice in a sidereal bastion of moonlit air. It was so conceivable, so easily imaginable that for hours after supper I played chess with my dreams. Wavering in and out of an image, some calligraphic lingering. Allain asleep. Ghisela's arm across my chest. And nothing, nothing to think about. "Did you hear something?" she murmured in a drowse. But I, too, was gone.

Splash! Hit right in the face. Ramparts of granite surrounding us. A rocket of sunlight overrunning the mind, heating the cheeks within seconds. On top of the world here. Our crest sidling both sides of higher peaks. We were all up gazing at the immense view before us. I put on the rope, took my camera, and Allain belayed me along the ridge. The full run out. Not enough. He came to me and I set off again, upwards, to get a vantage on the edge. Three hundred feet away. I turned around. There was no cornice. Only a rounded-off head·wall. Ten feet high. No more. A short rap down and we'd be on fourth class terrain.

I melted snow and made tea. We were delirious with joy. Floating in an oxymoron of fear compounded by the beauty and hard breathing. We decided to take all the gear though it would mean hauling it back again.

I set up the rappel and went down over the rim. It was a free drop-off for an instant, then dirt, snow and talus in a steep composition. We could unrope the entire slope. Cliffs and stretches of water-ice riddled the mountain but I could easily see a route through it all.

We made off carefully downwards, leaving a rope fixed off the edge. It was the windward side. The dirt was the color of basalt, swept over. No place to fall but no place to belay either. Precarious scrambling. Unthinkable exposure. Our ice axes were essential here. We went a thousand feet the first hour, traded packs, ate some chocolate and continued. The lower down we veered the more detail we could make out. The waterfall was huge. There was no monastery; in the shady edge, what looked like trees.

Our ridge was now concealed from view. The slope was breaking up into fast scree, and we glissaded, skiing riotously into the mirage of glacier and quadrangular verdure. Allain was way down ahead, stopped on what looked like a ledge from where there was no more anything.

We were on a narrow gravelly file. From here a rock wall fell off several hundred feet into the square. I could now see poplars. There was no other way around the cliff. The entire glacier below was in fact surrounded by such impenetrables. Like Kachatna in Alaska, or a glacial Monument Valley, it was a region that had escaped the notice of history.

I fixed the rope, tying off some large pitons to the ends to prevent my slipping off the rappel. Leaving my pack to be lowered afterwards, jumar belaying myself,

I swung free and descended over the bony wall. It was overhanging slightly all the way to the ground.

At the end of the rope I pendulumed back and forth to reach a flake. My right hand jammed in it. Expanding. "Shit!" I popped out backwards, rotten rock smashing into the talus far below. I steadied myself.

"You OK?" Ghisela yelled from the invisible above.

"Yeh. Give me a minute." I swung back and forth vertiginously, grabbing for another crack. The whole wall had leprosy and was peeling away. I fumbled against the one hundred degree face, scattering my swollen fingers all over the damned rock, dangling from my jumar. I went for a nubbin, pulled in, jammed the toes and frantically got out a small angle piton. Started to hammer and lost it. The pin twanged into space. I had two more. Concentrating, my jammed hand throbbing, I placed it carefully, tapped it once firmly and it was in. I bashed it all the way. Reveling in the high pitch it emitted. I took off a sling, checked the knot and snapped in stirrups to my harness. Stumbling in the air, I fixed two more pitons, secured the belay and screamed up to the others. "OK . . . lower the pack off another rope! Check the anchor! Remember, we're keeping the ropes fixed!"

Allain attached a carabiner to a nylon loop on the heavy pack and snapped it onto my rappel line. Presenting another guiding rope to the carabiner he then lowered it over the edge to me before rappeling himself. In this fashion we reached the ground after an additional two sling belays, fixing the ropes to the wall for when we'd reascend. There was a brief spell. Silent reunion. A thud coming from the earth's cool underneath. A rhythm that coupled with my soul.

We felt like invaders, thieves, astronauts. Not climbers. The amount of work required to get ourselves back up those ropes, then up the 6,000 feet of rough slope to the ridge, down the 2,000-foot face, across the glacier, down to Pemba's and the land-rover, with some one hundred-fifty pounds between us was a troubling prospect.

The humming was in our ears. In all directions. Like bees on the glacier. We sat chewing aniseed, drinking the ice water. I yanked off my clothes and dove into the pool formed by the waterfall. This was a mistake. Every muscle stopped. The water could have been thirty-five degrees, a bottomless pool, some seventy-five feet across. I retreated, clumsily, from the icy bath. The waterfall was heavy, a hundred feet high, plunging in a wide, white lineament. Its diaphanous veil of vapor drifted over black ice, then the garden, moistening the immense vegetables, which had all been neatly kept up. Rows of tomatoes, cauliflower, scallions, peas. There were melons and a small grape arbor.

It was a baffling conundrum. A half-dozen high lombary poplars, surrounding a run-down stone hut! And adjoining it, a single shiny apricot tree.

"How the hell do you suppose . . . ?" I was dumbfounded.

"What!" Allain shuddered . We all turned around.

A woman. Both old and young. Radiant. Walking over to us.

"Jeelai!" I called. She nodded, silently gesturing with her fingers to her forehead. Her age was elusive. A mixture of apparitions. In a goatskin shawl. Yellowish-white braids interlaced below her emaciated waist. She looked part Chinese, part American Indian. In her hand, a three-pronged staff. A few of her toes were gone where grey stump had formed. There seemed to be no flesh beneath the goatskin. And her face! Tight auric skin radiating over the pronounced boneware of her jaw and cheeks. She breathed slowly, each inhalation an act of near certain deliberation. And in her hair, a pink ribbon.

I looked for explanations. There was no breach in the walls. The glacier was nearly over us. How had she gotten here? And for how long had the hut stood over the garden in its inconceivable seclusion?

She bowed her head slightly that we should enter it. A stone door backed by teak. She lit a candle on a small table. There was an old yak hair quilt on the earthen floor. And in the corner, a small enclave of rocks festered with ash. An unlikely colorful thangka graced her otherwise barren walls. She took it down suspecting our interest and by the dim light we examined it.

"I don't believe this!" Allain exclaimed, fingering the worn silk brocade. He checked the inscriptions on the back and stared down at each appliquéd deity of the intricate iconographical design. "It's done in the traditional style of the Ghagyuba School," he said. "Boiled vegetables, minerals, and flowers held down with glue to a stretched canvas . . . Milarepa?" he asked the woman. She said nothing.

We set up the tent adjoining the trees. There were no stars, no moon. The sky was covered in cloud. But it was still warm, more mild than it had been even on the Indus. No breeze could penetrate this place. I thought I heard the echo of a whale's cry, mingling sorrowfully in the distant spray of water.

We sat around the tent composing dinner. The woman was in her hut. Our combined efforts yielded a yak-hair stew. The clouds hung prostrate, warming to us. It was as cozy as a Sierra campsite. We crawled into our bags. The ground was soft. The trees offered complete protection. The waterfall was as an ocean to my ears. I could have stayed in that moment forever. It was beginning to snow. Not a high mountain powder. Rather a wet Massachusetts spring slush that couldn't adhere. My head was spinning.

We were up late next morning. Allain went into the hut. The woman was gone. He took the thangka outside to examine it in the sunlight. The surrounding walls were caked in fresh snow, venting magical streamers. The enclosed valley, off the glacier, was dry. The heat poured in, and the reflecting effect of the ice produced a nearly stifling radiation in the air. That in combination with the mist from the waterfall engendered a most remarkable habitat for the fruits and vegetables. Ecologically, this portion of the earth seemed flawless.

The soil was replete with all the alluvial run-off of minerals. Rich, cloying, moist. Oasistic.

I wanted to explore the glacier. It looked like one might be able to climb up to it from the right side of the fall. There were large granite boulders, forty, fifty feet high atop a grassy area on the other side of the pool, but one would either have to go around on the glacier or swim to get there.

I went to check the last fixed rope. Somehow it had been secured too tightly. I let it dangle.

"Michael!" Allain called. "This thangka is unbelievable. You remember Milarepa?"

"The Tibetan poet?"

"I'm sure this is a depiction of his *Mila Grubum*, the *100,000 Songs*. It might be incredibly rare!" At least as valuable as a Rumanian rug, I suspected.

"The *Mila Grubum*?"

"A book. It was never thought to have been painted."

The pantheon of personages, landscapes and events was extraordinary. Hundreds of figures, cloud-swept mountains, bridges, caves, spires, cliff hermitages, saints, bodhisattvas . . . and circles geometrically affixing each portion of the large picture a special place in the rations of size, dimension and breathtaking color. It was about four feet by three feet. Allain was on his hands and knees going over it.

"All five thangka forms are displayed. There is the Buddha, surrounded by Arhats and Bodhisattva disciples. The Bhavacakramudra or Wheel of Life, showing the twelve stages through which people pass after birth. The *Intermediate State*, all those visions which take place between death and rebirth, the mandala, or mystic spiral, intersecting the whole design in symbolic patterns of the soul. One meditates upon these forms, enters into the divinity which is said to inhabit the point, the *Tig le* or *Bindu* of that intersection, the mountain top, and attains enlightenment. And there is the genealogical section, in which are all the lamas vertically disposed in their contemplative postures."

"But the Buddha is not on the mountain top. He's pictured as surrounded by the mountain?"

"Yes. I don't think I've ever seen a thangka where he isn't. The cave, the center, is symbolic of the top. It's the other extreme. And both are said to be illusory, or equal."

Ghisela photographed it. The woman had not returned and it was a mystery that we couldn't even begin to unravel. Surrounded on all sides by impenetrable rock and ice, the hut, the woman and her whereabouts were like some drug, asphyxiating enigmas, impossible conjectures.

Allain continued his story of Milarepa. I wouldn't be surprised if every Tibetan kid knew the same tale. He was a yogi, Jetsun they called him, the holy one. He was born in 1052 and disappeared around 1135. He studied under the great Sanskrit scholar Marpa who forced Milarepa to undergo a severe series of initiations. He had to build one stone hut after another on desolate mountain peaks throughout Central Tibet only to be forced to tear them down again.

For eleven months, and again for twelve years, living only on berries (I'd like to know which ones), he dwelt alone, meditating in a cave. He had already become something of a divine being. He entered the village of Nyanontsarmar from where he planned to visit the Great Cave of Conquering Demons. The devoted villagers prepared provisions for him, none of which he required and sent six disciples to accompany him to the cave. But the first blizzard of winter separated them. Two disciples died. The other four made it back to their village. The master had vanished in the whiteout.

In the spring the same four set out to find the body of Milarepa. They'd given him up for dead along with the other two. They discovered snow leopard tracks. For days they followed the paw marks over an ice field. Late one afternoon they reached the cave. The leopard's tracks had been Milarepa's own. By now he had mastered the *rlun* by which he'd penetrated the *Dharmadhatu*, the void, allowing him to become all bodily forms at will: Chinese Ch'i, Vedantic Prana-Mind. Milarepa had been out walking over the glacier, though apparently there are other translations which say that he was *climbing*. The disciples begged him to return with them to Nyanontsarmar. There are several descriptions of this return. One says he was a tiger with an ascetic's face. Another says he was naked. An edition by Evan-Wentz, published at Oxford describes him as clad in snowshoes, resting his chin on a headstick.

It was on the outskirts of the village, farmers weeping at his feet, that he sang the most famous of his 100,000 songs—the Snow Ranges. "To the remote Lashi Snow Mountain, came Milarepa, the anchorite who clings to solitude," the sinuous wail began. He referred to a rare body heat which kept him alive when winter struck and described all finitude as dissolving like water of the purest draught into one's being. He sang of his cave, describing description, catching his listeners in double linguistic binds that were bewildering, making them vulnerable to the "thirty-six essences." In similes that he insisted be memorized by the villagers, he said that if there be obstacles it cannot be called space. That the limit of definite things, their finitude, also limits our understanding of them. If there be East and West, there is no wisdom. That the sphere of awareness has no exterior or interior. And that the smaller we are, the more we come to participate in the greatness of Nature.

It was later in Milarepa's life, Allain continued, that he fought Naro Bhun Chon, the Bon priest at Mt. Su-Meru. And it was there that he disappeared, supposedly having flown to the summit.

I stared at the thangka. Other details, multi-headed monsters, tropical gorges, sacred articles, emerged from deep within its inaccessible symbolisms.

I thought back to all the sayings of the Fathers, the recitations of other lonely wanderers; to the numerous minds and fingers making up the web of levitation; the illuminati of the Gnostic Sects; Trismegistos and the Cult of the Hermetics;

Han-shan and the Cold Mountain mystique. A web of revelations all singularly triggered by the phenomenon of the vertical. The world seduced these spirits further and further afield into its beautiful, raw nothingness. Beggars on the Euphrates. Henchmen for Nebuchadnezzar; the St. Francises. And centuries of Chinese discontented sons, traveling with crates of jewels and manuscripts to outposts of celibacy in the forest.

"Michael, do you remember what Wangdu said as we were leaving?" I couldn't.

"Allain?" He came out of the hut. Then burst, "The fruits!"

"That's right."

"Kali! The old woman. He said to try her fruits!"

"And what else? There was something else?"

"I didn't catch it."

A blank all around.

And suddenly there was a flickering splash in the lake on the side closest to us. A piece of ice? And another. Himalayan trout! Here? But a more pressing conjecture still confronted us. Where *was* Kali?

CHAPTER SIXTEEN

A piece of serac collapsed in the night. My head lurched up from sleep. I stared out into darkness. The ice had tumbled with a violent crack over the waterfall into the pool where it sank like an albino hippo. My throat was parched and sore. We'd forgotten to fill the water bottles. Allain and Ghisela were asleep. I put on my inner boots and a sweater and slipped out of the tent. I went over to the moon-illumined pool, stooped down for water and turned to go back—when I saw it! Above the gushing spray. Moving swiftly through the glacier, indistinguishable from the shadow it threw off. The figure was on all fours, then upright. Its pace was bizarre. A large serac confronted it. And without altering a ghostly momentum it leapt a good twenty feet across a brink to circumvent the wall of ice. It was traversing the rim through deep snow, its speed flinging up bits of powder in the air.

I hurried to the tent, my footsteps absorbed in the greater din of the waterfall. From there I watched, standing concealed behind a poplar. Cumuli, splattered with a lunar alloy of light, swirled wind-stricken along Stok Kangri's sheer West Face. Adjacent to it on the north, a black rock wall, several thousand feet high, caked in verglas, rose shining like a diamond from the misty umber edge of the glacier. The pool was glistening.

The figure strode to the edge. I could make out a man. Naked. Loins dangling heavily. His face carmine and glowing, his arms and legs pallored by the argent filter of high clouds. His hair was long and his head strangely hydrocephalic. Facing outward, he descended the exact route, to the right of the waterfall, I'd considered earlier. But without using his hands! The ice nearly vertical. His torso was immense, and his legs monkey-like. He partly jumped, half downclimbed, nearly a hundred feet. Landing in a hurtling, flawless squat, emitting a rude grunt.

A sudden penumbra. Clouds passed beneath the moon. The pool blackened and I lost sight of him. Within seconds the cumuli had passed, and he was gone. I visually ransacked every inch of ground before me. Nothing! I remained standing for a good ten minutes, attempting to place the humming whose steady drone had not let up since our arrival. It was not clear that the timbre was issuing from under the glacier.

In the temperate late night I went out to the pool again and scrambled around the ice terminus. There was the spot where it had landed. And behind it, more markings, faint indentations in the scree, leading into the waterfall! I chimneyed horizontally against the first of the seracs and some boulders, freezing in the mist that covered me. I was climbing directly into the thundering cataract, getting too close, about to go back, when suddenly, an opening emerged. A sort of cave entrance going behind the falls, into the bottom of the glacier.

The humming was louder at the entrance, mechanical-like, and somewhere in the far submerged darkness deep in the cave's chilly bowels, a minute light, twinkling like a star, and no way to judge its distance from where I stood.

My teeth were chattering. I climbed away from the orifice, chimneying back to the edge of the pool. I returned to the tent, crawled into my sleeping bag and lay there, head heaving with notions. I emptied the water bottle, quenching my salty nervousness. The eyes would not close. And for hours I remained awake, staring into the midnight.

There was a faint morning chinook fanning the silvery leaves of the poplars. An alpine desert heat. The deep snowy edge of the glacier sparkling. A jumble of towers and soft, harmless-looking ruins deep in white. The ice couloirs were glittering and I noticed other cascades flowing down the black walls, and high strata of wind catching the veils and careening the loose strands of water out into the air. The rim, rectangular from where I stood, trembled in hard-etched mirage. This haven, trapped in beauty, a scent between two separate eternities grazing into each other, was like nothing I'd ever imagined. It was sunk, fixed in time, or resonating beneath all time.

My metaphors were failing me. I had not managed to draw a single connection all night. My senses were awake, my nostrils, ears, eyes—the world of my body was attuned alright. But my logic was gone. I couldn't formulate a *plan*. Staring at a piton. It meant nothing, nor did it even suggest retreat. To where? Back up the wall? It seemed impossible. Meaningless. And I was frightened. Not because of any idea. But because of the lack of them. A feeling in my body, a total something, calling to me. It was sensual, a totalness as vivid as my breathing. Like the first time I ever saw Yosemite Valley. But with a remote fear compounding the sensation. A tidal conjunction of mental listlessness and hypersensitivity. An instinct in every pore. The blinding snow. The swept stratosphere. A ripe vegetable garden, here, and the stone hut, surrounded by sturdy shivering trees. The towering walls, more forbidding than anything I'd ever seen. And the rims of overhanging ice! Breathtaking, against the aerial unknown of passing clouds. Like the storm-lashed golden seas Turner painted, elegantly agog in reflection, compassless purple.

I'd always felt a superb vacancy before nature, a consciousness happily endangered. As if my thoughts were unnatural excrescences, subjugations of the environment. But here the sensation of a vacuum, of a hollow cranium was like some pressing urgency, an extraordinary, uplifting fever. A merging with the real world. Of animals. I was quaking in the ingathering of my biologic self. My skin, my mouth, my vision—all going out to embrace something. And what?

But the mind was dumb to answer. I stood near the tent, Allain and Ghisela dozing inside, and I felt as if I were on an abandoned beach, the pebbles and sea carrying all my inwardness out to a horizon confused in the bright merging of cloud and water, where my intelligence drowned, freeing the senses in a sudden buoyancy of the spirit. Spirit? A combination, of intuition, reptilian ego, slimy, mud-caked volition. All earthbound. I was celebrating a limbo of myself. Rhapsodic with an animal parody so vivid, so alluring . . . Jeffers in Big Sur, Lawrence in Taos, Neruda on the beach in Malaysia, Kazantzakis in Murmansk, Shelley on the Mer de Glass, Lermontov in Tiflis, Basho in the far North of Japan, Sappho at the white cliffs of Lefkas (off which she jumped— *Katapontismos*—), Claude Gelee in the Campagna, Hokusai before Mount Fuji...with all my western enumerata, I felt firmly, squeamishly linked to a tradition of the hypnotic, the suggestive. But the magnetism was best characterized by the friction it generated. My mind tried to let go, haplessly. But it could not. If this was evolutionary biology, then I was finished.

This enclosure of frost and rock and glorious calm, like that sea, that ancestral beast emerging within me. I wanted to run in two directions at once. Backwards, up the rope, away from this unthinkable danger, and forward into the cave.

The old woman! Where had she come from? An alabaster sylphide crouched gingerly over a string of sweet peas. Working slowly in her garden. Aware of my presence. Unconcerned. In the silence, the yawning sky, the breeze. Two butterflies, picking up on the high currents, blue, and tiny neon, fluttering amidst the shining tomatoes. The cave behind the torrent of glacial run-off. That creature in the night. A sāddhu? An animal? Some form of ancient consciousness or mobility. Unfathomable spark, mineral. Instinct in precarious gestation.

I was losing myself to pungent mindlessness. The sea carrying me off, a canal, drifting on a boat, out beyond the harbor of control. No way to understand. Suddenly all the images of my past were floating away in the primeval apparition. Supernatant, without a name, ideas rising in a helium of surrender. Lost amidst the high snows. I was blinded, exalted in the persuasion of elements, of a simplicity as terrifying, as sensible as a live wire. I could stay here forever. A fulcrum stared me in the face, a gun, this glacier, this impossible gorge, this feeling.

"Morning!" Allain startled me, as he came outside to whiz. I was silent. I crawled into the tent. My head singed. My reverie was severed. I was a man trying to walk with his pants down, catching his knees. Ghisela was waking up.

"Hey, sleepy!"

"Michael, I, I . . . "

"You had a bad dream?"

She was groaning oddly.

"No! I feel terrible!"

"What's wrong?"

"You were gone last night. I thought you were Allain. Where were you?"

"Getting water. What is it?"

"Well, I wanted to touch you. I reached out, you know, under the sleeping bag. I fondled you. I was half-asleep. You, well you came. But it wasn't you!"

I was silent. It didn't matter.

"You're not mad?"

"Allain needed it. I'm glad."

"I'm sorry."

I shook it off. "Kali is back! She's in the garden." I went back out. Allain was standing next to her. They were each unspeaking.

"Jeelai, jeelai," I greeted her. She smiled, wondrously. I melted all over. Indescribable. Primal femininity showing itself through a vital corpse. "You sleep well, Allain?"

"Uhh . . . sure! You?"

"Not as well, thanks . . . Allain, something happened last night."

"Look, Michael, I'm sorry. Maybe Ghisela ought to explain."

"Oh, fuck that."

We went over to the tent where Ghisela had just gotten out. I explained about the creature, and the cave behind the waterfall and the distant light. Kali was looking over at us. Her lips closed. I sensed that she knew everything I was saying.

"I'm frightened," Ghisela registered.

"Allain, your sāddhu. Did he say anything about climbing?"

His mind hushed, then: "Yes. That I didn't need the rope."

Ghisela paused emphatically. "That's what it was!"

"What?"

"Wangdu's warning: To watch out for the glacier despite what *they'd* tell us!"

"Michael, we're going in there!"

Allain went over to Kali who had resumed her methodical work. She was on all fours now.

"Kali!"

She looked up. Allain pointed to the waterfall. "Déva?"

She didn't move. Staring up like a child at the bearded climber who hovered over her.

"Déva," she said.

"Damn!" She *could* speak! And her stare! Allain was struck hard, hanging in linguistic mid-flight. He looked over at me, his face a perplexity of motivations. Kali's angelic gloss under him; she stood up, went to the side of the hut and plucked some apricots. Then offered them to us. Those eyes of hers! Infinitely deep as they were suggestive. The color of an arctic wolve's. But there was also the confounding hint of civilization. Of disciplined restraint. And it dawned on me, as I took the offerings, that we hadn't thought to eat any of her produce since we'd been there. The fresh succulence was a welcome change after all the uniform freeze-dried garbage we'd been living on. She went into her hut. The stone door closed.

The food. It was . . . different. Seemed to taste like the *beginning* of taste. I sucked on a tomato and my thoughts seemed to fall backwards. The soil had leached an abundance of minerals from the ice; and with the perennial mist from the waterfall, a succulence otherworldly had been nourished. Like a drug.

We prepared rucksacks, broke open the bottle of kerosene we'd brought thanks to Tenzing, and doused some cloth with which we swathed three large boughs of poplar. We put on our crampons, took the axes and set off for the waterfall. It was awkward, stemming with all the gear. But we were quickly behind the downpour. We lit the torches. And climbed down the frozen steps into the entrance of the glacier. A huge arc of ice over our heads. A good seventy feet high, thirty feet wide. Allain went slowly in the lead. The ice, by the flickering of our scant flames was blue, unyielding in its bulging polish. The floor of the cave, or tunnel, was also ice, descending slightly into a ferocious cavity of black, a glint of wavering light in its center. A hundred years—or a mile?—before us. My hands were sweating, my mind reeling in an impulse, an excited claustrophobia.

We heard chimes! A slow egression of drums. And then the unmistakable chanting. That hum, bells and movement in the still air. For long minutes we waited, trying to grasp the noise. It was nothing like the symphonic cacophony of the Hemis raucous. It was deep, ordered, terrifying. A religion of caverned moans. Oracular fusions of rhythm, inwrought braying, and delirium. Seizure of many mouths. We advanced into the hypnotic cellar melodies of the underground. Millions of brilliant icy tons overhead. The light growing in intensity.

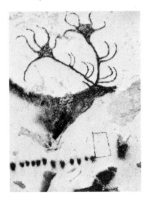

On the frozen wall, drawn with rich ochres in the carved veins, a series of designs. Extensive, colorful, like the Lascaux *Coat of Arms*. We stood before a shimmering link to Himalayan prehistory. A bear, risen up on its hind legs. A figure with the antlers of a spiral ibex dancing, cajoling the creature. Bare-breasted women in a circle, their legs spread and pulling unattached erections into themselves. Coupled with the deep blue of the crevasse.*

We continued down the tunnel, stooping under an abutment. Indigo, alkanet, umber—a flush of hues. Mottled squares in a design without meaning. We were just around the corner from the chanting. The tunnel turned. The three of us gripped our ice axes hard, and moved forward.

A sudden raging quiet. Pilose muscle. Beards. Big blazing eyes, as if expecting us. Naked. All of them. Staring indifferently, nonchalant.

It was dry. A chamber of painted rock. And exposed at the top. The double side of a crevasse, its icy edges dripping into the periphery of the pocket where painted amphoras sat collecting the water. A shaft of light was flooding the upper portions. There was a slow, sweet-smelling fire going. Instruments strewn about.

"Please, do sit down!" one of them gestured. We all three looked aghast at one another, like the Stooges. Another Wangdu! Fluent English. More than fluent. It must have been his native tongue.

I hesitated.

There was embarrassment in his voice. Seducing us into a dream as deep, as impossible as this tunnel under the ice. Again that sensation of the morning. Primal. The equation of animals staring back across time, over a mirror or transreality.

Calmly. "You are frightened. There is no reason to be."

We sat. "What is this place?"

"You know where you are."

"You are Hindus?" Allain asked.

"Not particularly."

There was panic in Ghisela's face. Her hand gripping my wrist. We were surrounded by half a dozen violent erections.

The man tending the fire noticed her alarm. "Don't worry," he said, with a grin. "Nothing will come of them."

I was amused, horrified. "You speak such perfect English . . . " I asked, my voice faltering.

"Some of us."

There were six men in all. Each was sitting in the lotus with a flat embossed

*André Leroi-Gourhan, in his book *Treasures of Prehistoric Art* (New York, Harry Abrams, 1967) has data-processed many thousands of Paleolithic cave images to better fathom the secret history of fertility. See *The Time Falling Bodies Take To Light*, William Thompson, St. Martin's Press, New York, 1981.

stone before him, some tablas, and bells, a crucible of ash and vials of what I later found out was Tibetan ginseng and asafetida. The walls were a maze of color, lichen mixed with painting. Animals, misproportioned yaks, mountains and clouds. The workmanship was all out of perspective but the color combinations, and the range of detail fantastic, intricate as the thangka, covering hundreds of square feet of wall. A glacial Sistine.

"You painted these?"

"No. Others. Before me."

"How long have you lived here?" He was submissive, governing my gained confidence. Intentional mystery.

"I don't know exactly. I come and go. And come again."

His English was as impeccable as Wangdu's. I decided there was no point in asking him about it. His eyes were following me. He caught my thinking.

"You liked Wangdu?"

My throat heaved shut. Another psychic. No way to conceal anything now.

"He directed us here," Allain said.

"No, he didn't," the man grinned. "Now did he!"

I wanted out. I wanted in. I couldn't go right, I couldn't go left. Whirlpool.

"No matter. You are here."

I couldn't think. Frozen on the man's twinkling eyes. Like Kali's, they were penetrating, inhuman. Bushy eyebrows. He was handsome, though not without peculiarity. His head was excessively large. Like C.S. Lewis. Patagonian. Heavy. And his hands, ungainly, dumb, prodigious bones, woolly. The brush of wind rushing across the crevasse, being sucked downwards into the circle. Silence. The other men were self-enraptured, faces of dark stone. Mute. Not one of them looked at us. Their penises were bristling, and Ghisela was transfixed. Allain concentrated on the man.

"What's your name?" he asked, faltering.

"Déva," he replied more soberly.

Allain was quiet. Great joy, consummated, unleashing a flood of questions which he was determined to slow down. "I met your disciple, behind Amarnath. He sent me here."

"So he has." He grinned wryly. "And what is it you require? Why such a long journey?"

"Require?" Allain asked.

"Yes! Why have you come after all?"

"We are mountaineers," Allain said, searching for a reason, an explanation.

"Also we love the mountains. But we live here." Courteous beguilement. Masterful Oxford English and Tibetan shortness-of-breath. Authoritative. Humble. Inquisitive. A dockworker's and a don's.

Allain looked at Ghisela and me. I shrugged. What *were* we doing here? The imposition of my *being* swelled up uncomfortably. We'd pursued a phantom. A rumor. And we'd pursued it hard, without knowing why. My plodding thoughts were checked, suddenly spellbound, unraveled like a yoyo. His fleshy gaze pierced my only certainty and I confessed. I *didn't* know. There *was* no reason!

"We're here, that's all!" I said.

"Good! Very good! Then we're all here together," he replied, glad to be over whatever obstacle he'd conceived that moment to be. "Tomorrow, you'll join me on the boulders beside the pool? For a little of your mountain climbing. Agreed? Very good."

We got up to go. Our torches were still aflame. We collected our axes that we'd set down and departed into the blackness. It was early afternoon when we got back to the tent. The heat was oppressive. I peeked in the hut. Empty.

We sat around on the file of grass that encircled the grove. Clouds were still hovering around the summit of Stok. The sun had exposed its entire West Face. A mammoth sheerness. Surely a great alpine route for some future generation of climbers. Or was it? I could not trust myself anymore. My head was aching from all the psychic backfire. I had felt like an idiot. Allain was wrestling with another rebus. He had aged in my mind. His face was harder. He had lost much of that fanciful gaiety. That extravagant elan which I once envied. More and more I was seeing him for the vulnerable man he was, expatriot visibly distressed, searching, confused by his quasi-findings. We all were.

Night, and with it, restlessness. I recalled hearing Louis Malle speaking of his five months in India, followed by eighteen months in a dark editing room. India—darkness—frightened him. He could not control his film, "Phantom India," for the very reason that he himself was out-of-control with all that the place elicited in him. Malle returned twelve years later and was, he confessed, even *more* terrified. India, he said, was travelling *backwards* in time, while we went forward. Einstein would have been supremely comfortable in Ladakh.

Disquieting alpha state. I see an old Egyptian anchorite. Shivering disciples, laymen and kings, bow down before him. He comes across the sands naked, dried lizards hanging from a loin-belt. Blackish-blue, a grueling ecclesiastic bitterness cleaves his wrinkled skein of a face. Titanic in his stride, like Frankenstein's monster descending the icy steppes of the glacier, he comes recklessly, deliberately. In that insulation, the flowers of cactus wilt by his shadow; the earth attempts to bar his way, unable to admit such ardent anemia.

Goat dung is smeared across his forehead, pin-holes scar his rotting cheeks; whiskers dangle from the sunken jowls, and urine, shit, and other acrid secretions fester cumulatively, dried and matted, on his thighs, wrangled in the crack of his deteriorated buttocks. His testes extend in slack skin from having been burdened by stone weights tied tortuously to them for decades.

He moves in a deadly zodiac of squirms, emphatic itching, insatiable contempt for mankind, vulnerable only to the scabies which have come and gone in waves for fifty years.

This great ascetic, of which history knows tens-of-thousands, lived most of his life in a putrefied dug-out of cliff. One radish a day was all he ate. He guzzled fetid water once in the evening and no more.

When he was eighteen, his first woman flittered off to El Giza without him. The tedious squalor of his slow life on the Nile compounded the frustrations of poverty and retarded manhood. He attempted to follow her. One night, whilst sleeping beneath his camel hair cloak on the road to the capital, robbers assaulted him. They were no robbers. Still, he murdered one, his dream heavy on the dagger which he drew in the midnight confusion. Heading eastward, he escaped toward Arabia. Never having made love.

Once, once only, he had been in the reeds with her, pulling open grimy legs, zeroing in on the one moist pouch that gave him evidence of God. Sex waged uncontrollable under gathering starlight. His tongue tasted a vaginal chaos that flooded out to meet him. And even before pulling it into place his semen wrenched to the summit of childhood, ending upon her belly. Fighting to get away—he wanted more—she hollered, ran splashing through marshes, flamingoes flying up to their halcyon fracas.

Were women different? He'd never know. The scar mocking his genitalia he transformed into an ideal of abstinence, the climate of the times. Others have killed themselves. But he locked himself up in the desert to appease the abyss in his loins, fingering long blades, lost dreams, first loves and other mishaps.

We stripped down and edged our way into the pool. It was easier in all the heat. Still the water was unbearable, dazing. A quick dunk, a swoosh of pain pinning the inner ear, freezing the genitals, and out again to bake off the water, one's chest feeling free, raw. Again it snowed that night. Again it was warm. Gutted morning. While powder avalanches careened off a hundred pedestals along the walls, our verdant enclave remained dry.

We'd made it through several arguments that night. I wanted to photograph these guys. Allain insisted we at least wait awhile. He was afraid to ruin anything.

We were restless. Sitting around camp. At noon, Déva sauntered out from behind the cataract. Stepping lightly through a rainbow in the deluge's fine spray and dancing, literally, through the cleft to the side of the pool. Naked.

CHAPTER SEVENTEEN

"Good morning!" he called, coming up to our campsite and studying the tent with amusement. Our large mountain boots must have seemed ridiculous to him by contrast to the fine apparatus of his long, slender toes. No frostbite I noticed. "So! You have chosen the best campsite in town!" he laughed. "And your names? . . . Well, Ms. Ghisela. You must spend some time with my wife."

"Your wife?"

"Kali. We were married in Lhasa. Quite some time ago, during the British inundations."

I flashed a string of calculations, placing men like Francis Younghusband and other emissaries into perspective. "But that was at the turn of the century?" I demanded.

"Never mind. She is quite a lady."

"Have you children?"

"Of course! But please. You have been to the rocks yet?"

"Pool's too cold."

"Nonsense," he chuckled, leading the way. In a long swayback dive, like some primal Johnny Weismuller, he plunged deep. Ten seconds later he stood facing us from the opposite shore.

"Shit!" I whispered to Allain. "It's too deep. Too cold. We'll drown." But he ignored me, already magnetized by Déva's beckoning presence. He fast removed his clothes, took several deep breaths and lunged. His muscle was frantic in the water. He bawled, thrashing to the other side like a man with red ants inside his gonads.

"I'm not going!" I yelled across as Allain dragged himself onto the bank, gasping.

"It's not so bad," he managed. I could see he was faint.

I looked at the seracs. The route I'd hoped to boulder was out of the question. On the other side of the hut, above the pool, vertical rock. Also no good.

"Come on!" Allain shouted. Ghisela had taken off her clothes.

"You're going?" I stammered.

"You bet!" And with that she was in the air. Smacking the water with a racing dive and a heart-rending cry. Swimming furiously to the other side. I stripped, contemplating the return swim, and tiptoed to the side like a poodle. Unbearable. Praying. And then blindly I wrestled across. Cheerless. Ghisela dragged me out.

Naked, the four of us stood before a thirty-foot-high granite boulder. Invested with crumbly lichen, steep, holdless friction. Next to it lay other huge boulders swathed in campion.

"So, you are mountain climbers. Well, show me!" Déva prompted.

"You must be kidding!" This was ridiculous. The three of us stared at each other, then at the rock, then at Déva. It wasn't a good joke to begin things with. "I'm afraid that's quite impossible," Allain began. "You see for yourself. There are no holds."

Déva moved to the central, silkiest section of the boulder. He stood probably five feet eight inches and his arms were long. I noticed the incredible development of his shoulders. And the thin but mighty legs. With the steel shanks of a horse. Or of a Burundi high-jumper. Without much to-do he put his fingers to the rock above his head, raised a foot, made contact with a toe, and moved off the ground. In that unlikely position he waited, his muscles unflexed, as we stood around him probing through the lichen to see what in hell he could be holding on to. But there was nothing. He moved higher. Hanging above us. We felt the rock where his toe had addressed. Nothing! Absolutely smooth.

"You can't do that!" But his face was serious now and he continued higher and higher, dead center up the sheer face. I expected him to lunge and mantle on the top but he face-climbed calmly instead. I moved around the boulder. Sheer or overhanging on all sides. Déva leaned over the top and chose a different, more difficult descent. We scrutinized his downwards arthropodous stride. There was no climber, in any country, who could have done what this naked old big-headed Tibetan had just accomplished with ease. It was impossible to know how old the man was. His musculature was timeless.

"But there were no holds!" I objected.

"No. Quite right. But there was plenty of rock!" he smiled, amused at my own mental belaborings. "Don't search for density."

I was consumed in formal inquiry. I had hit a wall, without meaning, as impenetrable as the boulder seemed to be. I repaired.

"OK. I'm willing to grant that you climbed the rock. But I can't *believe* you climbed it. I mean, I see you've done it, but I am unable to *know* that you've done it. Do you understand?" Actually, I didn't know what the hell such rhetoric, as issued from my mouth, was all about. Perhaps the final, insecure throes of narrow intellect up against all edifying feeling.

"Only that you're confusing yourself. But no matter. Try to climb it. Don't think about it."

But I wasn't listening. To make my point defiantly clear, I went to the rock. I stood precisely where he did. I raised my right foot in a simulating gesture against the exact smudge of lichen, my fingers up above to the same place, the same moment's pause. "Well?" I asked. "I'm raising?" Poised ridiculously on one foot, no possibility of getting off the ground. "I'm lifting and nothing's happening. How come?"

"Because you're asking me. Stop asking. Stop thinking."

"Bullshit!" I struck back.

Standing there like an idiot. My arm getting tired above my head. Playing with the lichen. Resting my cheek. "It's impossible!" And with that I stepped back down.

"But *I* did it?" he said.

"Yes." I stared impatiently at Ghisela and Allain.

"But your action lacks comprehensibility, damnit! I can't believe, I can't understand it!"

"Can you *imagine* it?"

"That depends on what you mean by imagine."

"Imagination exists without an understanding of it. I wonder whether you can imagine my action in absence of understanding?"

I couldn't get away. Both Balladeur and Ghisela watched on as he snared me.

"Alright, yes. You did it. I guess. But language fails to, I mean, no words can *convincingly—*"

I was bewildered. We'd gone from climbing to language speculation in an instant. I didn't know where we were.

"And what of metaphor?"

I calmed down, started to think, to extricate myself.

"A more complex means of establishing the invisible, the link between permutations. The thrust of analogy is always the same thing—a desire to connect, complementary colors, words, which function according to the underlying meaning." Intellect my only ammunition.

"So all words have a meaning?"

"If they are words," I resolved.

"And what about actions? Do all actions have a word?"

"Of course!" I stopped myself. He was smiling.

"Then, Mr. Michael, according to you, the impossible has a meaning. And what is that?"

I was lost. "The meaning of, of no-meaning, I suppose. I don't know. You tell me!"

"The way is in the last metaphor. On the edge, between two extreme pieces of thought. One is of yourself. The other is of the rock. Opposing hinges on a door which is your body. You must develop the mechanism, the muscle, the concentration to close and open the door at will."

"Huh? I'm sorry." I was gone. He was irritated. Not a very good teacher, I thought. But it was all a little much. Standing before a boulder that couldn't be climbed. And a naked yogi, or whatever he was, tripping me up. Allain was obviously more involved than I was. Following every word. We spent another hour or so among the boulders. Déva climbed half-a-dozen *impossibles* and each time he enjoyed himself immeasurably while we stumbled around at the bottom incapable of ever even lifting off the ground an inch.

"Tomorrow. From sunrise to sunset. I want you to stare at some lichen." As if I hadn't had enough of that crap. "Keep it close to you," he continued. "On your finger. Don't cease to concentrate upon it. Delineate its fine network of color and structure. Go back in years with it until that web of atoms is your finger, your finger your hand, and your hand—the idea of your hand. Start with the lichen. You should end with this rock."

"This is an ascetic technique?" Allain asked excitedly.

"No," Déva laughed. "It is no technique. I just made it up. I think it might work, that's all!" Allain's mouth turned sour, discomfited. "I told you, Mr. Allain. We are not Hindus. We are not Buddhists."

"Then what?"

I could see Déva, the glacial impresario, was just warming up. "Are you so blind? We all have everything and nothing. Choose what you will! You associate technique with advancement. With progress. But progress is only one mutant form of *significance*. Significance is what we're discussing after all. And it is always without meaning. The most simplistic words and symbols are so simple, so searing, that they are reversible with the unknown. Would you prefer to discover the known, or the unknown?"

"I, I don't know. What do you want me to say? I don't know!" Allain was bemuddled.

"We are of the same blood. The same bones. Only the hap displacements of time and space separate us. You agree? And now for this moment even those two aspects of being have merged. On the grass here. We are one race.

"America, Tibet . . . small variations on the same necessity. The same daily gripes, fears, exaltations, sleep. What are the essential differences? You claim I have displayed something impossible. And doubtless our species lays such claims to the universe every day. In the mating dance of scorpions. The path of comets. In rainbows. Avalanches. In the mind. The natural phenomena, of which the imagination counts equally, are miraculous to us. Science explains them away. But explanations, no matter how comprehensive, are sheltered from reality. We each have still to get through our lives as heartily, as merrily as we can. Regardless of new discoveries in space.

"I came from a large family. Twelve brothers and sisters. My father was a lama in the Potala. A great scholar who brought me up to be one as well. I was born in 1650. By the age of twenty-three I had been forced to read nearly all of the 333 Kanjur-Tenjur texts of Buddhism. Of course, I was far more interested in the village girls and it took me many years of fasting and running away before I could completely get that damned greasy religion out of my head.

"I wandered. Over the mountains. Always over mountains. Where the best water is. I met hundreds of masters. From China, Japan, Burma, Mongolia, Persia, Russia, even from Portugal. But none of them ever took into account the source of all their thinking—I mean the real source, which is glacial water.

"One man came from Abyssinia. I met him in Yarkand. He could produce things in his hands. Babies, tea kettles, even ants. I tried. I wanted gold. But gold he could not produce. I followed him across Asia. For ten years in a wagon we visited village after village producing things. I learned his tricks, and admittedly, some were not tricks. One night on the road we were attacked. His head was cut off. It was gruesome. And I was shackled and sold into slavery. Beaten mercilessly. I ended up, after years of hardship, in Peking. Serving the court as a dung collector. Forced to push my wobbly cart around. A beautiful cousin of the emperor persuaded him to give me to her. How she affected me!

"She introduced me to the cognoscenti of the period. All of them wealthy, with country huts, and all of them talking about the mountains. Since I came from Tibet, and was already considered to have mastered certain disciplines, I became something of a celebrity to them.

"With a small party one August morning in the Year of the Dragon we set off for Nanking by horseback. Scribes joined us. And whores. We took fifty chickens, ten sheep, flasks of wild ginger water, and bedding. To the famous T'ien-t'ai Mountain. There we set up camp in the ancient T'ung po tao-kuan temple on the steep slopes. But mind you, the mountain is a park. Not a mountain in the usual sense. One day we met a famous poet visiting there. Hsu Hsia-k'o. He had come from an immortal Taoist mountain near Chekang called T'ien Mu. What stories that man had to tell! One day we climbed to the Jade Terrace. On one side, a towering cliff. On the other, a high cascade. Hsu sat painting the scene. Suddenly we spotted a man on the cliff. Slowly ascending. I studied his smooth movements. The climber went to the top. I was entranced. I set off at a run through the banyans and found the baldheaded man bathing in a pool above. Soothing his sore feet, he said. He was Japanese and spoke of his Master, a man called En no Gyoja who taught a discipline called *sangaku tobai*, climbing as an act of worship. He was an ascetic. Had fasted like myself. For one month on T'ien-t'ai Mountain I learned how to climb. *First the boulder, then the moun-*

tain, and finally the boulder, he would tell me.

"Eventually I journeyed to Chengdo, past Mt. Namucha-bawashan, along the Brahmaputra and up to Lhasa. My father had been killed in a monastic dispute. My mother and several of my brothers maintained our small farm. I stayed for many years. Married, had children. Then a great plague came. Many people died. All of my family.

"The lamas confiscated all land and I was forced to flee to the West, along the road of my youthful exile. To Dí Se Mountain, Milarepa's mountain, I came. And it was there that I first encountered the Deva. Things really got wild!

"For over a century my body got stronger, drinking of the pure water—and ascending the mountain. Partaking in the sex of the Déva and the fruit. There were ritual orgasms and months of continuous bouldering. They were mountain wizards. They could fly. Drank only ice water, and had drawn up a veritable history of ice water. They moved like the water.

"One year I went alone to the largest mountain between the Pamirs and the Himalayas. Far removed in the Kun Lun Mountains. For ten months I climbed. The most difficult face of the high peak. Without eating. Drinking only ice water. There were many nights when I *knew* I was dead. And with that knowledge I was able to generate new life. Ongoing, day after day, until I generated the movement in my legs, and brought the surface of events—my body—into harmony with the environment. I returned to Dí Se a full-fledged Déva. Or so I was told. Still I am unsure.

"But in the last century many were coming to the mountain. A New Zealander discovered our cave. He published his findings and others came. They called us a sect, confusing us with the Sanskrit Śiva. Not understanding that Śiva is no God—what is a God?—but an idea, a discipline. We practiced *shambhuvi* in an allegiance to Parvati. We hung on our cliffs, hiking through the deserts around the mountain, making *parikrama* past the glittering blue lakes, visiting the ancient Gumpas for prayer, and taunting the tourists and pilgrims who would come from Taklakot, from all over India, hoping to purge themselves in a week. There were bandits, smugglers, and wild-asses. The immense mountain Gurla Mandhata rose over us and to the north, the mysterious Aling Kangri range. There were abandoned gold mines there.

"Mountain climbers also came. Though they were not looking for anything more than a summit. None of them were able to climb the peak. I even grew fond of one Welsh fellow in particular. We ascended to the top of Mount Everest—Jo-mo glang-ma—together in the late 1800s. He then went on to Inner Mongolia.

"Eventually I returned to Lhasa. But the town was infested with other tourists, all wheeling and dealing. Politics, opium, women, musk . . . my beautiful Lhasa was no more. I met Kali, who had her own story to tell. And within a year we were on the road together. We came to Leh. Where other Dí Se Déva had migrated. We had two newborn at the time."

I was staggered. My mind reeling and riddled with unaccountable suggestiveness. *1650?* Was it possible? It seemed normal. Absolutely normal. And a solo ascent of Everest in the 1800s?

I was bloated. His words were like some fable, softly, calmly eliciting my gullibility. A resonance of verbiage like music. His platinum ambience. Intoxicating imagery. The sun had gone down. Before things got any worse I decided to get back across the pool. I dove in. But to my amazed relief, I found the water almost tolerable. As if the past three hours of nakedness had prepared me for easier re-entry. I stumbled out of the fish-laden water as Allain and Ghisela followed.

Our clothes back on, we looked across. Déva chose the glacial route, climbing a high serac, adhering in the twilight to nothing.

We wearily made for the tent.

In the middle of the night I awoke. By now nocturnal restlessness had become a habit, a mental and thoraxic pressure.

I wanted to believe, and I couldn't. I couldn't let go.

CHAPTER EIGHTEEN

Up at dawn. Queasy. A dream of a long road, hewn from a cliff side. It never ended. And it never got dark.

As the light entered the square and powder avalanches started up, I went out and scraped together bits of lichen. Exhausted. Relieved to be off that road, for the moment. The earth was cold and stiff in the last breath of darkness.

I placed the lichen beside my parka pillow, eyes fixed on the darkly growth. I lay there comfortably.

Allain went into the empty hut, placed the lichen in his palm and sat on the quilted floor. Ghisela lay out on her foam pad along the banks of the pool. It took only five minutes before my restlessness compelled me to shift. I spilled the lichen, gathered up its remnants, sat, lay down, and sat up again. Over and over. I didn't go in for this sort of thing. Of course I was also impressed enough by Déva's performance on the rock to give it a try. If I could climb like that! And I stared, trying not to blink. But then tears swelled, and another break in concentration. So I blinked whenever I damn-well pleased and things got better.

My mind drifted. I recalled Allain reciting Milarepa. *If there be East or West there is no Wisdom!* What did that mean? Should I think about it, or about the lichen? Or my finger? Or my hand? Or as Déva summed up the process, about the *idea* of my hand? That is, ponder the pondering, in my hand, in my hand, ad infinitum. All by the way of the act of holding something. It didn't need to be lichen I assumed except that lichen existed on the rock; I would try to climb the face again and all that lichen would merely serve as some convenient vehicle for my mind and my hands to unify unconsciously over the platter of their mutual memory, and I would climb. The point apparently was not *difficulty* but *medium*, for it was clear to me now, on the phenomenal evidence of that boulder problem and the serac afterwards, that Déva could probably climb anything. And his insistence that it was physical skill, not mental cleverness confused me. For what was I doing meditating then when I should really be out exercising?

His comparisons between language and mountaineering particularly threw me. All evening I had considered the unlikely relationship, positioning the action against its words and trying to feel the etymology, the acceleration of metaphor between them. To see whether or not the analogy, the symbol, contained an equal amount of action, and of word. I had remembered St. Augustine's incitement to mankind: *Men go out to wonder at the mountain heights, and the tides of the sea, but they ignore themselves.* It was the first form of psychoanalysis. And it also equated wilderness with imagination. Language seemed lodged somewhere in the middle, between necessity and desire, famine and plenty, love and hate. But climbing had no basis in the world, no *real* reason. And no one had ever come up with an answer other than *because it's there.* Like language. A nebulous origin. Sure, children climb up trees, out of their cribs, like monkeys. Everyone thrills to hang off a limb and swing, to feel the rush of muscle stretching in the air, and the sudden dizziness before leaping off into deep grass. But that's its extent. The pleasure of the yawn, resuscitation of muscle half-atrophied during the night's refrain. If poetry, as Verlaine described, was the "prolonged hesitation between sense and sound," then climbing, I could see, shared tacit structure, made it appealing to pure land Buddhists, and Taoist herb collectors. There was, to be sure, a certain Zen that linked the two pursuits—climbing and language. But Déva was too steeped in his *Wittgenstein*, his polemics, to make it work for me in my own mind.

To climb a holdless rock trespasses on an area of the mind which has no equivalent option. Granted, one can read a great work, the golden flood of Cicero, Wang-Wei, Shakespeare and have no idea where such words came from. "The Great Wall—a thousand miles of moonlight!" Such connections are alchemical. But assuredly the words were there, somewhere. Whereas Déva said that he was not looking for holds, but for the absence of them. It made no sense.

All afternoon I sat fidgeting with the lichen. My thoughts traversed a sizeable terrain and put out a lot of unanswerable questions. But I certainly did not grow fond of the lichen. Nor did I come to associate it in any way with myself, except that it resembled shit, a little. People always assume that a master is synonymous with teacher. But I was beginning to feel, by late afternoon, that a master might not be worth beans—or even lichen—when it comes to imparting technique.

What, after all, was I really supposed to do? Immerse my powers of intellect into the earth? Indwell on the lichen? What the hell for? To climb a rock? I knew what I could climb, and I climbed what I knew. OK, so it sounds pedantic. But awareness of my own limits, as frail and as difficult a recognition as that is, had always provided me the greatest pleasures on a mountain. Knowing when to come down. I was a coward at heart. I knew how to save myself up on a wall when the going got rough. By getting the hell off. Fast. The Assyrian verb *to die* translated as "to clutch at a mountain."

It was sunset. Allain and Ghisela returned to the tent. There was academic conspiracy between them. Gullible assholes.

"Oh, come on. You aren't really serious?" I said angrily.

"Did you stare at the lichen?" she asked.

"Yes, and nothing happened."

"I don't believe you."

"What the hell *could* happen?"

"Michael, you're impossible!"

"Look, I'm tired of this . . . " I became somber, threatened. Had I really failed to do something? I was on edge. For it struck a deeper chord than merely the ability to derive whatever from lichen. I'd always secretly feared my intellectual limitations. It was hard for me to read a book without skimming it matter-of-factly. I mean, even if I tried to read each word, I'd invariably start skipping again, half-a-sentence at a time. I had no patience. And consequently I knew very little about any one thing, had great difficulty learning new languages. Friends had misinterpreted my breadth of *knowledge*. But I new better. And it was a painful domain. I was overly sensitive, easily intimidated, incredibly snobbish—all acts of defense. No one! No one must ever know my real ignorance. However, this fear had the advantage of yet deeper misgivings . . . I didn't really *trust* intellectuals. I trusted nature.

As far as I was concerned, existentialism—the very nadir of academic despondency—was situation comedy.

In fourth grade I had a social studies teacher who said Franklin Roosevelt killed himself because of his incurable syphilis. She used to say the Jews had existentialism, as if it were cancer. I examined the word and conferred with the definitive text.

A hairy, grimacing Frenchman, naked, with bullet holes for tits. This searing image of ennui, of a man desperately trying to hold his fart, affected me at a scrawny, opportune age. I still resembled Shirley Temple, wore braces and could roll up into a ball to bite off my toenails.

La Nausée struck me profoundly, particularly the French title with its air of learnedness. A devious nine-year-old, I rapidly figured how to feign philosophic depression, Oriental mononucleosis, I called it. Sartre's book provided me the surest vehicle for intimidating schoolmasters and the girls. A humanism indebted to despair, ontological dyspepsia, transcendental Bobsy Twins, Betsy Ross minus panties—it was all there. I could say, do anything with that book. Even drop out of school and go skiing with a free conscience.

A woman's nipples, German chocolate cake, sunset over the Pacific—these masterpieces of nature I knew from the beginning were what really counted for something in the world. Not Anselm's proof of god or Mill's Utilitarianism.

Yet, I was existentialist to the core. An outdoors existentialist.

We went into the tent. A cricket was cheeping in the garden. I took out our aluminum pots, boiled water on the rusting stove and prepared dried vegetables, adding sunflower seeds, garlic and raisins. We got some onions from the garden. Had hot chocolate and dug into our bags. I loved going to bed just after sunset.

It procured a certain freedom of the night, elongated dreams.

Ghisela and I stared pulsing at one another. I felt estranged, unable to grow with her, at her own fast clip. She was gullible, I told myself. Gullible, no thanks to me. There was lewd levitation in my sleeping bag.

"You're angry with me," she sighed.

"Not angry."

"What then?"

"I feel a little remote. That's all."

"That's a lot."

"What are we going to do?"

"I don't follow."

"What's happening here?"

"He's incredible."

"You believe him?"

"You don't."

"Do *you?*"

"Yes."

"I don't know what to say. How to secure this thing. I have a craving to consolidate, fortify, to make sure of it. Like there are still unsigned papers."

"We've got time, Michael. We just got here."

"I'm . . . frightened."

"At least you admit to it."

"It's just a gut feeling."

"The gut can be wrong."

"I have to tell you something. I slept with a Tibetan woman."

Ghisela didn't react. Then, "I know."

"What?"

"I smelled a woman."

"I met her in the bazaar. I mean, I didn't even meet her. It just happened. She was young."

"How young?"

"Young. Very free."

"So am I!"

"I'm sorry."

"Don't," she turned.

"You really smelled her?"

In the morning we went out to the pool. Minutes after our arrival, Déva emerged from the cave, accompanied by Kali, whom we hadn't seen in days. They made a curious couple and I was eager to know why she had aged so much more than he. I could understand a young man's passion for an older woman, but this was something else again. Was I dreaming? We all watched, amazed, as the tortured, arthritic immobility of the Kali we'd first met, moved towards us as fluently as her husband, with sprightly muscularity. The age difference was there. It was something in our own orientations which was missing. Her lengthy hair was tied back. Barefooted, in her shawl. Déva was naked. I noticed three lateral dots painted on his stomach and a tight-fitting gold band around his neck. His dark chest and arms had been rubbed down with oil and were gleaming, almost incandescent. Kali smiled at Ghisela.

"My wife will join us today. She does not often ascend anymore. She is much older than all of us combined you see. Please. Why don't you remove your clothes. It is important to do so."

We did as instructed. Only Kali remained in her garb. I questioned Déva about it.

"Mr. Michael, my wife has forgotten her English. But no. She does not take off her clothes. There would be no point. Nor does it become an older woman." His tone was gentle, humane, accommodating. "Let us go on to the glacier. You have a name for these towers?"

"Seracs."

"Good. Well, now. To climb seracs is an easy matter. Three points to remember."

I rose in panic. He wasn't really serious.

"And swiftly, like grain sliding through one's fingers," he continued, "to forget. First, our discussion of seracs, the words around the seracs. Think of the words as a drifting cloud. Then the idea of this serac attached to those words. The words around the ice. The words as a cloud. We walk to the base of the ice and our momentum is as a wind that carries the cloud away, and with it the words, and with the words the idea. So that we can speak unriddled by the opposition, the conflict of desires our words are bound to incite. But never get confused, especially during the climb. The idea is not the same as the action. Don't forget that. But don't remember it either. And when we have let all our clouds pass over us, through us, we can climb the serac. Shall we?"

He and Kali strolled over to the ice. The cold misty spray from the falls was piercing and painful this time in the morning. For the sake of maintaining calm, I had vowed to suspend all skepticism. But not if it meant doing something crazy, dangerous. Kali took Ghisela's hand and I admired how firm her thighs had gotten. Pressing her palm, their eyes meeting over minutes, Ghisela began to undulate. An energy, or radiation, like a mirage between them oscillating feverishly. Kali was moaning softly in alternation with her breathing, like someone dying of congestive heart failure.

Suddenly Ghisela went up, ignited on her toes, her eyes still fixed on Kali's. I thought her skin tone darkened slightly. I don't know what I thought! As if a real cloud had passed beneath the sun. But the sky was clear, a vibrant Himalayan mauve. Ghisela cried out in pain. Her buttocks twitched violently, a tic in her ass, her back muscles flexing in a spasm of expenditure. Still on her toes. Sweat pouring from the small of her spine. In a sauna of mental exigency, holding her, branding her, Kali looking demented. I'd seen a similar ritual in a French porno film. There was a drop. A total release. Ghisela sank back off her toes. And I breathed again. Allain stared expectantly.

"That was incredible!" Ghisela gasped. "What was it?"

"Forced gtummo," Déva explained. "Good heat. You must learn to produce it yourself. And then to do so instantly, as if it were an idea, an image of itself. Then you must know how to discharge it as quickly onto a single spot. The ice, for example. Watch."

He walked over to the blue hanging pinnacle. A good eighty feet high. I'd practiced aid technique about such walls on the glaciers of Mount Rainier. Déva stood quietly before the ice. Like the day before, on the granite boulder, he raised a foot, then his arms. I watched closely. His fingers touched the ice and at the same time water ran from the point of contact. He pulled up. Water pouring off a toe hold. And burning his way in this manner he fashioned his own ladder, all effortlessly, in silence. He climbed all the way to the top. Where it overhung and looked dangerously thin, snow-covered.

Now I was beside myself. We all were. He downclimbed the same route. His bare toes adhered miraculously. Even granting this spectacular heat-generating ability, I still could not understand holding on to the holes, without crampons, daggers, ice hammers.

"It's impossible!" I vowed.

"Don't say that!" he threatened with his finger, back on the ground, the ease of his breathing undisturbed. All I could think of was how on earth I'd ever describe what I'd just seen. There was no possibility of imparting the information, the experience. There were no words for such a feat. Perhaps they'd understand it in Hollywood.

"Mr. Michael. Nothing is impossible. Watch!"

He took Ghisela's hand. I'd stop him. She was still trembling, epileptic-like in the ague of moments before. He led her to the ice. Was she hypnotized? I couldn't tell.

"Now, Ms. Ghisela. Transmit your shivering to the ice. Let it become a locomotion of steam. Think of the lichen as your hand. Remember your hand. And what its size, its fine fingers, its strength consist of. You are the cloud. You are the ice. You are your hand. And very shortly, you are the top of the serac. There is nothing in your head." He held her palm as Kali had done. The sweat was streaming from all over her body. She shook. He held on. Up to her toes. Transfixed. I wanted to grab her. To stop it. But I had to see. Her foot went up. She touched the ice. Perspiration dripping from her crotch. The ice was dripping, too! Her back flooded with red. She cried out. Her head twisting down. Grimaces shooting through her neck. Off the ground! Impossible! Three feet. Her toes bearing one hundred twenty pounds, sticking to the moisture of a trance. Out in the air. It had to be a trance! But how did that explain it. I was breaking. But there it was. Ghisela, the woman I slept with, climbing a sheer serac, naked. Thirty feet above the ground. Her back no longer flexing. Smooth now. With a tempo. I was there spotting. But it was no longer unbelievable.

I stood back to take it in. How many years had I fantasized such a climb. Just touching the wall and ascending. I had to ask her how it felt. But before I could speak, Déva pierced me with his look, gesturing that I mustn't say a word. Ghisela continued. Now on the overhang. She didn't even seem to notice the change in degree, her motion as even, as effortless as Déva's. And she disappeared over the top. I collapsed. Terror stampeding through every pore.

"Who's next?" Déva smiled.

"Allain, please. I . . . I can't." I'd never been so scared. It was really happening. Every conviction I'd ever had regarding all the hundreds of cults, hermetic societies, Jesus freaks, astrologers, UFO's, T.M., Gestalt . . . in one bleak, disturbing blow, all flashed into me with atomic feasibility. My whole life had been mistaken. My Ph.D., my acquaintance with the world, all the thoughts and values I'd secured—gorged with exploding contradiction. In a disarray of depression, I sat down.

Allain went to the ice. Embalmed in seriousness. The same process. Déva imperiously holding his palm. His frame wracked with convulsion, whimpering. Sweat oozing down his crack.

And then he started, as if upon an invisible scaffolding. Burning holes, ascending in a tantalizing, nearly sensual rift of stupor, elegance, and impeccable control. Allain doing that! It seemed so natural. So conceivable.

I watched his every flex. Abandoning control and controlling abandonment, his body was like idea turned flesh. Resplendent, ephemeral, a god riding the stark cobalt barrier of ice like a child on a bull's back. Raw, orchestrated in the oblivion of the surroundings, I saw in him a sudden hero that was universal. Or was it self-pity that moved me to admire the impossible spectacle? I was thinking hard. My heart churning. A desire as pure, as unmistakably animal, was overpowering me. A humanity of ascent. This was real passion, I thought. Aboriginal philosophy in motion. Expedition of the senses, it was the going that astounded me, the movement beyond persuasion, beyond the dialectics of quality.

I saw the journey blazing over Allain's body. No longer was he desperately squirming. Now the fire was a science which he easily converted into ascension.

I stood up, wiping the tears away, ready, embarrassed, drugged. Allain had climbed over the top. Not a word from him or Ghisela up there. I stared at Déva. That radiance! Somewhere between Leibnitz and Jesse Owens. And Kali's devilish grin. Like stepping into flowing lava I went to him. I extended my palm, no longer frightened. As if I'd already died.

The heat came through me. My chest was like a limekiln. The tip of my tongue shot back against my palate. Heat poured in through the buttocks, coming up the spinal cord, a tingling, a heavenly shush, resonating like a snake which crawled up the back, each nerve blossoming in the exfoliation of inner pressure. A hot, painful concussion. Mountains coming inside me, the glacier moving over me, into me, a river, uncontrollable in my loins. Déva's hand had disappeared. A tiger beginning to pace in my fingers. My fingers! Moving, like just being born, like lizards on a steaming binge, their heads looking upwards, their throats bobbing. Alpenglow amassing over my senses. My rear end stiff, starting to ache, down the andiron legs, a fire in my blood. An island. Suddenly alone. My thoughts rearing back. All sensation now. The foot, each toe alive and bending, and *feeling*. My breath somehow maneuvering a logic in the skull, but empty, a great, clutching pendant segregation of myself, from another self. In high Gothic schism, two arenas of intensity, one lounged in a supple duration of pleasure, the other rigid, flexing hard, going for a spot on the ice. A channel flowing with combinations throughout myself. My heat burning, down my arms, into the fingers. No ideas left. Nothing, pure, pure, pureness speaking.

Against the ice. Like a current in the sea, like deep rocking sleep. Water under fingers. Serene, pliable invigoration looking upwards. No who I *am*, or who am I. Nothing. Only sensation. Natural apocalyptic direction aloft, towards the image of a cloud. At once, aerial, melting. No question of confidence, inconfidence, of ego. Nothing. Just rhythm, remote, growing closer, blending, higher, higher, into the mouth. A climax in my mouth. An allusiveness—great lyric poetry—pierced the discs. The surrounding ice was some ether of matter afloat—hazes—collectively disappearing in my greater emerging psyche. Leading down the neck, swaying thoughtlessly. A timeless river eating me alive. Leaning out over nowhere. Seventy or seven hundred feet up. Snow, glittering, a glacier, a glacier. Dry ice burning sweetly against the fingertips. When I remember.

Falling! . . . Falling! No . . .

Collapse. On the glacier. Blinding. Ghisela? Allain? Sitting beside me. Each of us alone, blinking dumbly.

I fell back into deep snow, the pounding waterfall now hidden under us. What if I had remembered a moment before I made the top? A detonation of ego too soon? Was it getting to the top that did it, being exhausted? "I'm hanging. Naked. I'm going to die," I had remembered. "No!" a second residual self said. "You are fine."

We grabbed on to each other. Ghisela was crying. Allain epileptic. Madness enshrouded our threesome. And then Kali came over the lip of the ice, pausing out on the edge, looking upwards, hanging by the frail umbilical cord of air. She came over to us, the fresh powder sucking up her ancient scarious limbs. Déva leaped like a showman, a Tantric comedian over the top.

"You did alright," he said. "You enjoy it?"

I blurted out nonsense.

"Good! Now to keep gtummo you need only act gtummo. By act I mean move. Once you stop for too long, once you break up the rhythm, the heat will naturally leave your body." But I felt like I'd already lost it.

We stood up and set off across the ice fall. It looked treacherous now. Hundreds of seracs hanging tenuously, sunk at their bases in deep, unknowable white which concealed crevasses. Surrounding us, a half mile in front, a thousand feet on the sides, were walls, obscuring the arc of sky in a vertigo of granite complexity; shards of cornice above our heads. Water churning deep under us. The snow blinding my eyes. I still couldn't believe it. I'd been hypnotized.

"Now. To check for crevasses. Attune your ears to the gurgling water. Get it down so that you understand the liquid angle. Decide which direction it is going. Follow it. We'll go to the rear peak. When the sound of the water suddenly stops, you must stop. Always follow the sound. Never contravene the angle of echo. The glacier is only water after all. Where you hear it, the glacier is solid. And where you don't hear it, there are crevasses."

He led. Kali stayed in the back. Across the amphitheater of silence. At times we were up to our genitals in snow. Déva stopped. Took some steps backwards, moved to the left. Then forward. We followed right behind him, every step. A crackling! Suddenly a strip of snow thirty feet across to our side caved in with a monstrous deep crash, exposing a blistering black gape. We were standing precisely where the crevasse pinched to a close!

Déva led upwards. The glacier was steep here, confounded in a chaos of broken, or nearly broken seracs. Some were freshly shattered.

"Again, follow the sound of its reverberation through the towers. But do not touch them. Move slowly. If one collapses onto you, there is little you can do. Tighten yourself. Generate heat furiously. There are three nerves worth mentioning. The *sushumna*, the *pingala*, and the *ida*. The *sushumna* must not be damaged. Your body is as an aircraft with many engines. The *sushumna* is a glider. Even when death is upon you. Go with *sushumna*."

"But where is it?"

"The heat in your back. Let it leak out any injury which might befall you. It will flow out as easily as blood. It is your decision to concentrate on the blood, or to go with the *sushumna*. *Pingala* and *ida*, they will help you anticipate events."

"But where is the sushumna?" I asked.

We passed through the head of the ice fall. I had never felt so free in my life. This wasn't soloing. It was floating. An airy deliverance. Anatomical license to discharge one's being with pleasure, without meaning, in the same direction. It was *anti-symbolic* motion. Unmuzzled consciousness. I could be careless. I could lose myself. As long as the sound of water was in my ears. As long as I kept up the heat in my body. It was so natural. It was immunity, gorgeous, perfect. A song that denied all those prior tears. I'd abandoned that suffocating ardor to delineate the contradictions between belief and the senses. No care for anything else. I'd broken through. As clear as a Big Sur firmament, I thought. Or did I remember? I stopped. Beginning to ponder, to battle the song. What did I just think? Where was I that instant? The sun confusing my vision. The others suddenly well ahead. Kali waiting wisely behind me. I set off again. Nothing.

We stepped off the glacier onto rock. We'd been in the snow a good three hours. Yet my body was perfectly comfortable. Warm. Not the slightest discoloration. No more fatigue. No fear. Only vital breathing and the sense that I could burn up a newspaper simply by touching it.

I took Ghisela's hand. A calm warmth. Now a fear set in. No amount of heat would make holds on rock. Had I failed yesterday? The lichen. This was different. My head began to throb.

"We have created a path of memories through the glacier," Déva began. We all stood at the end of a narrow ramp which led from the ice to the beginning of a crack system. The wall disappeared a good five hundred feet above. But I knew there was another mile of alpine face above that. Leading up to the 20,000-foot Northwest ridge of Stok. It seemed quite normal in my present state to have climbed the serac and traversed the glacier. Now he was proposing something utterly out of the question. My mind raced to grab details, linguistic defenses.

"You must relax now, beyond the symbols, behind the memories. In other words, squeeze the morning and the night, your sleep and your waking, your dinner and your breakfast, your penis and your vagina into the *Now*. Take the cliff and the glacier. Encircle them with your heat. Lean out. The real mountain is the imaginary mountain and vice versa. Because you have encompassed everything, absorbing all differences into undifferentiation. Out of control with consumed details. All of them neutralized in the furnace of your omniscience." His voice was inutterably calm, masterminding eloquence with humility, clarity with poetry, seductive poetry. He was not pushing too hard, not yet. And I felt placid beside his windlessness, his meaning inside no meaning. "You see you are not living in space. It is space which resides in you. Fill out such space and eternity is yours in the here and now. Draw a picture of this mountain-water eternity in your head. As you did the cloud. The outward must possess the inward. Until reciprocally you are able to read the environment by reading yourself, without confusing the ego for that environment. There are two of you. The reader, and the being. The mountain water is also the being. You see, water is alive! Did you hear me? *Water is alive!* To read the mountains properly, that is safely, you must do so without infecting that space with the act, the *will* of reading. In other words, don't let ego slip between the lines, the talus, the horizon. Keep them pure, free of yourself. If you have fallen, if you are civilized, it means you have taken the signs of nature—the mountain-water picture—to be exclusive metaphors for your experience of *yourself*. That is the selfish, western mind.

"That is pathological. A lexicographer must act that way. But not a man in love, a dancer. And never a mountain climber. When Kali and I first came here from the city—and believe me, Lhasa is immensely urban, social, religiously festering—it took us a decade or more to lose the stifling residue. To reacquire those things I had attained at Dí Se. I hadn't lost the image, the vision, but I had ignored it. The heat had long before cooled. My three nerves had lost their sensitivity; my mind was filled with things, things—yaks, butter, spools of fine thread, with raising my daughters, growing food, with daily living in other words. But I was not entirely happy. Because I, too, carried a special fondness for the cliffs.

"I gathered the lichen, drank of the ice water, concentrated. I thought back to my initial lessons at T'ien-t'ai Mountain. And I entered this cycle into my life as I had done on and off for so many years. It is not easy to make readjustments like that, in the course of one's existence. It requires sacrifice, and courage. But real passion is synonymous with such courage. Within only a few months it was apparent that I coud concentrate, and still do all the necessary life-preserving tasks. The sacrifice, in other words, was minimal. *Sushumna* returned. And in the company of other Dévas, old lovers of the glacier . . . "

"Watch it!" I screamed, lunging off the wall into the ice-fall. In a split-second we were shadowed. A rush of whizzing rock bursting off ledges up above, crumbling masses toppling in titanic flurries, catapulting other pendant hulks of verglased granite. Clinging in my veins, slumped and dizzily digging in the snow for cover, I waited while the torrent rained down, splattering with resounding crunches into the glacier.

And then it was over. A surcease, total silence. I looked up in the now calm air. Allain and Ghisela were deep in snow. But Déva and Kali had not moved. "Why didn't you jump?" I protested.

Déva grinned unalarmed. "When the rocks came you failed to remember the fact that we are standing under an overhang."

He was right. All of the rock had smashed a good hundred feet above, on the lip of the concave declivity, and from there, in an illusive battlement of spray, had fanned out well past our position amongst the seracs. His acute foresight was phenomenal. The sudden fear had plunged me into mindless panic. But Déva experienced no fear. His intelligence—focused in the present moment—saved him. My instincts jeopardized me.

We climbed back on the ledge. In the distance, three men, like wolves, were traversing the glacier in great easy strides.

"Other Dévas?"

"Friends."

"They've fallen!"

"No. That is the center of the glacier, remember? Where we first met. They have descended. It is late. We ought to return as well. Tomorrow, I will show you the pause between thought and action, the space between meaning and no-meaning. The object itself: the rock!" With that he leapt off into the snow, and disappeared with a *scream*!

"Déva!" Kali cried, leaping after him like a wild doe. She raced, downclimbing out of view into the crevasse. Moments later Déva climbed out, his forehead bleeding, Kali right behind him. She pampered him. He was greatly embarrassed, and lucky. The crevasse had not been deep.

"There are no formulas," he laughed loudly, wincing as Kali rubbed the wound with snow. "The paradox is never physical. The finest mysteries always exist within the most sudden of realities, in the purity of the unexpected."

"Could you have died?" Allain asked him.

Déva thought for a moment. "No. Life is a wink and then a grimace . . . But always another wink!"

We traversed the seracs following the subglacial troughs of water flow. Kali left our group in the center, disappearing into the painted cavern. The four of us continued to the drop-off. I'd been contemplating it nervously for an hour.

"Now. This will be interesting. And I warn you. A fall is a *real* fall!"

I was sitting in the deep snow along the rim. My heat was still with me but it seemed normal now. Like 98.6. I knew, I knew at the bottom of my heart that I could not downclimb it. I was not in the trance. None of us were. And Déva's unexpected warning. What was going on?

Suddenly, as if tempting another crevasse, he jumped off, yelling like a verb-in-motion. Over the waterfall, seventy feet into the pool. A splash. And his shouts of merriment below. We gaped wide-eyed at one another. It was either downclimb, or jump. I went to the edge, using his footprints. I stood there looking. He had swum to the left bank and was washing the dried blood from his forehead. I couldn't bring myself to do it. A sick up-shot in my stomach. "Ohhh . . . " flailing in the air as the snow underneath broke off. Smash! The cascade pounding on my back. Shock! Delight. I swam ashore. The water was as mild, as pleasant as a heated pool.

And Allain came running off, his skinny, ridiculous legs still bicycling through the air. Swoosh!

Then, bathed in velveteen glow, her breasts taut, her hair wild, Ghisela plunged off the snowy edge after us.

CHAPTER NINETEEN

By now we knew what was coming. But none of us knew if we could have downclimbed the serac. During the night my body had cramped up. I took two Valium, but still could not sleep. By morning every muscle was rigid. Wasted. As high as the trance had elevated us, its nocturnal cessation had taken us down. The speed of our desensitizing was too great, and the imbalance, the trauma was critical. Migraines, vomiting, severe muscle spasms in every part of the body. There was not even time to discuss the actual events of the day. But all of us were feeling the cumbrance of a new threshold.

Déva appeared at the top of the serac in mid-morning. This time he descended very slowly, as if demonstrating something new. We watched phlegmatically from outside the tent where we convalesced, sipping on hot chamomile tea. The sight of a human being downclimbing overhanging ice naked and unroped was as unreal, as fantastic, as it would have seemed weeks before. He had this in-furiating ability to anticipate our thoughts and rejoinders.

We sat unspeaking. The sky was dotted with high white specks of cloud. A snow plume had blown up around the summit of Stok.

Déva was staring down at the tea Ghisela offered him. He was a delicate anachronism aware of itself I had determined; not what he appeared to be. All of his techniques, his lifestyle, the extraordinary coincidence that we should find him, and his brilliant control of the language and of philosophy—it was too markedly modern. And his story about being born in 1650. What did someone *do* with such information? Yet the explanation for it all, the nature of the trances, of his nakedness, was a mystery no less arcane. Somehow we were being manipulated; a rare combination of events, of subtle psychological manifesta-tions, imponderable glacial eddies suspending us in some other system of seeing: the apposition of *context* which intellectually was credible, with individual events of the body that could not be explained. Déva represented the link. We did not. And so our thought processes were being continually frustrated against the wall, the impossibility, which his professed metaphors consummated. In other words, he was able to *do* what he said. And though we could also say, and think those things, there was no way to do them. Or such was my recollection of everything that had happened.

Though I had ascended the serac and spent hours in the glacier, my memory of it was like the faint ache of a near accident in one's past, the loss of a loved one. No real connection to the present, no reliable meaning. A noumenon of intimation as disturbing as a spectre, ready to strike at any instant, a nail in one's shoe.

Déva slowly looked up, as if probing obliquely back in time. I saw the suggestion of wrinkles, like a second face waiting underneath his surface sheen.

"I must know what you are able to say about *extreme mountains*," he began.

"What do you mean?" I deferred.

"What is the furthest thought you have of the mountains?"

"Furthest from?"

"Yourself."

"I'm sorry. I don't understand."

"What does your supposed *love* of mountains mean to you?"

I shrugged. I didn't like the tone of this. "I'm sorry. I still don't know what you're asking."

"Alright. Why are you here? Mr. Balladeur first told me that you are mountaineers. But it is obvious by now that there is some additional reason."

I didn't want to think against him. Not this morning. "Look. I enjoy climbing. Getting away. Sleeping under the stars."

"Would you enjoy it all of the time?"

"No. Of course not. I relish other things as well; food, women, the ballet. That gold of yours."

"And what do you want in fifty years?"

"Ask me then!"

"I'm asking you then!"

I looked impatiently at Ghisela. "Look, Déva . . . " but he was waiting for an answer. Impish. "I don't know."

"What do you do with yourself in America, Mr. Michael?"

"Well, I'm a writer, occasionally."

"Of?"

"Whatever works."

"And it relieves you?"

I was surprised. "Rarely. Writers are as desperate as readers."

"Do you write about the mountains?"

"Sometimes."

"And what else do you do, tell me?"

I was perplexed. What the hell *did* I do? My days slipped by in meaningless dalliance. Plans, hopes, fevers. Watch the news. Write letters. Solicit. Dinner parties, climbing with friends.

"I try to build the next day, sometimes the next month before it eludes me. Dream a lot. Constantly after magazines for a commission."

"Not very complex."

"No."

"And what does your intuition tell you?"

"That you can't fight the imponderable."

"And before the mirror?"

"The mirror?"

"Looking at yourself. What do you see?"

"What do you mean, what do I see? Me!"

"You?"

"Of course!" I was angry. Being baited.

"Then let's start with you. And with the mountains. For they seem to be your two exclusive sensations. The mountains allow you to escape yourself. And you allow yourself to escape the mountains."

"Why call it escape?"

"You have a better word?"

I couldn't think. For I wasn't entirely certain of his purpose. "All right."

"What other creatures go on escaping things?"

Again that tone, *creatures*. "Slaves escaped their masters. Gazelle, they escape lions. And meadow mice escape hawks." He was grinning at me.

"And your two escapes are asymptotic?"

"I'm sorry. Your English outclasses my own."

"You never see the mountains in the mirror?"

"You mean think of them as intrinsic to myself?"

"Yes."

"Sure I do. But it's always fleeting. More like a recognition. A statement of belief. The mountains, unfortunately, don't solve my greater dilemmas."

"Which are?"

"Survival."

Balladeur shook his head. He looked ill, disappointed.

"I see. Do you feel confused at this moment? Does my erection frighten you? Or this glacier?"

"Your cock is a trifle blatant. And I don't particularly enjoy being toyed with. You're not the only one who's been around." I shrank at oncy by my sheer stupidity.

"How old are you?"

"I'm twenty-five." I was feeling a strong urge to let him satisfy himself. But I felt I was winning. Hitting him with a little of the mundane. I wanted to tell him of my revelation the other day. Of that prehistoric feeling. Of floating away. But he needed to be contaminated with the simple truth of myself. And so did Allain. Ghisela couldn't conceal her simplicity if she tried to. I suppose that was her greatness. What I envied in her.

"You do know that you are still a very young man?"

"Yeah, sure."

"Very young, indeed. And I take it you have not established yourself?"

"Not entirely, no."

"And you are married?"

"Not yet."

"So your responsibilities are only to yourself?"

"I wouldn't say that."

"What do you *really* want?"

No one had asked me that in a long time. And I hadn't even posed it to myself. It had always been a relative conjecture before. What I wanted from a job. What I wanted to do for the summer. Déva waited gigantically, his conscious manipulation burning my insides. He knew everything I was thinking and, it suddenly dawned on me, everything I could possibly think. His look was unrelenting. Like Caesar's.

"I don't know."

"Then it would seem you have little control of your existence. You are floundering a long ways from home. And because you have no control, you are missing out."

"On what?" I stammered indignantly.

"Completion."

I was irritated. I didn't need this.

"Your beginning and end."

I had the image of those paintings in the tunnel and suddenly saw myself as sitting before some febrile wraith from the Middle Ages. A vestige of Neanderthal tempting me back over millennia. Or deep, too deep, into myself.

"You are obsessed with yourself. But your obsession is without real happiness."

"How can you say that! You're off-the-wall!" which inadvertently ignited a grin, relief, from one camp.

"Because you are sitting here before me, Mr. Michael. Don't think there have not been others like yourself, all roaming restlessly. Archaeologists of themselves. Sifting through dead clutter. Rummaging to discover the abracadabra of their lives. Unmindful of the years squandered in the search."

I hurt. Like frostbite in the mind. He was not going to let up.

"You are cut off from happiness because you are divorced from purpose. You groom your intellect, your desires, and are titillated by the excess leisure of your selfishness."

"Fuck you!" I blasted.

A brutal doom surfaced in his expression. "You are the same cynic. You'd best listen!" He turned to Ghisela. I was numb. Somehow he seemed to be generating theories off the syntactic intricacies of the conversation. Inciting me to break through my own hangups by penetrating our dialogue. But words were words. I was caught in the melée, powerless to analyze.

"Ms. Ghisela. What is worth talking about after all?"

"Love!" That was Ghisela all right. Not a moment's hesitation. I knew other women who used that route.

"Good. One's family. The weather. And adventure. It has always been so. The source of language. Of art. Of human nature as we are able to perceive it. You are comparing me to others of your own culture. Don't! You maintain ambassadors. Airplanes. Frequencies in the air to establish immediacy. I must confess. I have partaken of your world . . . "

I knew this was coming.

"For a brief period, with Wangdu. I went in many airplanes. I received letters. Despairing audiences. Saw your TV. Heard the radio. Took trains under the ground. Even tried your ice cream. The chewing gum, the escalator. I walked through Saks Fifth Avenue. In New York I saw a range of mountains! Or so I thought at first. I could not breathe, there was no drinking water. Wangdu had led me into hell. So many people confusing their culture with their existence! I went into samādhi, and got out. A big jet in the night. So I am quite familiar with where you are coming from. Do not be discouraged. You received the gtummo. There are many who could not."

"But what about the immediacy?" I broke in, wanting to establish a connection between his kind of instantaneity, and that of New York. It seemed like one possible access that I might understand.

"It is an interface. For you in America, and for us, speaking about it here. Remember the disjunction I described. The words *around* the serac. So your memories—your path of memories—surround you at this moment. And you know remorse in the uncontrollable engenderment of details and comparisons—tramways, social gatherings, job raises—which you cannot let go of, which prevent you from engaging this moment completely. Even my erection, a custom of Dévas, how can you understand, as long as you try to understand? For what does your kind of understanding consist of after all? More comparison, exponential enumeration, neutron bombs. Let me remind you, as you said yourself, that this moment, and always this moment, is your *only* purpose. Your fullest existence. The *only* moment. That's all there is, kid!"

"So you're saying to abort the past, and all comparison, memory, for the future?"

"I am asserting rhythm. A combination of the past and the present. A swift confluence which is entirely deliberate. And as wild as the Blue Bear.

"The Master of T'ien-t'ai Mountain called it *Nyubu*, entering the mountain. Proceeded by *Suzukake*, lowering over the cliff. This is a very different feeling and significance than the samādhi. For there is the sting of cold air in one's nostrils. The pounding fear in one's heart. The blue and white and black of Himalayas all around. Nothing more satisfying, more implicitly religious than a lifestyle which works. I have a friend, a Hebrew Déva. If you are ever in Jerusalem, go see how he lives. I am referring to a technique. Yes. But I only call it technique so that you will readily apprehend it. Actually it is a lifestyle, like water. We call it *tsa*. The people of the Vedas knew of something similar—their Karma. Tsa is the perfect proportion. The reason for all *backwards*, for memory, nostalgia. In essence, it is the whole, the life blood of the Himalayas.

"Tsa is the substitution of gravity for ego, spawning salmon. A friction of conjugations. It is, above all, a history of ice water."

"What came before history?" Ghisela asked.

"Ancient lifestyle," Déva said calmly.

My body had relaxed. The sun was directly overhead. My tea had been cold for hours.

"What is ancient lifestyle?" Allain asked.

"Simply unencumbrance," Déva said.

"But what of disease? Ignorance? Cruelty?"

"Progress has not eradicated anything. Concealed, complicated, yes. Destroyed, never. Cultural man is domesticated, not civilized."

"But progress has yielded, for many of us, a more comfortable compromise."

"I am speaking of the one-in-the-many. Of ourselves. Do not resort to social simile. It is a useless deferral. An illusion which betrays your own uncertainty. The Buddha knew nothing of labor unions. He was, after all, the supreme narcissist. Rich. Confused. Stubborn. Introverted. Somber. Forlorn. Weak. He professed an ultimate model of himself. He was an artist. And like other artists, he relied on his emotions. And was easily able to translate the tenets of his neurosis, his inspired egotism, into principles. Compassion. The politician promises comfortable compromise. Unencumbrance is something else entirely. It means *wildness*. The world in the brain of a snow leopard. Not your American breed of wildness, however. Surely you have noticed how odd it is that you Americans, who have come to suspect all preservatives, go on speaking of the preservation of wilderness. I am referring to the impact of the glacier on your senses. To the gtummo. To our presence here together.

"We are doing what my own ancestors did. Drinking tea. Chatting. And getting ready for an adventure. You have come around the world to do what has always been done. There are sīddha ashrams everywhere, Mr. Allain. In villages throughout Tibet. And Oklahoma no doubt. Vortices of community interaction. Not progress. But stable places where fathers and grandsons, mothers and daughters, like prismatic beads of dew on a spider's web, collect over centuries. Hauling up water. Washing clothes. Telling stories. Burying the dead. Morality is not sudden. It accrues over a life. And morality is what we're discussing. Not mountain climbing. Not enlightenment, as you have been assuming."

Allain was perturbed. Engrossed in a mystery which was now glaring, almost amusing. "Déva, how are you able to *speak* this way? I mean surely, you see how unlikely, how odd . . . I mean here, in this place?"

"Don't forget, Mr. Allain, I have lived and studied for more than three centuries. And I have known your language for many, many years. Do not compare me with your New Yorkers, with the stories of your novelists. With the trends in your thinking. Nor to Wangdu, who is of an entirely different breed than myself. I am naked before you. Expressing myself as a man. Not an animal. You are confounded not because you cannot believe I am as old as I say, but because you are unable to believe in *anything*! You are, furthermore, far away from your normal place. Not so much in miles, which the world's technology has falsely reduced, but in your expectations. *You hope for instant knowledge.* And this rage for immediacy is what forces you to distrust age. I have resolved some fundamental dilemmas which you have not. I have chosen the simpler of two worlds. Where as you are undecided. As it should be. Perpetual wanderlust, exile, youth—that is the good fortune, or the fate, whichever you prefer, of a mountaineer.

"The spiritual melancholy, the acute song, the Pyramids of other ages—this is the fresh air, the ease about which I am discussing. All the first impulses, grunts, jokes and mythical viscera—here is where you must place your trust. Society believes it has survived the ancients, not wishing to suffer ever again the primeval awkwardness of mystery. And subsequently, society's musculature is better suited to pushing shopping carts than climbing mountains or worshipping the earth.

"But again, we are not society, you and me. Or not wholeheartedly, anyway. But you are unsure. And since every idea is neutral, you are grappling twice-over. I am not. The impasses you have been feeling have an exact analogue. Which is the futility of arguing one's own happiness over another's. All beauty, truth, pain—they are equal if they are real. My content is your anxiety. The normalcy of my world, is the phenomenology of yours. And my age is your youth! I have spent three centuries acquiring certain techniques. You expect to gain them with a word, a touch, in a matter of days. That's alright. I help you all along because I like you. I feel that you mean well. But don't be fooled. Technologies are only useful insomuch as they are properly, integrally applied. You have a lot of work ahead of you yet. Your civilization is an immoral one. I think I'm old enough to be opinionated on that matter."

I was all vexation. Morality? It seemed we were in limbo. Why *had* he helped us? And what, *really*, had he done, said? I was suddenly unsure. Did I truly *believe* this man? I mean, *did* I believe in anything? Shit! How does one *know*? The Chipewyan Indian word is *inkonze*, meaning "to know something" about spiritual nature, which is synonymous with self-knowledge. But sieved through my pyrotechnic being, such words have little purchase. I *feel* a lot of things. But the mind, or my mind, anyway, ultimately dictates. Little fucker, it is. But Déva was absolving my mental rights, insisting I give them up for morality's sake.

I looked at Ghisela. She was burned like a Cretan muleteer, reddish, standing firm, both feet on the ground. I think she had decided, and looked as tranquil as I'd ever seen her. Something separated us at that instant and I felt that I'd been suddenly trajected into space, lost from those in whom I had a stake, a footing. And it was her faith. She had simplicity. I was the urbanite, the screwball, the ambiguous one. She had the *wabi*, the psyche, whatever it's called; whereas I was all prisoner of notions. The closer I came to giving up, the fuller was my grasp. A drowning man, a desperate man, an abstract man with hunger.

"We have our affinities then," Déva went on. "Stop transforming your pangs of conscience, your aspirations, into greed. Your penchant for wandering will save you, unless you expect it to. Open up the floodgates of passion." His words were raining down on me.

"Tsā is for you and me. For anyone who has embarked, in any century. It is freedom."

"You're suggesting tsā as a solution to all dichotomies?"

Déva looked down. Discouraged. "Why must you seek answers?"

I stood up. To stretch. To get something. I went into the tent. Allain joined me while Ghisela stayed with Déva.

There was urgency between us, the sense of things closing in.

"How does he compare to your Déva at Amarnath, Allain?"

"Different, radically different. The whole mythology of Śiva was so crucial then. It's not now. I was a detective. Younger! Yes, I was alert to clues then. And the Déva didn't deny them. Though he never relied on them. But this Déva . . ."

"There's something of Wangdu in him," Balladeur went on. "What do you think about Kali? Her climbing that way. And their age? I'm not saying they're contradictions. He's convinced me they are not. I mean I was the one who first believed in the sīddha ashrams. Yogis living to be nine hundred. I guess I expected something different. His logic, his English, the trances, or whatever they are. I'm feeling cornered. There's more here than I'm willing to admit. It's inside. I can't escape that fact about myself."

"What do you mean *inside?*"

"I mean my own mental map is breaking down. I don't trust anything anymore. I can't work it out. It's as if my mind has become malicious against its own instincts."

"I thought you were the true believer, Balladeur?"

"I am. That's what's frightening me. The way we climbed the ice. Do you realize what we did? That was for real! How the hell are you going to go home again?"

"Look, Allain. I'll grant you his powers. Hypnotic. Sagacious. Otherworldly. Call them what you will. I can't understand them. I've been trying. He's remarkable. Agreed. The whole place, an extraordinary accident as far as I'm concerned. It's happened too fast. I'm scared as hell. But I know how to get home. And I know that's where I'm headed."

"Well, there's the difference, Michael. You've got a closed and ordered society of knowledge, whereas I'm scattered. And you've always had a Ghisela, in one form or another. Your cynicism saves you from the labyrinth.

"I'm scared. I want to stay. I want to take off my clothes, for good."

I knew this had been coming. Balladeur's perturbations were famous for their conspicuity. I wanted no part. He was right. I *was* cynical. I'd acquired a taste for it after suffering successive, half-light futilities; of discerning my limits, in my inability to love responsibly, to make new friends, in all my sweet, mellow, fucking degradatory, derisive, endless *normalcy.* I might be as unspectacular as a worm on those days. But then I'd be the first to smell the resonant earth after a rain. Such compensations saved me. More than ever, I needed to hold on, to clutch to what was behind me, and to where I'd be headed. Balladeur had exercised his full allure on my life. I'd followed him. Indulged his antics throughout the poet walks of New York; and come hapless to Asia after his geese. Now I had the distance. He seemed pathetic to me just then.

That big, big world was not so glamorous, perfect, dynamic as I'd once thought. Things happened by way of hard work, and unaccountable anonymity. Lots of loneliness out there. Disappointment. Whole generations of hang-ups. No guru, no matter how searing, how relevant, how fantastic his metaphors, his silence, his acrobatics, could change the way the world was. So yes, I was something of a cynic.

Allain and I talked for a short time. I tried to calm him. I mentioned other climbs we might try. But he was inconsolable. We went back out.

They were gone! Ghisela's clothing on the ground! Not in the hut. On the glacier? No way to see up there. The cave. "Let's go!" It was the first time Déva, with his hard, ascetic cock, had been alone with her.

We'd only been in the tent twenty minutes. Why hadn't she alerted us? We made torches and ran around the pool. Behind the waterfall. There was light coming from within the center. We moved carefully, quickly.

Kali was there. Lazily tending a fire. Munching on some radishes. Three sād-dhus were sitting in samadhi against the rear wall, motionless, eyes glossy and affixed dead-center inward.

"Kali! Where is Déva?" She shook her head and pointed up through the opening in the crevasse. Blinding sun above. I yelled at the zombies. "Where's Déva, you bastards!"

Suddenly, we heard screams coming down through the crevasse from the glacier over the tunnel. "Ghisela!" I yelled, grabbing Kali for an explanation. It was like touching marmoreal granite. Her eyes wide, immutable, as if to scold me for manhandling an old woman. I kicked rocks into the fire. "Let's go!" I felt certain we could get up to the glacier quickly. I'd find the bastard!

Her cries were still coming down. We ran out through the tunnel, tripping over our crampons. "Allain, he's raping her!" My lungs were hoarse. There was no question of going after the ropes. It was either repeat the gtummo or wait, helpless. "He'll kill her, Allain! Jesus, he'll kill her!" My eyes were bursting. Allain's story of that goddamned pervert at Amarnath. And then these shitheads, walking around with uncircumcized schmucks.

We both stood at the ice. Breathing fast. Do it! Goddamnit, DO IT! Blood curdling in my veins and blood-squealching cries continuing from above. Nothing!

"Shittt . . . Déva, I'll kill you! You fucking sonnufabitch . . . " My world spinning. I was crying. Unable to get off the ground. Burning up. Ghisela screaming and no way to move. A dumb cripple.

It was all over. The side of my fist banging the serac. And then silence. Allain leaning against the ice, his head slack, dizzy in the outbreak of this new insanity.

I sat down, sobbing. There was nothing to do. "Ghisela, Ghisela!" Silence.

We went back to the tent and waited. "I don't believe he'd do it, Michael," Allain said.

"I've never heard her scream like that."

"I know."

We waited. All afternoon. I couldn't stand it. I went back to the cavern. Kali was gone. And so were the other sāddhus. I came back to the tent. Allain was writing in his notebook.

"Why? How could he? If we don't find her we'll get the military. A helicopter."

"No helicopter could clear the ridge. And no Indo-Tibetan police would risk their necks coming up here. Besides. You realize we're beyond the inner line. We'd be arrested."

There were butterflies drifting over the garden. A nightmare. Darkness came. The whole morning had been a philosophic seduction, prefigurements for the murder. "He's psychotic. A devil!" I lay back in my bag. Thoughts moving fast in shock. What were we really going to do? How to explain it to her parents. To mine? To the authorities. To ourselves? That we'd been learning about the wilderness from a naked Tibetan on a glacier? That he went crazy and dragged her off? Raped and murdered her high up on the snows? Had he hypnotized her back up the ice? How could I be so blind, so unabashed. To let those perverts come anywhere near her. "Allain, I can't stand it!"

We plundered the garden.

"I think we should try the gtummo again," Allain ruminated out loud.

"I don't want to hear it!" We ate in silence. I got into my bag. Allain sat out by the fire we'd built. I was terrified. Asking how, how it could have happened. It was late.

"Ghisela!" I dove outside the tent. Ran to the pool where she'd just emerged from behind the falls. Her hair waxy by the moonlight.

She fainted in my arms. I carried her back.

"Oh god," she murmured, waking twenty minutes later.

I lay her in a sleeping bag, and slowly she came around.

"We're listening."

"It was a test. Déva conceived it."

"I knew it!" Allain exclaimed.

"And you didn't pass."

"Don't give me this shit. You were screaming like a dog with a sword up its ass!"

"We were near the center of the glacier."

"How did you get up so fast?"

"Gtummo. When you went in the tent. It was magnetism. He leaned over and touched me. I was burning. I understood what he wanted to do. I left my clothes. Somehow he knew you'd be in there long enough. We went to the ice and climbed it as we all did. Quickly. Mindlessly. I followed him across to the top of the cavern. He explained to me his purpose at that point."

"Which was?"

"To make you think precisely what you did think. To forget everything he's told us. To wipe it out. Of course, we heard you from up there. When you threatened to kill him he even apologized to me."

"Ghisela, did he fuck you?"

"Michael!"

"Ghisela!" I grabbed her wrist.

"Of course he didn't! He never layed a hand on me. I screamed. But I was acting. I was hot. And he wanted to see—we both did—if either of you could generate your own heat and climb the ice after me. Do you understand?"

"You scared me to death. You know that?"

"At the time, I didn't consider it. You experienced the *sushumna*, the overpowering, unbridled flow. That thing. Don't you understand?"

"OK. But where were you all evening?"

"Well, my head was going crazy. Thinking you'd come. I think he thought you would as well. When you didn't we traversed the glacier. Back to the cliffs behind the last of the seracs. Michael, we climbed the entire wall!"

"You're lying!"

"No she's not!" Allain broke in.

"He showed me the technique. And he plans to show you. When you've simmered down."

"It really works?" I pleaded, feeling like we'd maybe—just maybe—pulled off a coup.

"It accomplishes what it's supposed to."

"Getting up the rock?" Allain ventured.

"Well, yes and no. There's the inside of the thing."

"What are you saying?" I raced. "What?"

She hesitated, still in a state of adrenalin addiction.

"It's another form of *gtummo?*" Allain asked, pressing my query.

"It's well, it's sexual."

"He didn't touch you, huh?"

"No! It's internal."

"Most orgasms are." I was repulsed.

"We were on the same ledge. Under the crack. He described psychic junctures, the genesis of OM. He called me Devi."

"Did he have an erection?"

"Yes. And he came!"

"Oh no!"

"He ejaculated off the ledge into the snow."

"You watched!"

"It was beautiful."

"I can't believe this. That bastard masturbated in front of you. He got you on a ledge to jerk himself off . . . "

"You will too! Both of you! In front of me!"

I was faint. She wasn't the same woman. And I was excited.

"Listen. Déva called it *Maithuma*. He said it was a symbolic union. He came gloriously, groaning like you do. But what a show. He shot his semen twenty feet. I was hallucinating, it went so far. And there was so *much* of it! He sat down and looked up at me. Blushing. Happy. And I understood. I rubbed myself. It was outrageous with Déva next to me that way. But it wasn't a real masturbation. It was . . . I don't know. An energy. Every inch of my body heaving with pleasure. But he never touched me. I wasn't at all concerned about it. There were other things happening."

"Other things?"

"We stood up, touching the rock face. The *gtummo* was inside me. And the crack was not that difficult. Certainly nothing like the serac."

"But the burning. How could it bore holds in the rock?"

"That's not its purpose it turns out. The purpose is thirst!"

"Thirst?"

"You get so thirsty you can do anything; you *become* water."

"The *tsā?*" Balladeur motioned.

"Yes. I felt this tremendous gladness, an affinity with the world. The mountain was alive under me, and everything in my life peacefully directed up that rock. I stepped into . . . the wave of myself. And the moment I did I was carried. There was control and there was no control. I was free-falling upwards. I was soloing."

"And how high did you really go?"

"All the way."

I noticed a dark burn on her palm. "That's no climbing wound. What happened?"

"We touched hands during the gtummo. To remember him by."

It was his blessing.

CHAPTER TWENTY

I was ready to make my reconciliation with Déva. It had never occurred to me to equate sexual orgasm with mountaineering. Though certainly the metaphor, the ascension of body, is precise in both cases. The fundamental act of hugging rock, sticking hands, fingers in cracks. But I'd never thought to climb in any *reliance on*, or in *conjunction with* the sexual impulse. And while I had done it one windy spring afternoon off the top of the Lost Arrow Spire, the greatest phallus on earth, in Yosemite, I never thought to do it at the bottom.

All that afternoon I tried to think back over what Déva had told us before he set off on this *test*. He might have done it differently. Though the theatrics, the illusion, was so frightening, so frustrating; it had indeed demystified me, temporarily. God knows I'd played my own ruses. Though never with such flourish.

He was coming the following morning and I was determined not to bring the whole affair up. Ghisela described Stok's Northwest summit, the hanging glacier on top and their incredible descent by moonlight to the cavern where Kali greeted them with food and a hot fire. I figured her solo would probably rate as the greatest mountaineering feat in history, among mortals anyway. We stared at the wall through our zoom lens. It was a good 4,000 vertical feet. As high, as sheer as the walls of the Baltoro, Patagonia or Romsdal. Caked with ice, with overhangs. And she'd downclimbed it as well, naked, at night, from over 20,000 feet! It was an instant legend in my mind. One of those miracles better not repeated, nor described. There was no *access* to believe.

Déva arrived early. Kali was with him. For protection, I assumed. Our greeting was strained, civil. And for the first time he was wearing a loincloth.

"You cold?" I asked. He bowed his head. And I registered a grin to keep us afloat in the ribald morning.

"Gentlemen. We have some interesting ground to cover today." His appearance was particularly austere. Serious, or defensive. "You needn't undress. I suggest you wear what you wore when you first arrived here." I searched Allain's eyes.

We followed Déva and Kali to the serac. Again it seemed impossible to climb. Now it was really absurd. The ice was blue, overhanging, wet. A flawless sheen.

I had on my wool trousers and cramponed double boots. My two ice axes were in hand. After having first ascended it naked in gtummo, these accoutrements felt ridiculous.

"So climb, Mr. Michael!"

I was not good enough. Even with a rope I wouldn't have been strong enough. I looked at Déva. Remembering how I was also unable to do it the day before. His blue eyes were sparkling. I threw down my ax, my serrated ice hammer, unstrapped my twelve-point crampons, took off my boots, my thick Austrian knit socks, and touched the ice.

I felt a sudden surge of friendship for that unlikely couple. I wanted to hug Déva. To thank him. To prove that his brief teachings had not been wasted on me. And I felt nearly confident. Ghisela and Allain were behind me, beside the pool. I turned and faced the serac, standing six inches in front of it. There were high cirrus above, in the edifying thin air. The cascade was thundering white froth, pouring from the rim of another world. And I wanted to get there. As if everything in my life suddenly depended on it.

Déva stood. I felt his breath. And skinny Kali with the ribbon in her hair. I touched the ice. No thought of possible or impossible, of me or it. But of the whole unreal scene, all its connections, a slow motion of wind, of ice water and of the glacier. Déva's image was like a glare in my mind's eye. Salient, crisp, inspiring. I gave in to it, like someone gulping down a drug to alleviate pain.

And I was hot, my penis stiffening in my underwear. A sensual wide-eyed recognition adhering in a friction of calm. Happy. Until completely at one with the cold, mute circumstance. Ascension at my doorstep. The alphabet of elevation implicit. A reality that was pellucid, tangible, erotic. Until, still on the ground, every detail of the landscape perfectly formed in my head, I opened my eyes.

THE WATERFALL WAS DEAFENING! Mist on my face. Wind through my hair. A frenzy of ice threatening to topple over me. Hard to breathe. I was high. There were cliffs surrounding me. The pool. Clouds. Two miles above. An old woman and an old man. That hut. And Ghisela. With not the slightest reason for any of it. Except that it was beautiful, exhilarating. My blood circulating hard and snow hanging over me. Dazzling! Marble-white and forbidding. I'd never been here before.

"I don't have to climb it!" I said, turning, exalted, to Déva. And I felt great love, kinship for the sly debauchee. I was breathing relief. My stomach churning. A sudden renascence of unrestraint. Building like a furnace. Free. To climb or not to climb. I again faced the ice. Blindly, dazed, indifferent. I went to the glacier. I could go anywhere.

Within ten minutes, Allain had gone through a similar reunion with Déva's natural cycle. We'd both been spawned. And soon we were all sitting around on the ice fall.

We headed to the side of the glacier. An obvious route above us. I'd been looking at it for several days. A vertical rock wall, as large as the one we'd rappelled, breaking up into a convergence of mixed rock and ice, a steep couloir, and a grey band of overhangs. All topped by cloud-engulfed cornices.

Kali was eyeing Déva and there appeared to be some nervousness between them. Allain, too, looked worried. I stared at the immense wall, straining to perceive it as I would have the previous year. But I could draw no comparisons. My body was consumed in the ride of self-possession. Nothing, not even my eyes, could thwart it.

"Rock is the beginning and the end of everything," Déva began. "And for our purposes, so is the human being. By tsā, by gtummo, you must affix your own beginning, the bottom of your origins this minute, to the rock's own beginning. Then you can climb *as* nature. You may accomplish this link, this interembryology, in two ways. Obliviously, with your genitals. Or mentally. By simply conjuring the image of that harmony. As you did with the lichen, transmuting it into your fingers, your ideas, and finally giving it back to the rock. Of course we cannot *know* the geological beginning of the rock. But every time we approach a boulder, each new encounter, is a beginning. Aboriginal and unqualified. You must inhabit this mystery of the eternal beginning. Bring your home into the sovereign resolution of the image that gives you the most pleasure. If it is ascent, then consider your home as such."

"Live on the wall?" I asked.

"Yes. The human being can adapt to any dimension. And in that assimilation is a *new* dimension, an unexpected possibility. Consider the Tibetan yak herder. His amenities are meager. His lifetime a simple register of deliberations no more intricate, no more pressing than the whimsies of his yaks. He needs little. His musings are as much an escape from the wilds, as they are a function of the wilds. His survival is a system of disciplined nonchalance, ruthlessness, tranquility. Hunting activities are conducted up high, where he stalks bharal and wolverine, pica and wolf. He engages in minor agriculture, maintaining cultivation from late spring, when the soil starts to thaw—potato, maize, barley and wheat being sown—until early autumn, when his vegetable gardens are pulled up and the yak herds brought down, wool manufactured and hay stored, while his woman harvests the ripening grain following the crops steadily up the mountainside. Plants are ready at delicate intervals, each foot separating the fruition period so as to allow his family time to bring it all in. The herd grazes on the emergent stubble and manures it, enriching the fallow. In winter there is great intercoursing, smoke in the eyes, cereals, bear's fat, millet, star anise and masala of currants. He dances a chant—sad and wild and learned centuries ago—beats on crab tree drums, sings boisterously and stalks the leopard by moonlight, setting out through golden barberry and primula Tibetica, up to the silvery snow. In bamboo panniers he carries one hundred fifty pounds of food back to his people. Children manage half of that. His oldest son stays with the herds up high. The boy grows up, surrounded by the amiability of mastiffs, clean wind, roots, tubers, rice, the sweep of mountain and incessant time, time to believe in the substance of days, in the giving slope and the soil. He returns to his father, one day, a father himself. The Tibetans vanish into one generation after another.

"The mountain promises the worth of all endeavor. And the Tibetan yak herder knows this. Which is how he so easily survives in a harsh environment. There is nothing *really* to think about! But human beings are easily embarrassed. To live on the ice is to be naked, regardless of the paraphernalia one drags along with him. But there are two forms of nudity. One is real, the other is imagined."

I was confused. "Which is the imagined?"

"The one you are aware of!" he grinned.

Allain stopped short. Thinking. And then he looked at me as if to point to some past assertion now affirmed. He was nearly blushing. With a dubious consecration flooding the red of his face. A huge gap had opened between us. As if he'd been carried away and I was still at rest.

"What's going on?" I asked Déva.

"That's up to you, Mr. Michael!" he said.

I stared up at the wall. I did not want to climb it. Though I think I could have. It was a laziness, an ease which prevented capitulation. It was like a trail, an easy feeling. But there was no reason to *hike* up there. No. No reason to do anything. My testes were rising and sinking to my deep breathing. I felt strong, incomparably powerful. Déva was looking at me strangely. There was suddenly nothing left to say and we all felt it in a unison of emptiness. I could remember nothing, nothing. The word naked. What did it mean? What was it? Like a gem of syllables whose emblem had been lost to the ages, whose lustre had dulled, or washed away in the river of time towards some other shore, some other settlement of meaning.

I was marooned. For the first time in my life I could not move, pinned by the invisible. No hunger. No cold. Only calm volitionlessness. I had not a single motive nor idea in my head. Nothing! Like the child in the mirror, repeated infinitely to himself, without a demarcation zone. All was surcease. The air still. And silence between us for hours it seemed. Until Kali stirred. Standing.

There was Ghisela, thick-crotched, strong-boned, her flesh burnished, her hair long, caught in the gossamer uplift of light that penetrated the enclosure. Her head was at rest, eyes set peacefully like I'd never seen them. She was a marvelous creature and I loved her.

Balladeur, too. He'd gotten me here. For all his rash turnabouts the man was genuinely gifted, soft spoken, feeling on a high level. What could he do now; what could any of us?

I was, perish the word, stoned; as dizzy with this newly discovered architecture, this ecology, this balance in myself, as bees in nectar. For a long time we all lay quietly in the snow.

"What was it?" I asked, as if awakening.

"It was you," Déva replied calmly.

An equation of being, of my whole life, had been solved in a flash. Or like Alice probing the looking glass, I'd reverted to my oldest fantasy. Staring across a creek-bed in my upbringing, under the stars, to the line of evening fireflies glowing in an electricity of the natural world. Hoping to be saved, firmed up for eternity.

It was a contradiction—to be completely satisfied! Hoping for nothing, having no other wants but the present. A yielding, commodious quiet. I had to be crazy to feel so good, so complete. In such an environment.

And it lasted. Almost into fear it stayed there, a separate recognition between us all, for so long. A fear of really giving in to it. *Giving?* I asked myself. Of giving *me* away to it. Genes, past habituation, past knowledge—I was weighing the pro-spects of self-immolation on an invisible altar. For there was no future; only the snow of the glacier, the strange friendship with Déva and Kali.

It was a decision that had nothing to do with the molten liberation, the *gtum-mo,* or with the *ideas* of this deliverance. It had to do with my ineluctable disposition. They *were* ideas, with which I was free to sustain a dialogue or not. I'd not been conquered altogether. I was still outside of the forest, staring with cognizance into the trees. I could go there. The path was open to me. I was pinned by the options. We want to see a beautiful butterfly tremble in the air, its gold and lavender wings shimmering. And we also want to pin it down. Analyze it, rhapsodize it. I wanted both worlds. Success, *and* disappearance. Were they so incompatible?

Suddenly I looked clearly into the heart of urban crisis: pollution, masses, poverty, disease, violence, treachery. Of course people died in their seventies! The more complex the material—artificial—stimuli, the more strain on the system. The more complicated the food intake the less likely the body was to govern itself naturally.

So people jogged along waterfronts. Joined tennis clubs. Went camping three weekends a year. Played golf. Ever since the Jack London genre, Westerners assumed that simply by taking a big breath of *fresh* air, and forgetting their sor-rows, they were momentarily returning to nature. And there was consolation in that. In a bed at night, alone, with a book in hand, the mind spinning its own delectable webs.

It was just that. Mind! Mind and little else. Mind sabotaged each day by the vaster onslaught of unwanted images — billboards, emotional intrusions, newspapers splattered with the spectrum of gores our civilization craves. Déva spoke in platitudes. And at first I'd found him heavy and pedantic. Lacking any humor, his one-liners full of bromide. But now I understood his necessary method. Of enclosing what it is he felt with words which, admittedly, were mere semblances of the heart's images. Like terms of anatomy, of the galaxies, of a mountainside.

But Déva's life was the *context* which verified those words. And his life was right there. If this was education, it was also personal conservation. With Déva the legend was fact. His biographer would have a hard time!

I had been demystified only to believe all the more. That was apparent at this point. Delineations had slipped by me. I'd loosened my grip on all definitions, so thoroughly that I'd managed to climb the impossible. Not because I was climbing any better, but because I now accepted the idea of impossibility. The context to lose myself that way was the decisive factor. But I wondered the consequences of losing myself in Union Square? Of course even Déva had his defenses. Samadhi, the impenetrable shield which Allain asserted had saved Christ on the cross. And which Déva amusingly implemented in confrontation with the Avenue of the Americas. So it was not inconceivable to survive in a dual role as Wangdu did.

I had everything in Big Sur. The wild sea under me. The endless stars overhead. My health. My family. My cottage. Ghisela. That semitropical lusciousness, those delicious mists, the wild strawberries, blue sky and eucalyptus. I had the mauve, sea-grazing kelp to meditate upon, right under my window. And the continuous enrapturing smack of arcing waves against the beetling cliffs. I had some dear friends. Hot water. A stereo. A thick foam bed. Despite some sordid essentials, life was easy for me. I had eluded all its difficulties. I had secured no routine, no enemies, nor any future. I was free and wild. And I had nothing.

I had to make a decision and I already knew what my answer would be. There was no escaping it: I was not, after all, a Tibetan. And that mattered. If ideas didn't matter, if, in the end, it was lifestyle which would save or ruin someone, then I would have to admit it, sooner or later; that I was who I was.

There *were* solutions for someone in my boat. The world *was* beautiful after all. Though it wasn't the beauty. But becoming immortal, then dying.

If I wanted everything I would have to cultivate the completion Déva had shown me, but in a different context. This was obvious to me all along. I wanted to climb mountains, yes. But I also wanted to browse through bookstores. And if I had a craving to wander across a desert, I could be sure that I'd want one hell of a celebration dinner afterwards.

If that's the essential penchant of civilized man, to despoil, to crown the purity of his heavenly flights with good old bantering, and french-fries, so what! Commerce with the banal, daily chores, the comedic—these were critically *human* modes. Contrast was the essence of doing anything. Even tsā. No, *especially* tsā! Water against rock. Rest and exhaustion. Thirst and quenching. All motion conspires to create life in the restive epicenter of each passion. The lemon sun across overhangs in Bellini; rapids plunging through the gorge; surf against the coastal cliffs. Two bodies.

What?

Kali was taking off, smiling, touching her fingers to her forehead in the tradi-

tional Ladakhi manner. We stood with Déva as she made her way slowly across
the white drifts for the central crevasse. My heart pumped. I knew what was
happening. And there seemed suddenly so much to say. So many questions left.
Déva's face was savory, far off, no more than a rumor.

I was forgetting everything. Surrounded by the mountains. A breeze coming
from the South. Like the rush of emptiness, wordless agitation in my chest.
Allain's beard had grown. And so had mine. Ghisela was tan, beautiful.

Déva was flooded with calm; he beamed, undistinguished from the intense
glare of the sunlight on the glacier.

"We're going," I said. Ghisela didn't move.
"I know," Déva responded. "But be careful!"
"Careful?"
"There is a certain danger I have not mentioned."

My fears coming back, I could have easily shattered. I held myself. Allain
stood innocently. Waiting out his time as if it were some death-sentence which
he was certain would be commuted.

"The real risk, the only mystery of mountain climbing, of all love, is the first
move. For he who ascends, ascends forever." He bowed and set off for the
crevasse in his easy Neanderthal stride.

"Wait!"
"Let's go," Allain choked.

So we headed back towards the waterfall. Throwing our clothes off the serac
and plunging over the edge. Completely at home now in the divine pool. "Why
didn't we invite them for dinner?" I suddenly flashed, as we dried ourselves off.

"I have a feeling they wanted to be alone tonight," Ghisela grinned, and we
made for the tent, very tired.

We were up early, stuffing the sleeping bags, already nostalgic, deflated.

"I'll go check the ropes," I said, as Ghisela and Allain went to the pool to wash
out our pots and pans. I hurried up the talus to the base of the cliffs. Confused.
Where was that crack? I moved along the jagged bottom. I couldn't remember.
Back down, where the overhang was most severe. Nothing! The ropes were
gone! I moved out away from the wall, scanning the higher dihedrals. Empty.
All our fixed ropes. Vanished! "Allain!"

The three of us stared dumbfoundedly at the sheer, rotten wall we'd rappelled.
A tumult of orange lichen, overhanging fingertip cracks, dangerously loose
flakes. We got out the telephoto. Even the pins, the blue slings and the
carabiners had been stripped.

We stared at the amphitheater of ice couloirs soaring in the early morning
light thousands of feet into the ashy clouds of the pinnacle rims. Stok Kangri's
razor summit was obscured in the makings of a storm. And to our left, above
the glacier, the undeviating wall of ice and overhangs we'd looked at the day
prior. We had not a rope between us.

I scurried for the tunnel. There was no light. I moved over the ice to the clearing. The eerie grottoed echoes of water dripping in the shadows. Sun flooding over the dead embers of a fire. Empty.

I ran out. Up to the hut, shoved open the door. Gone. The thangka still on the wall. An ethereal repose of paints and symbols. And candles, burnt on both ends, strewn about stone. My head was bursting. "Déva!" I screamed. "Déva . . . " my voice bounding off the walls, absorbed in the infinite brilliance of the glacier. "Déva . . . " But only yawning silence, of time which had been sleeping in secluded courtyards. I was back to stage one. None of this existed. No square. No techniques. Only my voice mocking me, defining in the highland tide a supreme soliloquy.

"Some quip," I flustered, slumping in a frustrated muddle of dirt and ruined hopes.

I surveyed the square, miles around.

"Are you ready to go home?" Ghisela weighed.

I stood up. Renewed vigor.

"We'll have to leave everything. We can't climb with the packs." I leaned against a poplar whose leaves quaked like aspen. I was faint with a dry mouth, a dizzy head. "Three pitches and we've got it!" I mumbled, totally unselfconscious, urgent in absence of alternatives.

Coming back would be easier, I dully ruminated. Coming back? The thought surprised me. I had had to come this far to see just how far I was willing to go. Such confusion of priorities—testy paradoxes—courted addled ambivalence. Where was I *really* going?

"Not pitches. Just rock," a voice continued.

We left everything. Recorder. Nearly fifty rolls of film, most of it exposed. My Leicaflex. Ice axes. Even the ounce bottles of iodine. Our parkas, sleeping bags, double boots, socks. Everything. And moved back to the cliff. I pleaded with destiny. Against the rock. Looking at my two comrades. Forcing the new warp of circumstances out of my mind. *Pick up the image. Get it. Get the image.* My breath heavy. And then Déva. His eyes. The stern muscle in his back. The whole behemoth of body. That hieroglyphic erection. The dots on his stomach. The taut gold veil of skin and his voice. In a combustion of memory. Sticking. Water in my toes. Water in my veins. Fire from the sun. Down the arms. Into the legs and up the spine. Into the rock. Airborne! Slowly. Steadily. Losing the world. A blanket of mindlessness behind. And then a breeze, a stop in time.

Thunder, accompanied by lightning. Caliginous vapors hurtling in whorls over the mountain, admitting in an instant the gold-emblazoned square, now lost beneath the mantle, years away below. A dozen mountain goats, racing across the talus venting a volley of rolling stones. Something altered. I shook my head. Grabbing. Something wrong.

"Help!"

We stared, in last second fixity. I'd lost it. Allain grabbing my forearm.

"Hold, don't let me go!"

I squirmed over the edge and lay face-down, panting on the giving turf, my eyes squeezed tightly shut.

We waited as I regained the wherewithal. Snow flurries swept the face. I clutched on, benumbed, ebony. Suffering.

It took time. The day feigned in and out of cumulous nimbus, I slept. I stared, I let go. My two friends said nothing, waiting patiently. The goats reappeared, gazing across the wall at us. Startled. Craning white necks in dazzlement, ears lynx-like and heavenly perked. Two kids whinnying.

I got up. Warmed. "What time is it?"

Ghisela burst out laughing.

"Come on!"

We embraced on the ledge. Allain remained gazing on the lower world as I renewed my ascent with Ghisela.

One final wall to surmount. I bouldered it. No other way. Thrilling to the risk I now courted.

I pulled up on a block of quartz. Clear glacial crystal. It broke off in my hand. I was in ecstasy. I'd been climbing for twenty, thirty minutes. In an instant I'd gotten there. I handed Allain his peradam.

Up the talus. Without looking back. Warm. Physics. Skeletal. See-through bodies. The snow on the ridge. A thousand feet at a time. The prow, five hundred feet more.

Scrambling in a jailbreak of freedom, every upwards heaving step was some collision with insatiable longing. To escape the enclosure, to climax in the momentum of Déva's magnetic residue. It was bursting in my nudity. Admixing with my breath in aerial, unleased toppling. A sling-shot in my loins. The skin on my arms was platinum black, the hairs golden. My face was hot. Wind curdling the cheeks. Ghisela and Allain, plying on all fours through the slipping scree of the upper steep slopes, were blushing red with the intoxication of our ascent. It was physiological fanfare, pure soloing. My memory had no stable ground. I could not equate my past with the present. There was no way to grapple meaningfully with what we'd accomplished and for that reason I could truly enjoy myself.

Under the burnished silver-blue sky there was high-voltage in my veins, each passion, each coming day, every conceivable act of my horizon wrung out, at once, into the essence of myself. I continued to climb dizzily, borne upon invisible seconds which seemed to separate two immutable sides of the world, lolls in eternity. And I was the shaft of trigger-happy delirium in-between. Stains of paradise on the balls of my feet, *frisson* in my soul. Blurred whispers in my consciousness. And a trail of perfect movement behind and underneath me. I was devouring the cold air.

We were a tandem passion in flight, the three of us. It was ultimate sensuality. With a parched throat. Calloused skin rubbing over stones, my penis swinging to my tempo. Like sudden nomads. Déva's world had disappeared from an explosive independence I was now feeling.

It was akin to weeks-worth of debauching, to months of concentration, to years of urbanity—all in a matter of hours, in those several thousand feet. The freedom was accentuated by the dim recognition that I'd passed through death, had escaped falling, and was thus reborn. It was the total mountaineering reincarnation. I remembered clinging to the overhanging lichen, my fingers unconcerned with the rotten crack they indifferently fondled. At times my legs had hung free as I hand-over-hand climbed upwards in the ever spiraling morass of bulges, ceilings, narrow fissures, and impossible smooth faces. I had not only left the logic of my body, but had, again effortlessly, suspended awareness—civic, or reasonable awareness. There had been an achievement of the senses. Somehow they had overpowered all consciousness, reducing ideas to feelings, and charging me with the certainty that I could live in no other framework biologically. Now I was unsure, my reaction melting away the easier the terrain became. I was pinioned in cold sunlight, beyond entropy.

Allain was next to me. Ghisela below. Not a sound between us. It was colder. We were higher. In my head, a cold-sweat. I felt at one with the dusty talus of the mountain. My toes seemed to reach out to caress sharp rocks, to doddle in the cold slush of melting ice ribbons. Water was trickling down the face in hundreds of runnels. There were snow plumes above, and wind ripping into the corniced summits of the surrounding peaks. I could see the thinly strewn edges, snow in tidbit flight, piercing comet-like the stellar altitudes above us.

I was naked. Naked! The sensation was utterly glorious! To be alive that way. To have been so for days, in snow, over rugged territory. And no reason. No meaning. No plan!

The three of us stopped to look back down from a perch that angled off the edge of a fierce couloir. The square was now a discernible formation, over a mile below us. The poplars had disintegrated into a general humus of color, set back against the waterfall, now plunging creamily in a silent, steadfast whittle against the earth. Shock searing my memory. The night had been a compulsion of sleep. We'd not eaten. My mind had literally burned its way into sleep. And now, exposed on the high ridge, it was steaming, airing out. It was over.

A rope. The first we'd left, in place. Over the top. The wind nearly knocked us down. And then the view!

Desert. Sasur-Kangri. The Karakoram. Clouds listless over hundreds of square miles of glacier and sand. The Indus Valley. And the green composite painting of Leh. Unreal . . . a metropolis. Swarming with other-dimensional forms.

And we turned. Like the satyrs of Mount Pelion gazing from their highest precipice to the far gone ship of Athena, we looked down to our tiny Arcadia, the square of glacier. Minute now. Dwarfed in the onrush of 10,000 other squares, and vaster ranges. All without name.

It was noon. The ice screws I'd fixed had long ago come out and we were without a hammer. But a snow picket was in place. Instinctively I doubled the rope around it. Threw the two ends down the descent route and started off in a dulfersitz, over-the-shoulder rappel. I slipped. Uncertain what I was doing. And instead of holding onto the rope—the first lesson in rappelling—I went for the snow, digging in animal toes to the sixty-degree hard surface. Leaning against the slope. Staring down between my legs at the 2,000 feet of white face falling into glacier. And desert hills below that.

I flung off the rope and downclimbed. Over the ice steppes. "Come on!" I shouted up. "Forget the rope! I'm going down."

With gtummo. Melting large footholds. Half-floating, and in controlled free-fall, glissading down the lower chutes. Within an hour we all reached the glacier. The old wands were nowhere to be found. We crossed over to the shoulder. But the ice had changed. New crevasses had dramatically closed and opened. More nevé had collapsed and a frozen cone of shard had formed at the base along the scree. We downclimbed the two hundred feet of rock, traversed the upper slope and skied barefooted the loose slope. All the snow had melted over the rocks.

There were yaks grazing. And smoke faintly rising from a low mud bungalow in the green sward. In the distance, our beloved Indus Valley.

"Hello, sab, hello, hello!" Pemba, followed by his cheering children, was running down the slope to greet us at the original Base Camp site, goat cheese in his hand. And with him, their young full breasts swaying under black velure blouses, his lustrous Tibetan women.

CHAPTER TWENTY-ONE

Jerusalem
Autumn, 1976

It was a long shot. But neither of us had ever been to Israel. We'd called the international information operator from Delhi. In the Jerusalem phone book, a Mordechai Déva. We placed the call. Waited hours in our room at the Akbar. And finally got through. A young woman's rash of guttural Hebrew. Mordechai was in town. Yes, he had spent time in Asia. No, hesitantly, Déva was only an affect, what he liked to call himself. The real name was Schwartz, Dr. Mordechai Schwartz.

It was enough. We exchanged air vouchers and flew to Tel Aviv via Istanbul. We were splurging all around and when a vacant double occupancy was discovered at the King David Hotel, unheard of during the High Holidays in September, we entrenched ourselves.

To backtrack:
Allain was gone. We had slept on the yak hair rugs at Pemba's that last night on the mountain, children curled up all over us. The sunken habitation reeked of heat, incense, and the smoke of a slow dung-burning fire. It was exactly the paradise, the safety, the social commingling—hot breaths and all night goosing—that I required. By the time any of us were awake, Allain had gone. Back up the mountain, two of Pemba's children reported. They had followed him in the pre-dawn hours as far as the bottom of the scree.

We worried and waited the entire day, and again that night. But by the third afternoon our anxiousness to get down prevailed. We left a message with Pemba though there was really little to say. Then we set off along the dry river gorges. It was dark when we reached Stok and we were shivering. Barefoot. We'd truly come down by that time. Pemba had given us woolen robes to cover our nakedness.

The land-rover was there as we'd left it. Parked in the hard mud along a wall of prayer stones. Tenzing, despite our insisting he take it to get himself to a hospital, had not touched the vehicle. The key was still hidden under the wheel. Our wallets, passports, the gear we'd left behind—everything was in place. The battery had gone dead, however. So we continued by foot across the rubbly salt-flats of the upper Indus.

Across the bridge, we made for our tentsite. A slip of paper on the inside. Tenzing was putting up at the Yak Tail Hotel in Leh. The next morning we inquired after him.

Remarkably, neither Ghisela nor myself had noticed the signs. An unfamiliarity with Tibetan seasons, perhaps, or simply the exhaustion, the physical transformations we'd undergone. But Tenzing was no longer residing at the Yak Tail.

My heart has never leapt as that morning when we were told Tenzing had left many weeks before for Srinagar.

Ghisela and I seized tourists on the streets, plucked newspapers, racked our memory, attempting to recount the calendrical sequence of our past days. It didn't work. We were scared. I could vividly enumerate the day-by-days, and there were only eight in Déva's company. But by the *Herald Tribune's* estimation, it was early September. Somewhere, we lost nearly two months. Or gained?

I was wholly incapable, at that time, of dealing with the implications.

Along with a message to let Allain know where we'd deposited his passport and Swiss traveler's checks, we left the zippered tent standing along the river, facing out to the white Trident. Someday, we thought, he might need it. Two days later we bummed a ride on a military convoy and plowed through diesel clouds four hundred and fifty kilometers into Kashmir.

Dr. Schwartz' house was deep in the Mea Sharim, the old Hasidic quarter. It was mild and breezy and the narrow cobbled alleyways were alive with payosed children playing soccer, hunched vendors pushing their carts and elder men strolling quietly in groups, big-bearded, with black top hats and coats to their knees.

The air was nippy. The middle-eastern sun, a flat radiance which absorbed the landscape rather than assaulting it, vague and mellow, shone overhead. There were rows of three-story apartments constructed from Jerusalem's own lime-curdled stone, interspersed with wooden stalls still upright from centuries before when Saffad, in the Galilee, and the Mea Sharim were thriving centers for the study of the mystical Kabbalah and its scared book, the *Zohar*.

Schwartz was probably in his mid-forties. Medium height. Clean shaven. A healthy crop of reddish-brown hair. He was muscular, good looking. Fluent English.

"You are a doctor?"

"Actually a medical researcher, at Hebrew University."

"And do you go by Dr. Schwartz, or Déva?"

Off his guard. He looked hard at us both. Then smiling, "Schwartz professionally. Déva to my friends. You are Jewish?" he went on.

"Yes."

"Both of you?"

"I'm undecided," Ghisela volunteered.

I was at home in his eyes. Had been raised under its wing. The easy openness. And the Yiddish, a mixture of impatient gruff and clairvoyant, affectionate sonority. "So, what brings you to Israel?"

"It's the first time for both of us. A convenient short stop. We live in California. Been mountain climbing all summer."

"In India?"

"Yes. In Ladakh."

He became still, immersed.

"I see. And what is your opinion?"

"You mean, do I believe it?"

"Yes. Déva. What do you think of the Déva?"

"So . . . you *do* know of him?"

"You didn't see any other Dévas in the phone book, I hope? Good!" he chuckled.

"You spent time with him?"

"I sought him out. And spent the good part of a winter in his company. Many years ago. I wasn't much older than yourselves."

"A winter? You were snowed in?"

"There was no civiian access into Ladakh in those days. No road. And of course the Cold War had not yet broken out. I went in the year after William Douglas. Three weeks from Manali. We were fine where we were. You must know the place. The poplars, the warmth. But Ladakh in winter is inaccessible. A Himalayan arctic. We stayed through the spring."

"How many of you?"

"Just two. Another woman and myself."

"And where is she?"

"I don't know, frankly. We lost contact years ago. Déva called her Devi. She was Swiss. From a wealthy, religious family in Basel. Her name was Naomi. What a climber! Only twenty-two at the time. About a year after we got back, she went alone searching for a psychotropic vine in Brazil. I've heard nothing from her since then."

"I think I have the right mate for her. Problem's going to be getting them together in the same crevasse."

Mordechai drove us all around Jerusalem and down to the Caves of Qumran on the Dead Sea. Behind Jericho we climbed to the precipitous Monastery of the Mount of Temptations, nestled on the edge of the cliff. Christ supposedly fasted for forty days and nights on that ledge, four hundred feet above the talus, looking out to Mount Nebo, where Moses was said to have disappeared, on the edge of Canaan. Mordechai loved the place for it resembled the Buddhist prototype.

He was a member of a *Hevra Kadisha*, a sacred society among Jews concerned with the proper burial of the dead. Only the most pious members of a community were called upon to render such services. It is a mere coincidence that Jews term the period of mourning Shiva. Mordechai was also engaged at the University in the study of longevity. He'd hiked throughout the Caucasus and Hunza. But it was among the Déva, he told us, that the possibility for long life had truly been realized. "And among the Jews!" he laughed, toasting with the traditional *l'haim*, to life!

"There is a physics that baffles me," I went on. "How, *how* did we lose two months in there?"

"You didn't." And he stopped me short of further conjecture with a gaze of guying clarity by now not unfamiliar to us.

"Déva reads the landscape like an x-ray, the way we read a book," Mordechai continued. "He voices an active trust in the healthy body of nature each time he goes out on the glacier. This health is his own health, which people fortunate to have been reared in wild places come to bask in. There is nothing irrational about it. Nor is there any demonstrative science to the association. Granted, Eskimoes, Bedouins, Laps, Hopi, have each a nomenclature for Nature as intricate and rigid as any botanist. What separates the *primitive* classification system, and subsequent willpower from Lamarck's is its context, this inbred notion of health in the cloud-wrapt summits, down every cataract, the focalization of all things. This is no anthropomorphism, no religiousness. But praxis, symbiosis, the soul of man entering into working agreement—call it communion—with the environment. Mbuti, Igorot, Sherpa—the same communion.

"This generation of Tibetans who have come of age might end up in Bombay, even London or Berkeley for that matter, while their parents remain traditional, with nightlong lovemaking among kith and kin, deeply recessed oblivions about which only far-off wanderers know; with yeti lore and that crystalline air towards which philosophers on all continents in all times have raised their nostrils. But even among the older generations of Tibetans—of all Central Asians—the Déva are uncanny.

"The mind of Déva, it seems to me, is in itself, a species of wilderness, an unending process not obvious to the eye, internalized. Civilized savants have this boring penchant for idealizing the backwards peoples associated with history; people, in turn, rooted to a specialized and uninhabitable terrain. Nostalgia for arcadia, for the happy shepherd musing on his hillock, characterizes every age which has succumbed to the seduction of its fonder memories. Like his hunger, his caudal tail, man's inner urging, the soul in him that has waited its turn five million years to sprout wings, Déva is that constant summons to beginning impulses, of which surely a foremost one is moving, disassembling camp and commencing a journey into the unknown.

"Mountain people themselves have always received scant adulation amid this intellectual hubbub. Déva's *kind* of life—the nitty-gritty details of it—might be verity enough to inspire the map-reverent, Everest-dreaming wanderlust of city children on all continents. But his world, like the Sherpa's, the Bolivian Runas, the Monpa, Hmong, Wakhi, Balti, whatever tribe you consider, that real world of theirs has been abstracted into an *idea* of such a world, a place unpopulated, where only this *idea* of sanctity and surreality—verdant pinheads of gossamer cloud, ink blot pinnacles, nobles in their Taoist condominiums—can live. Not real people."

He showed us Samuel Beal's two volume *Buddhist Records of the Western World*, published in 1884 in which there are references to numerous Déva Temples and naked ascetics, as seen and recorded by early travelers, foremost among them the famed Chinese scholar-wanderer Hiuen Tsang of the seventh century A.D. Tsang describes a stone palace, high on a mountain to which devotees risk their lives in the act of climbing. At one temple a group of "heretic ascetics" have erected a high column which they climb each sunset, hanging by one hand and foot at the top, "turning wonderfully" throughout the dusk and descending "refreshed" in the dark. Tsang discusses hundreds of such practices, all based somehow on the notion of a vertical aesthetic in combination with *hard primitivism*, asceticism. In Hebrew such practice is called *Zumzum*. Such Dévas he calls "rupavacara" meaning that they mentally and physically inhabit the summital realms of Mount Di Se.

We looked through a translation of the *Vedas*. As Allain himself had shown us, the *muni* or ascetics were first described in the *Rgveda* as having magical powers, pursuing the wind and flying through the air.

The four *Vedas*, or hymn collections, represent the oldest extant literature of Indo-European languages, composed by Aryan nomads who drove their cattle down through the Northwestern Himalaya during the second millennium B.C. The fourth, or *Atharva Veda* deals extensively with theories of love and marriage, citing numerous magical charms, enchantments, eugenics and conjurations for the successful maintenance of a happy family life. And it is also in the *Atharva Veda* that the Sanskrit word Déva is employed. A muni who has become "divine"! It is important to note that such ascetics marry and sire offspring.

Mordechai had made a study of the mountain over many years and had circulated among friends a tantalyzing essay, "The Codex Onesicrytus." Nearly every culture on earth appeared to have its own mountain god, regardless of the horizontality of that culture's real environment. And each culture had its own *access* to symbolic heights. There was a photographic reproduction from the Louvre of an Akkadian King, Naram-Sin, shown climbing a sharp peak embossed on a stele found at Susa and dated 2150 B.C. Mordechai considered it the earliest known representation of a human being confronting a mountain.

He'd discovered genealogical ties to the Virgin Mary in the ancient Phrygian mountain goddess Cybele whom he compared to Pan, and Rhea. There were charts of symbols—mastabas, stuppas, Taoist Huts of Silence, references to Renaissance iconography . . . the exquisitely detailed peaks hidden mysteriously behind the Mona Lisa. "The Renaissance, first in China, in the 11th century, then in 15th century Europe, was founded on the allusive impetus, the subconscious embrace of Nature," he said. "Mountain nature. Cliffs. Wilderness. Horizons."

But there were hundreds of other figures: from Hsieh Ling-yün, a fourth century Chinese apparently responsible for the invention of primitive crampons, to Percy Shelley, the poet laureate of Mont Blanc. Mordechai's thesis stated that the mountains promoted wildness. And that wildness was immortal. Both Ghisela and I were startled by the similar scholarship of Mordechai and Allain. But then, of course, it was Déva who prompted them. The facts, the myths, were obvious ones.

But one thing still puzzled me. "What is Onesicrytus?" His face lit up and he recited a tale.

" Onesicrytus was a Greek officer, a disciple of the Cynic philosopher Diogenes. He had accompanied Alexander to India in 325 B.C. At Taxila, Alexander had heard that some famous mountain ascetics were meditating at the far edge of town. He sent his officer to investigate. Onesicrytus found fifteen of them, sitting naked, motionless, in the burning sun. He addressed the first of them and the ascetic bluntly answered that 'no one coming in the *bravery* of European clothes could learn their wisdom.' "

We met Mordechai's wife, Rebeccah, some of their friends, and went to a Friday night service at his synagogue. He was orthodox, deliriously religious, a family man. Josh, his payosed little darling, was something of a devil. And already adept at climbing over the rickety apartments of the Mea Sharim. He said he wanted to scale the Wailing Wall one of these days. Mordechai's synagogue was presided over by a Rabbi who had been "dead" for three hundred years. After the service we all drank sweet Israeli wine and went dancing in the cramped streets of the Hasidic quarter half the night.

We were leaving for New York the next day. He took us to our hotel and we all embraced.

"Mordechai," I asked him. "Tell me. In your scientific opinion, will Déva ever die?"

He thought a moment, leaning against his small compact, an expansive grin brimming in the mosaic of his eyes. "Yes. Of course he will. But with balls like that . . . he'll live forever before he does!" And his fleeting laughter was inside me for hours after.

AN EPILOGUE

Big Sur, California
Autumn, 1976

The same kaleidoscopic path down to the ocean. Topophilia. Like the back of my hand I remembered it. For all its scent, serenity, and rich texture. The trillium, the hummingbirds and sea-wracked steeps. But it was not to last.

Ghisela and I migrated to the city for the winter. Renting a three-room flat across from Golden Gate Park where I could run our Samoyan Husky, and begin reassessing everything, everything! Nothing fancy. Just learning people anew. A very different kind of wilderness, one in which I was a beginner. In as much as I found more in common with a herd of deer than with most people on the street, I had a long way to go if I was ever to feel comfortable in the necessary company of others. I judged people according to their relationship with the natural world. If there was no such obvious relationship—and of course there was, if you speculated, went cosmic, perceived life in its larger circle—then it was doubtful that I could ever warm to such a person. Feeling misfit, sapient without purpose, in tune with shadows of an earlier sun, I needed to work through the conflict which welled up insistently, flared my nostrils, struck a grimacing countenance, made me sullen with perpetual flight, and the secret urging, albeit sublimated, to love others as I love the hills. Such dualism was perhaps the cleanest form of narcissism. But no matter its name. I needed to talk and that was something. Call it human ecology. It was a beginning of understanding. I'd gotten to shore. Entangled in gleaming seaweed.

Ghisela was participating in a neighborhood theatre group. Dancing. Studying Chinese brush painting. Working for Greenpeace. Struggling with detoxification. Climbing regularly, where she wasn't likely to be seen.

And I was trying to write. A few months' hectic exposure revealed to me the erratic, dismal sense that I was in trouble. Aflame with restlessness. An alien saga in my veins.

The summer, to coin a cliché particularly unsettling in our case, was but a dream. As remote, as painfully unclear, as our future.

Until one late evening. Arriving home from a *feverish* five days in the Palisades Glacier cirque. We had been alone. Once denuded, the body remembered. It all came back. It was real!

And then the letter. It struck to my depths; corresponded with a decision soon to be fructified. I knew, I smelled, I went for it. From somewhere in Asia. Thread-bare, baroque, scribbled hastily, Mongolian for all I could decipher.

A contagious smattering of emphatics: YOU MUST COME! And a photograph, weathered and out-of-focus. Of Déva. Naked. Erect. Making a face at the camera.

GLOSSARY
OF CLIMBING TERMS

Belay   To protect a second climber by keen manipulation of his rope

**Bergschrund
(schrund)**   Crevasse or large gap at base of mountain face

Bouldering   The art of vertical T'ai Chi, ballet, upon severely difficult rock, ice, or snow sections (primarily upon boulders themselves) in which the climber may sustain a fall with little likelihood of injury

Carabiner   Metallic oval snap-link through which a rope passes, and by which a climber can be supported through a variety of tie-ins

Couloir   A steep, narrow ice shoot on a mountain. Good for ice climbing, or scouting spectres

Fixing Ropes   A practice instituted by nervous expeditioners to place ropes on a mountain in advance, retreat back down them for one last look at the weather, a comfortable meal, a good night's carouse, before going back up the mountain for good, using ascenders to regain the previous high point quickly. This practice often gets the climber to the summit, and back down again, more safely, as well as fostering photographs of him on top for the folks back home

Gaiter   A full wrap-around fabric, with zipper to keep snow out of the boots

Ice Screw   A piton hammered and screwed into ice

Jam   A rock climbing technique of wedging the hand, or other portion of the body, into a crack for support and upwards mobility

Jumar   A handy pair of devices—size of a small lady's purse—which are snapped into a rope, and into the climber's waist, thereby allowing him, in essence, to effortlessly ascend a full length of rope (165 ft) in a matter of moments

Lieback   A rock climbing technique of counterforce between the hands and legs

Pitch   A section of a climb involving a belay at both ends. This section can be of any length, according to the length of the rope, and the demands of the section, i.e. availability of a safe belay

Piton   Any of a variety of metal spikes hammered into holes and cracks of rock for the purposes of attaching sling (rope) materials, carabiners, ropes themselves, and, naturally, desperate climbers

Rappel (rap off)   A fast, often times essential manner of quickly descending a rope via the use of concocted friction-giving systems of carabiner entanglement at the climber's waist level

Serac   A large, ready to topple, piece of ice. They stand, or lean, like sentinels in gleaming arrays, sometimes a hundred feet high. When they crash, capriciously, it's no place to be

INDEX